I0579244

A NOVEL BASED ON THE LIFE OF

ST. FRANCIS OF ASSISI

SINNER
SERVANT
SAINT

Margaret O'Reilly

Barbera Foundation, Inc.
P.O. Box 1019
Temple City, CA 91780

Copyright © 2021 Barbera Foundation, Inc.

Cover photo: Chronicle / Alamy Stock Photo

Cover design: Suzanne Turpin

More information at www.mentorisproject.org

ISBN: 978-1-947431-37-9

Library of Congress Control Number: 2021940247

All net proceeds from the sale of this book will be donated to Barbera Foundation, Inc. whose mission is to support educational initiatives that foster an appreciation of history and culture to encourage and inspire young people to create a stronger future.

The Mentoris Project is a series of novels and biographies about the lives of great men and women who have changed history through their contributions as scientists, inventors, explorers, thinkers, and creators. The Barbera Foundation sponsors this series in the hope that, like a mentor, each book will inspire the reader to discover how she or he can make a positive contribution to society.

Contents

Foreword

First and foremost, Mentor was a person. We tend to think of the word *mentor* as a noun (a mentor) or a verb (to mentor), but there is a very human dimension embedded in the term. Mentor appears in Homer's *Odyssey* as the old friend entrusted to care for Odysseus's household and his son Telemachus during the Trojan War. When years pass and Telemachus sets out to search for his missing father, the goddess Athena assumes the form of Mentor to accompany him. The human being welcomes a human form for counsel. From its very origins, becoming a mentor is a transcendent act; it carries with it something of the holy.

The Mentoris Project sets out on an Athena-like mission: We hope the books that form this series will be an inspiration to all those who are seekers, to those of the twenty-first century who are on their own odysseys, trying to find enduring principles that will guide them to a spiritual home. The stories that comprise the series are all deeply human. These books dramatize the lives of great men and women whose stories bridge the ancient and the modern, taking many forms, just as Athena did, but always holding up a light for those living today.

Whether in novel form or traditional biography, these books

plumb the individual characters of our heroes' journeys. The power of storytelling has always been to envelop the reader in a vivid and continuous dream, and to forge a link with the subject. Our goal is for that link to guide the reader home with a new inspiration.

What is a mentor? A guide, a moral compass, an inspiration. A friend who points you toward true north. We hope that the Mentoris Project will become that friend, and it will help us all transcend our daily lives with something that can only be called holy.

—Robert J. Barbera, Founder, The Mentoris Project
—Ken LaZebnik, Founding Editor, The Mentoris Project

*I have been all things unholy; if God can work through me,
He can work through anyone.*

—SAINT FRANCIS

*[I]n no one has the image of Christ our Lord, and the ideal of
Gospel life, been more faithfully (and strikingly) expressed than in
Francis. For this reason, while he called himself the 'Herald of the
Great King,' he has been justly styled 'the second Christ,' because he
appeared like Christ reborn to his contemporaries no less than to
later ages, with the result that he lives today in the eyes of men and
will live unto posterity.*

—POPE PIUS XI, Encyclical *Rite Expiatis*, 1926

Chapter One

FRANCESCO, SON OF PIETRO DI BERNARDONE

"Francesco di Pietro di Bernardone, pay attention! *Attende, attende, attende!*" This had become a familiar refrain for Francis at San Giorgio, the little school outside Assisi's south gate. Sometimes he awoke at night from a restless sleep with those words ringing in his ears. He knew too well the scowls on the faces of the dons when he made a mistake in his sums or misspelled a word on his wax tablet.

The six and a half years that Francis spent under the tutelage of the dons at San Giorgio passed quickly for his parents, who watched their son shoot up into a stripling. To Francis the years seemed to crawl. His days spent in school were uninspiring at best; dullness alternated only with exasperation. Don Sylvester was a stern teacher and the other dons at the school followed his lead.

Francis had come into the world in 1182 with an amiable awareness of others and a love of all things beautiful. As a small child, he delighted in tales of chivalry, spending tranquil afternoons playing that he was Roland at Roncevaux Pass defending

Charlemagne's army against the Basques. He knew by heart all the French poems and songs that his mother could remember from her youth in Marseille, and he loved to hear the stories and *chansons* of the troubadours who passed through Assisi. He memorized them all and entertained his parents and their friends with them. But the dons at San Giorgio were not so readily impressed.

"Francesco!" the don snapped, so that Francis stiffened. "In Book Five of the poem 'Tristia,' Ovid wrote '*Rident stolidi verba Latina.*' Parse this saying and translate it accurately." Francis had no difficulty understanding poetry, but his grasp of grammar was shaky. It took more than one attempt to parse the sentence. He redeemed himself in the end with a satisfactory translation of the saying, "Fools laugh at the Latin language," but he thought, *At least they laugh, which is more than we may do here.*

Francis did not care whether a particular noun was in the dative or ablative case. He rarely remembered which was which; it did not seem to merit much attention. He did his schoolwork most of the time, and he tried to conceal his apathy. However, when the sky was clear and Francis could hear the city's fountains splashing in the piazza, his thoughts soared with the birds outside.

By the time he was thirteen, Francis had had enough of education. His mother could not persuade him otherwise and his father did not try. Pietro di Bernardone had little education himself and he noticed that his business did not suffer for it. Besides, he thought, he could use his son's help around the shop. Customers liked Francis; he had a way of putting them at ease. He had learned to write well enough to satisfy his father and he could do the simple computations required to keep reliable records of sales and purchases. What more did the son of a successful cloth merchant need?

Reinforced by his father's opinion of education, Francis expressed it in his own terms. "School is a waste of time," he said to his friend, Benetto, on the way to school one morning. "There is so much more we could be doing! The world is teeming with excitement while we spend our days listening to Don Sylvester prattle on about things that have no relevance to life."

Benetto was the son of the town's tailor of the same name. He was an amiable lad, stout, friendly, and untroubled by ambition. Benetto was inclined to agree with Francis in this opinion, as he did in most any other idea Francis expressed. "I can surely make a living just as well without reading Latin and Greek! Simple arithmetic and common sense are about all we really need," he concurred.

"For myself," said Francis, "I will earn honor one day as a knight. Horsemanship, tilting, and archery are skills worth cultivating. Chivalry is what we ought to be learning, Benetto. Honestly, the troubadours have more to teach about life than the dons."

"You speak wisely," said Benetto.

"Let's take the day off then, to enhance our education!" Francis suggested with a devious gleam in his eyes.

The two friends turned around without a backward glance at the school gates and sauntered over to the Bernardone stables. Francis offered Benetto the use of his Spanish pony, and they went out for a day of hawking and fishing, finishing off with a leisurely swim in the cool water of the Chiacasco River.

Late in the afternoon, Francis flew into his mother's kitchen, "I'm taking some of this, Mother!" he announced as he placed slice upon slice of roast venison onto a platter.

Lady Pica objected, "Your father will be home any minute and then we will have a family meal. Stay with us this evening."

"No," he told her, "Benetto, Lapaccio, and Roberto are waiting outside. We are preparing a little feast of our own!" He gave his mother a fleeting smile and peered into the pots. Into a bowl he heaped some gnocchi that was simmering in a sauce, and then he was out the door with the steaming dishes. Dona Pica heard the boys laughing as they walked away together. She could only guess where they were going, or at what time of the night Francis would return. She shook her head and sighed.

Once, in the months before Francis was born, she had received a powerful premonition that the child under her heart would be a "Son of God" with some great purpose in his life. She recalled it often; the recollection gave her comfort on days like this.

When Dona Pica complained of their son's behavior to Pietro that evening, her husband merely snorted, "It is time the boy was finished with his schooling anyway. I will make an apprentice out of him. He has the wit, and with time and training, responsibility will come."

"I suppose you are right," Pica reluctantly agreed. "He would be free, then, to accompany you on your next trip to Provence as he has always wanted," she added hopefully. "It might spur his interest in the cloth business."

Pietro shook his head. "He's crazy to want to make that trip. It is grueling for a child, and fraught with danger. I am beginning to weary of it myself. Anyway, you can be sure it's not the cloth trade that attracts him to France. It's those absurd troubadours and lovesick poets."

Pica knew that Francis longed to go with his father to Provence and to the Champagne Fairs. She also knew that it was the romance of French culture and the Cote d'Azur that tantalized their oldest son, not the cloth business.

"As soon as I can," Francis would dream aloud, "I am going to travel all over France as a troubadour, performing the poems of Marie de France before spellbound crowds. Perhaps one day I will even compose my own lyrical poetry." Dona Pica smiled at her son's youthful enthusiasm for her homeland with its ideals of chivalry, its world-renowned tournaments, and the "courts of love" that flourished there.

Even if Francis could not travel with his father just yet, he considered working in the shop preferable to the tedium of school. He had met the minimum academic requirements, and on the side he had mastered the ability to juggle fifteen abacus beads at once while Don Sylvester's back was turned. There seemed little point to Francis in prolonging his education. Consequently, at age thirteen, Francis quit school and began his apprenticeship in the cloth merchant trade.

He lacked enthusiasm for the job, however. Over the next

three years he did only what he must to pacify his father, and nothing more. He focused much more on amusing himself with friends and dreaming of a glorious future. By the time he was sixteen, he was utterly unreliable and a source of consternation to his parents.

"Let's see what's happening at Campo di Sementone today," Francis suggested one late morning, forgetting that he had promised his father he would come to the shop after breakfast. His friends, Roberto and Benetto, sat with Francis on the balcony of Benetto's two-story home. From there, they could see the full length of the narrow side street below, leading all the way to the city's gate known as Porta del Sementone. They had noticed knights in full armor that morning passing through it on their way to the military field beyond.

Francis and his friends often went to Campo di Sementone to watch crossbow practice, sword fights, and tilting exercises. If they were lucky, there might be a jousting tournament that would hold them spellbound for the day. The boys made their own swords, spears, and bucklers out of wood scraps.

Francis had acquired some mastery with the sword and the spear by watching and practicing. He and his friends refined their skills with a lance and a makeshift *quintain*, a sawdust dummy they had made. It supported a thick wooden shield that spun on a pivot when it was struck squarely in the middle. Out of the top of the pivot pole a wooden arm projected at right angles from which the boys suspended a small sandbag. When the shield was hit squarely, the arm swung around, full circle.

The boys quickly learned to duck and dodge, or else to take the consequences on the head.

With the quintain playing the part of the imaginary enemy, Francis sometimes recited an entire battle scene from the ballads of King Arthur to the amusement of his friends. He attended every tournament in Assisi and in the nearby towns of Perugia and Foligno. Even if he was not born of noble blood, he could mimic the manners and bearing of a true knight until, somehow, someday, he could find a way to become one.

When Francis remembered his broken promise to his father that morning, he lightly shrugged it off. It was not the first time he had neglected his duties, nor would it be the last. He had begun to resent the work he was asked to do day in and day out. To his parents' dismay, he could no longer be depended upon to help at the shop for more than a few hours in a week. Neither did he help his mother with the burdens of household management. Instead, he slept late most mornings, ate whatever his mother had set aside for him, and then went out looking for his friends. He came home only when he felt like it. He preferred the company of friends to his fretting mother and his irritable father. He did not enjoy his brother's company either. Angelo, who was now of school age, seemed to Francis to be little better than a self-satisfied snob.

This morning passed like many others for Francis. For a time, he and his friends watched the knights spar and did a little sparring themselves. Then they squandered the rest of the afternoon roaming about town. As dinner time approached,

Francis remembered his broken promise again, and decided not to return home until everyone in the household was asleep. He could wait it out at the home of one of his friends or pass the time at a local inn.

Just as he had hoped, no one stirred when Francis crept into the house late that night. The hearth fire was out, but his mother had left a lamp burning near the door. He slipped into his bedroom and closed the door. He knew he would hear nothing about his absence from work if he did not emerge until late morning when everyone else was busy or away. He settled in for a long, comfortable night's sleep.

Although Francis was growing distant from his family, he was never lonely. He had friends in every walk of life in the small town. Lonso, the baker, beamed whenever Francis came in. Displaying his fresh bread and pastries, Lonso would exclaim, "I hoped you would come by, Francesco, I've outdone myself this morning!"

The farrier's stall was another regular stop for Francis. Simone, the farrier, shared with Francis a love for horses. Pietro had procured a Spanish pony, a jennet, for his son in a lucrative trade and the farrier assured Francis that it was the envy of many a nobleman in Assisi. To show it off, Francis sometimes rode his horse through the Murorupto, an affluent neighborhood that took its name from the ancient Roman walls partially surrounding it. Situated near Assisi's northwestern gate, Porta San Giacomo, the Murorupto provided a convenient shortcut when business or pleasure took him out of town. Francis tried to act as if he belonged there. His blasé exterior barely disguised his reverential awe of its expansive palaces and refined inhabitants.

Count Favarone Scifi and his wife, Ortolana, lived in the Murorupto with their small daughters. Their family lineage was as old as ancient Rome itself. Occasionally when he rode by, Francis saw the noble Count Favarone or his brother, Count Monaldo, on the broad staircase in front of the Scifi palace looking as important as Francis imagined them to be. The cloth merchant's son was not envious, but he was ambitious. Someday, he vowed, he would be just as important as they. And he would live in just such a home.

Late one morning when Francis was seventeen, he passed through the Murorupto on his way to join a hawking party in the country. He noticed one of the small Scifi daughters playing by the fountain that splashed in front of her home. She could not have been more than five years old and moved thoughtfully back and forth, placing pebbles in a pile on the ground.

"What game is that, little girl?" Francis asked her, pulling in the reins of his jennet.

"I am Chiara Scifi di Favarone di Offredicio," the little girl volunteered with a curtsy. Then turning to her collection of small rocks, she explained, "It is not really a game. You see, I add a pebble each time I offer a prayer or make a sacrifice for poor sinners."

"Your pile is growing large," Francis teased. "Are there so many sinners in Assisi?" The little girl sighed, casting down her eyes so that her dark gold lashes rested on her cheeks. She shook her head solemnly. "We are all sinners, I am afraid." Then she smiled up at him quickly to be sure she had not offended him.

Francis returned a reassuring smile and restrained his laughter at such an unusual pastime. *Anyway,* he thought to himself as he rode away, *her prayers and sacrifices are not wasted. There is more sin in Assisi than such an innocent child could possibly guess.*

After a leisurely day of hawking, Francis threw a small feast for his friends at the tavern of one of his favorite inns, The Silver Stag. They loitered long over the wine until the night grew late and their jokes ceased to seem clever. Chiara's pebbles came unexpectedly to Francis's mind, and he decided it was time to go home.

He stepped out into the dark street with a few of his friends, nearly tripping over a man asleep in the gutter. Francis recognized the beggar, Albert. Unable to pass without giving him something, Francis fumbled in his leather pouch, took out a few coins, and placed them on the ground beside the man.

"God's blessings upon you!" said the beggar, stirring from his sleep. Then, to everyone's surprise, he got up and spread his threadbare cloak on the ground in front of Francis as if he were royalty. "I revere you now, Francesco, son of Pietro di Bernardone," he announced, "and one day not only I, but the whole world will revere you as one sent by God!"

Flustered by the unexpected prediction, Francis treated it as a joke. He walked over Albert's sodden cloak grandly to the applause of his companions. The beggar took his coins and cloak and disappeared into the night, calling back to Francis, "You'll see!"

While he made his way home, Francis puzzled over what Albert the beggar had said. It was such an outlandish claim, yet something about it seemed authentic. He had always had an intuition that he would be great one day, but to be "sent by God" was not how he thought of it. What could it mean? Since he could not solve the puzzle, Francis decided to ignore it.

Chapter Two

"WHAT ARE YOU DOING, FRANCIS?"

"What are you doing, Francis?" his brother asked when they met on the street by San Giorgio one afternoon a few weeks later. It was a question Francis heard often. Today though it was followed by another that was unusual. "Why do you look so green?"

"Hush, Angelo," Francis hissed. "Do you see that wretched man across the way?"

Angelo turned in the direction Francis was looking. "Yes. His leprosy is advanced," he said as he stared at a disfigured man hobbling across the street. He carried a bundle of old rags gathered from the shops to use as bandages at the leper hospital on the outskirts of town.

"How disgusting!" Angelo added contemptuously.

"Hush," Francis insisted again. He did not want to give offense to the sick man but, at the same time, he did not want to be anywhere near him. Keeping one hand over his nose and mouth, he pulled a few coins from his pouch.

"Here," he said to his brother, "give these to him for me, will you, Angelo?"

Angelo snorted at his brother's squeamishness. Taking the coins, he stepped into the street and tossed them in the direction of the leper. The sick man picked them up and made a sign of the cross to show his gratitude, since he had no lips or tongue with which to speak. Francis was nauseated but acknowledged the leper with a nod. Then, taking Angelo by the arm, he scuttled away.

If Francis was generous toward beggars and lepers, he was more so with his friends. As he grew older, he became more extravagant and his popularity among the young men of Assisi increased. Any one near his age, from any social class, was welcomed by Francis as a friend and potential party guest. Bernardo was the son of Berardello, one of the wealthiest noblemen in Assisi. Benetto was the son of the well-to-do tailor whose shop stood next to Pietro's on the Piazza del Mercado. Lapaccio was the son of Lapo, of the imperial guard stationed at the Rocca Maggiore. Roberto, his closest friend, was a neighbor on Via San Paolo whose parents, Pasquale and Nofra, worked in the cloth trade as journeymen assisting local merchants with sewing and deliveries. Although his friends represented a wide range in social class, they were united in one objective: to have a good time, day and night.

Francis continued to view the cloth business as an interruption to his social life. He was beginning to realize that there was a great deal more to it than he had previously assumed. On the days when he came to work, he had to note the inventory and balance the budget for the shop. He filled letters of debt when agents came from other merchants. Sometimes he was allowed to represent his father on short trips to collect debts from cloth merchants in Gubbio and Perugia, or to choose wools from the local mills. His affable manners made him a valuable asset in the shop and that is how his father made the most use of him, on the occasions that he showed up to work.

"No wonder he is often preoccupied and cross at the end of the day!" Francis mused one day as he observed his father with a difficult customer.

"This fabric is uneven," the man was complaining.

"What do you mean? It is a fine raw silk, I assure you," insisted Pietro. "The varied texture is considered a desirable feature. One can see from a distance that it is genuine silk of the best quality."

"It is uneven. I don't like it. Do you have any that is even?"

"I have shown you three varieties of silk, in five different colors." Pietro betrayed the slightest irritation. "Perhaps you want a different fabric? A smooth satin?"

"No, I want silk. It must be silk! But this is uneven."

The customer was not satisfied, but not inclined to move on either. Other customers were waiting.

Francis had been entering inventory in his father's books, while his friend Bernardo leaned against the wall waiting for him. Detecting his father's stress, Francis came near the customer who was pondering the many silks, thus freeing his father to attend to the others in the shop. "This is the most striking one of all," Francis said as if to himself, taking an edge of a deep crimson silk in his hands. Turning to Bernardo he said confidentially, "This is the fabric I will recommend to the Duchess of Urslingen. She will be wanting something suitably elegant for the baptism of young Frederick Hohenstaufen next month. The Duchess will be hosting the celebration, naturally, and will want to be as refined as the Queen herself."

Bernardo, who knew nothing about fabrics, and cared less, looked blank until Francis winked at him. Taking the cue, he looked at the cloth and said, "It appears very rich, indeed; like something suited to nobility alone. Perhaps my sister would like some for the same event. I suppose she will be attending. Is there enough?"

"I am not sure," Francis considered. "I will check the inventory."

"Don't trouble yourself!" interrupted the customer. "*I* will take that one," he announced imperiously, ". . . all that you have of it!"

"Oh, sir," said Francis, with an air of good-natured resignation, "you certainly have a sense of quality. This is, without doubt, our finest crimson silk."

This was true, as a matter of fact. Francis understood human weakness and was not above manipulating it to advantage, but he would not lie. Like his father, he recognized excellence, and he was honest. Francis was confident that this man, whose finicky ways spoke of newly acquired wealth, would be a returning customer.

"Thank you for your business! The recipient of this cloth

will be fortunate indeed," said Francis amiably as he completed the sale.

"Thank you. I was perhaps a trifle difficult, but one doesn't want to settle for anything less than the best."

"How true!" said Francis.

With this transaction concluded, Francis and Bernardo hurried from the shop before Pietro could object. There was to be a play that evening in Assisi, the first of its kind, written and performed entirely in French. After the performance, Francis planned to treat a large group of friends to a banquet of foods and wine that his father had procured from France. Naturally, Francis had preparations to attend to, so Pietro was left to deal with the customers by himself. At the end of the day, Pietro locked up his shop and went home alone.

Francis came home from his party much later in the night. The house was dark except for the small lantern that his mother always left burning for him. Francis tossed his cloak on the back of a chair, took the lantern, and flopped on his bed. He would not go to the shop in the morning, he decided; he was too tired.

How good it was, Francis reflected, to be free to come and go as he pleased, to do whatever he liked! He was lavish with everything: clothes, food, and parties. He knew how to have a good time. He had plenty of money, and he spent it. Occasionally his mother reminded him that he was the son of a merchant, not one of the grand nobility. But why shouldn't he live like a nobleman? Was he not just as good as they?

Some of his friends were noblemen, some were not, but they

all treated Francis as if he were. He played the part well. He had the most expensive clothing, the best horse, the most ready money, and more freedom than any of them. He was generous, easy going, and chivalrous in public, with the confidence of a natural leader.

Pica often wished her husband would curb their son, and in fact Pietro, too, sometimes grumbled over Francesco's behavior. "You are no prince's son, Francis, to throw away money as though it were water. Must you feed so many parasites at our expense?" he exclaimed. His father harbored a certain detectable pride, however, that his son knew how to behave like a prince. The rare scoldings he gave his son were unconvincing and, consequently, ineffective.

Occasionally Francis did push his parents too far, however. He awoke the morning after the play to the unaccustomed sound of raised voices outside his bedroom.

"He asked his friend, Benetto, the tailor's son, to do it," he heard Angelo whine.

"Why did you not tell us?" came his father's angry voice.

"You didn't ask me," Angelo answered. "Besides, I didn't know you would mind so much."

"Oh Francis, Francis," he heard his mother murmur.

Hmmm, he thought uncomfortably, *I wonder what they are all ranting about?*

At that point Pietro barged into Francis's room. He pretended to be asleep, but in his father's agitated state, that ruse went unnoticed.

"Francis! What did you do to the expensive velvet cloak your mother and I gave you last month for your birthday?" Pietro asked through clenched teeth.

Oh, is that all it is? Francis thought.

Aloud he said, "I did that days ago, Father. I wanted to play the part of a traveling minstrel. I thought the rough patches sewn into the velvet would startle people. It was supposed to be funny."

He could see that this did nothing to placate his father. "Anyway, I can still wear it with the patches on. I wore it last night. It gets attention." At the time he asked his tailor friend, Benetto, to cut up his cloak and sew in the patches, it had seemed like a great idea. Now, under Pietro's glare, it seemed regrettably absurd.

His father was unimpressed by this feeble attempt at flattery. "I'll bet it gets attention," Pietro growled. "It has certainly gotten mine. I bought that velvet myself in Paris, I know how exceptional it is . . . or was, before you destroyed it! You, the son of a cloth merchant, ought to recognize its quality. How could you just cut it up and patch it with rags? Rags!"

Pietro tossed the adulterated cloak on the floor and stormed out of the bedroom. Francis, groaning to himself, muttered an irritable but refined, *"Mon Dieu!"* and covered his head with his blanket.

I guess I will get up, Francis thought at last. *I will take a walk first and go to the shop later, once Father has had time to calm down. Maybe.*

Francis left home feeling some remorse, but not much. True, the cloak was expensive, but his family had plenty of money.

Francis thought his father was unduly frugal. After all, he was probably the wealthiest merchant in Assisi! He had his own shop and several properties in the surrounding valley. His home stood on the most valuable real estate within the city, apart from the estates of the nobility. Oh, he knew his father worked hard, but Francis was not convinced that he needed to work as hard as he did. Of course, there were expenses if one was to maintain a suitably high profile: servants, horses, imported furniture, and exotic foods. These were costly. And there were heavy taxes to pay. Francis had heard his father complain about them.

With already wounded pride, the indignant Francis turned his attention to the injustices of the social system in which he lived. Although the Bernardone family was wealthy, he knew they could never rise to the level of nobility, which was almost exclusively hereditary. Nor could they expect to hold high political offices. As a burgher of consequence in Assisi, Pietro sometimes represented the merchant class in town council meetings, but that was the most political status he could ever expect to achieve.

Francis had heard other merchants and tradesmen in town grumble about injustices. They were especially resentful about their lack of freedom under the watchful eye of Duke Conrad of Urslingen, the German lord whom Emperor Frederick Barbarossa had installed in the Rocca Maggiore above the town. The foreign duke had been named "Count of Assisi and Nocera." The title alone was cause for indignation. How could a German lord be Count over the heart of Italy?

Why should my father slave away to pay taxes and quitrents, just so that a few noblemen can build their high towers, and lord it over the rest of Assisi? thought Francis. A bitterness festered in his impressionable mind, along with a hatred for the higher class. He was fond of his friends who belonged to that class—but that was beside the point.

As the face of imperial oppression in Assisi, the duke had never been liked. After Frederick Barbarossa's death, the new emperor, Henry VI, depended on Duke Conrad to maintain order in the region. The nobility, who served under him as a kind of political police force, built their lofty towers above the common people as a well-intended reminder of their protective presence. Yet this, too, aroused indignation. In Assisi, as in most of the towns of Italy, rivalry existed between the noble classes—the *majores*—and the class of serfs—merchants, and craftsmen, called the *minores*. It was a place ripe for civil strife.

In September of 1197, Emperor Henry VI died suddenly and then his wife, the Empress Constance, died soon after, leaving their three-year-old son, Frederick Hohenstaufen, with the wealth and responsibility of a vast empire. Pope Innocent had been entrusted with the boy's upbringing, but Italy was on edge without a viable emperor.

The gap in imperial power inspired uprisings across Italy. Long-held resentment in Assisi, too, reached the boiling point. In the spring of 1198, Duke Conrad left his post in Assisi to pledge allegiance to the pope and his imperial ward in Narni. As soon as his back was turned, the lid was lifted and hatred spilled into the streets of Assisi.

"Conrad has gone to Narni!" a loud cry came from somewhere. "Storm the Rocca! Storm the Rocca now!" Shouts echoed through the streets. The resentful *minores* saw their opportunity to free themselves from all over-lordship, and they grasped it. After the first cry reached the Bernardone household, Francis raced to the latticed window that looked onto Via San Paulo. Pica watched him.

"What are you doing, Francis?" she asked, her voice full of apprehension.

Without a word, he charged out the door. Pale with fear, Pica followed as far as the doorway and then stopped. Pietro shrugged his shoulders. Angelo did nothing.

Pica watched the gathering young men of Assisi, wild with mindless hatred and lust for revenge. They charged toward the citadel as one mob. "Please, God, protect my son," she murmured.

Sighing, she turned back into the room and closed the door behind her.

"The boy will be fine," Pietro said. "He knows how to take care of himself. He is a better fighter than most young men his age."

That is little comfort, thought Pica, as she returned to her work. The dishes were unfinished, the hearth was dirty, but in her state of distraction, the servants irked her. She dismissed them for the night and then scrubbed and cleaned long after Pietro and Angelo had gone to bed. Dishes that had never even been used except as decoration were polished to a high gloss. Francis did not return that night, nor for many nights after.

Chapter Three

> "*Hath any loved you well, down there,*
> *Summer or winter through?*
> *Down there, have you found any fair*
> *Laid in the grave with you?*"

Francis worked mechanically while his musical voice resonated above the drone of a dozen trowels, scraping against limestone blocks and patting down mud. The clanging of hammer and chisel provided a somber background to the popular French love song.

"Who are you thinking of, Troubadour? Is it the vile garrison we dispatched to the dust? Or was there a sweetheart among the dead *majores* that you had set your heart upon?"

The question came from a burly man who chuckled at his own wit while he worked alongside Francis. The victorious revolutionaries were building a defensive wall around the city to replace the mighty fortress they had torn apart stone by stone. Duke Conrad of Urslingen had already threatened to fight back and if he managed to gather reinforcements, the prospects were ominous. The nearby town of Perugia posed an even more imminent threat. A long-time enemy, Perugia had formed an alliance with Assisi's ousted nobility to aid in a full-scale retaliation.

Francis shrugged his shoulders and kept working, "I'm just singing, that's all."

On the night of the raid on the Rocca Maggiore, Francis and his friends had formed a well-coordinated cohort to assist in the attack. They had not been required to do the killing themselves but only to divert the attention of the imperial soldiers, so that the Assisi militia could carry out their brutal work. After the sentry guards were out of the way, Francis had stayed through the night to help demolish the Rocca. The proud fortress was reduced to a pile of rubble. Everything happened so quickly; there had been no time to stop and reflect.

After the initial bloody work was done, graves had to be dug—many, many graves. A military patrol was hastily established. Guards were stationed at posts throughout the city to prevent news of the raid from traveling too quickly to surrounding landholders or hostile neighboring towns. Sometimes it was necessary to "silence" would-be informers. The patrolmen were also vigilant for signs of organized resistance. Certain families among the nobility might need to be "dealt with," lest they try to prevent the rise of the new government.

For days after the revolt, small units of militia were sent out on raiding parties. All of this inevitably required more graves to be dug. Francis never saw the faces of the victims. Their corpses were wrapped in their own cloaks or blankets and dumped into the graves. He had done his task and had asked no questions.

Francis stopped singing and set down his trowel. He went to the back of the Rocca where he used to sit with his friends to look out over the wide valley below. A feeling of emptiness replaced the peace he used to find there. Dirty orange smoke from fires hung in the air. The towers of the nobility that had so irked the townsmen no longer marked the skyline. They had been looted one after another, then burned out and leveled. The Murorupto neighborhood was a shell, with only a few homes still standing. His picturesque town, its landscape once fragrant with orange blossoms, stank of decay, ash, and smoke.

Francis knew that soon the wind would blow away the pall of smoke. Children's voices would ring in the streets again and people would return to their mundane occupations. But for now, everything was ugly. It had been necessary, he told himself over and over. This was what the city needed. This was the birth of independence for Assisi!

At the same time, questions haunted him. What had become of Lapaccio and his father who lived at the Rocca? Where was the Scifi family, whose little girl marked her prayers with pebbles? Some of the bodies he had buried were small, weighing little more than a few bolts of cloth. And what of his friend, Bernardo? The magnificent Quintavalle house was empty and there had been no word of him or his family.

"Hey, Francesco!" His neighbor, Roberto, approached.

"Good morning, my good friend!" Francis shook off his gloom.

"Nothing like a little civil war for a change of pace, eh?" Roberto quipped.

Francis became serious. He searched Roberto's eyes. "Do you think it was necessary, Roberto? Was it truly a civil war, or just a rampage?"

The same question had troubled Roberto enough at the outset so that he had decided not to take part. He could not offer Francis consolation.

"What brings you here, Roberto?' Francis asked.

"Your parents are asking after you every day," Roberto said. "I can't walk in or out of my front door without being hailed by them. Stop by your house and let them know you are alright. Your poor mother looks like she has been through a whole year's agony in the week and a half since the raid."

"You are probably right, Roberto. I was thinking about heading home anyway. I am tired." Francis stared thoughtfully at the heap of debris that had once been a part of the proud fortress. Somehow it brought to mind Chiara Scifi's pile of pebbles again.

Francis went home as soon as darkness fell. His father spoke with him briefly about the turn of events in the town. Needless to say, business had suffered during the uprising but Pietro was confident that this was a temporary setback. He had locked up the shop during the worst of the violence and intended to have it open for only a few hours each day until order was restored.

As a burgher in Assisi, he told Francis, he had been called upon to support the new government. Already the Palazzo dei Consoli, the headquarters of the new popular government, was up and running. A podesta, the first political officer of the commune, had been placed in power. This was news indeed!

Neither Francis nor his father spoke about the murders, or about the families who had been forced to flee their homes. Francis felt his head pounding and a few times he closed his eyes to try to shut out the images of the shallow graves on the hill.

After Pietro went to bed, Dona Pica hovered about her son like a mother hen. Although it was long past dinner time, she prepared a meal for him and sat down beside him at the table. They spoke about many things, but not the raid. He ate only a little and then got up to go to his bedroom. She realized that his face was flushed. Since early childhood, Francis had been prone to fevers and she recognized the signs at once.

For the next few weeks, she cared for her feverish son. She brewed willow bark tea and cooled his hot forehead through the night with damp cloths. While the fever was at its worst, she sang old Provençal songs softly in her beautiful native French as she stroked his forehead. Ten-year-old Angelo was kept busy doing errands for his mother. Through it all, Pica's every thought was of her elder son's welfare. All her worry for him she laid before God in prayer until, at last, her prayers were answered.

"Are you finally getting up?" Angelo asked Francis one morning after more than a month had passed since his return.

"I am going out. Want to come?" Francis said.

The brothers exchanged few words as they walked side by side. For the first time, Francis saw the effects of the rebellion in the streets of his hometown. Debris from the demolished homes had been gathered into disorderly piles and cleared to the side of the road. Beggars lighted on them, searching for anything of use. Francis noticed that there were more beggars than there had ever been in the piazza. Even they had been displaced by the raid. Many shops were closed, some permanently. Without the towers of the nobility surrounding it, the town looked flat. People milled about as they had always done, but they were more reserved than before. The bond of trust within the commune had been shaken.

Francis did not linger anywhere until he and Angelo came to the Cathedral of San Rufino. He went in and stood in the back for a long time. Angelo looked in, uttered a quick prayer, and stepped out again. Eventually Francis emerged and they walked on. He did not stop to greet anyone and barely looked up. Angelo did not know what to make of him.

"Look at the filthy beggars," Angelo casually observed as they drew near to a group of lepers begging by the roadside. "They should earn their pay like honest men!"

"They are lepers, Angelo," Francis said in a hushed voice. "No one would pay a penny for an ounce of their sweat." He skirted the group of lepers, instinctively holding the corner of his cape over his nose. He was carrying no money so he could not help them. "It is a shame," he said. Angelo shrugged. "Let's go out into the countryside, Angelo," Francis suggested. "The air is stifling here." But Angelo was irritated by his brother's melancholy and returned home instead.

Continuing alone, Francis passed through Porto del Sementone and heard the familiar sound of men jousting. His attention piqued, he turned his feet in the direction of Campo di Sementone. Sure enough, foot soldiers and knights in full armor were drilling on the large, open field. They looked proud and strong. They bore themselves with dignity and confidence. Francis stood transfixed.

At dinner that evening, Francis announced, "I am joining the new militia. The town needs a good defense if Perugia decides to attack, or if Duke Conrad tries to make a move against us. And I will be among the defenders!"

Pietro was enthusiastic. His son could win great honor, even knighthood. That would elevate the name of Bernardone to nobility—true nobility, not by mere inheritance, but by valor in battle. Pietro would make sure that his son was outfitted as well as any knight in the land. The two began an animated discussion about where to obtain a good battle charger and what kind of armor would serve best.

Dona Pica sighed. She did not want Francis to be a part of this. Although it was good to see her son's energy return, she feared for his safety more than ever.

"It's about time you did something interesting," Angelo put in.

The next morning, Francis returned to the cloth shop to help his father, but at the end of the day he left to secure a mentor to train him in the arts of war. It was easy to arrange since his purse was ample.

Francis showed promise with a sword—his experience with the homemade quintain had not been wasted. But he was slight in build and clumsy with the heavy lances, spears, and mace. It would take time and a great deal of patience to become a competent soldier. There was not much time, however.

Ostensibly peace was restored to Assisi, but the common folk were savoring their long-delayed revenge, feeding it with the blood of the feudal lords and their families. The nobility was no longer safe even on their rural estates. To protect themselves, they allied themselves with Perugia and prepared an armed assault.

Francis trained for conflict with a sense of urgency. Each day before and after work, he practiced on the Campo del Sementone. His routine made him far more reliable than he had been before, and his father began to depend upon him in the business.

"I will be leaving soon for the Champagne Fair at Lagny-sur-Marne," his father told him one morning on their walk to the cloth shop. Francis's heart pounded. Instantly, all his enthusiasm was diverted from Assisi to France. Was he at last to see the country of his childhood dreams? The land of poets, unrivaled beauty, and romance?

"I will have to cross the Alps with some of my best merchandise. You must begin to take stock of it, and set some aside," his father continued. "On the return journey it will be easier to go by way of Marseille, don't you think? I can do some trading there, and then sail to Genoa. The entire trip will naturally take many months."

The Alps! Marseille! Lagny-sur-Marne where the famous international tourneys were held! The Champagne fairs with all their tantalizing sights and sounds! Francis's imagination came to life while Pietro droned on about business details.

"I will take Pasquale with me," the oblivious Pietro continued. "He is knowledgeable in textiles and hard working. It helps me to know that you will be running the shop in my absence."

Francis grit his teeth and frowned. Glancing sideways at his son, Pietro shook his head unsympathetically. "There will be plenty of these trips for you in the years ahead, Francis, after I am gone and you are running the business." Pietro went about his work, oblivious to his son's disappointment.

That day it seemed to Francis there was an unreasonable volume of business and a high level of irritability among the customers. One nobleman returned a length of cloth that had water damage. Francis replaced it, but the customer left angry. A short woman wanted a bolt of cloth that was resting on the highest shelf. As Francis stretched to reach it, she complained that the shelves should be better organized. A couple wanted one bolt more than there was on the shelves. There was more bickering over cost than usual until Francis felt he could tolerate no more.

"Alms! Alms! I beg you in the name of God, give me something. A small coin, or a crust of bread. I have nothing to eat. Please, in the name of God," a beggar called out as he entered the shop. Francis looked up irritably from his books where he had been double checking the cost of a skein of wool for a skeptical gentleman.

"Oh," he rolled his eyes when he saw the ragged old man. "Not now!"

The beggar turned on his shaky legs to go out.

"Wait," Francis relented immediately, but the old man was evidently hard of hearing and continued on his way.

"Will you please complete this transaction? I am a busy man," insisted his customer. Pietro shot his son a sharp look. Francis showed the customer the price of the wool yarn, accepted his payment without stopping to write it down, and thanked him. Then, without giving a thought to the line of waiting customers, he ran out of the shop.

"Wait! wait!" Francis called to the deaf old beggar who by this time had made his way across the piazza and was turning onto a small alley. Francis followed until the man disappeared behind a tall building. Finally, he caught another glimpse of him milling among the crowds of vendors and carts on the Corso Manzini, the central thoroughfare through town. At last, the man seated himself outside of San Rufino Cathedral in a shady place on the grass with his back against its high wall.

"Old man," said Francis, standing breathless in front of him, "here is an offering!" Francis smiled at the man's surprise. It was the first time since the night of the raid that Francis felt like smiling. The beggar looked uncertainly at the large sum of money.

"It is for you," Francis assured him, "all of it! In the name of God!" and he placed the coins in the man's lap. The beggar looked up at Francis questioningly, and for the first time Francis wondered why it had mattered so much to find this man whom he had rebuffed.

The beggar shrugged his shoulders and thanked him with a simple, "*Grazie*." Francis nodded, smiled again, and walked away. As he made his way back to the shop, he remembered the line of customers he had left. He knew his father would want an explanation and he tried to come up with one. *If anyone had come into my shop in the name of one of the nobility I would have been as polite as I can be and given him whatever he asked. But this man came in the name of God, and I brushed him off.* Francis thought about this for a while. *Maybe it was the injustice that bothered me so. I will not let that happen again.*

When he reentered the shop, Pietro gave him an angry look that Francis knew boded no good. He stayed just long enough to gather his cloak and leather pouch, and then he left. He walked into the closest church, San Nicolò, and begged God's forgiveness for his rudeness to the man who had asked for alms in His name. Then he got his horse from the stable at home and rode out the gates of the city.

"I will never be a cloth merchant," he said to himself with certitude as he rode through the cool, late afternoon. "I know that I was made for greater things. Oh God," he prayed, "show me what it is I should do. I loathe this business."

Francis looked up at some cypress trees at the border of two fields that towered far above the landscape. *That is what I will be like!* he thought. *In good time I will rise above all this. I may have to bend for now, like those trees in a strong wind, but I will bounce back up and stand taller for it. Is that arrogance?* he wondered. *I don't think so. I have always felt that I was born for some great purpose. I just don't know what it is.*

Francis had agreed to help in the shop while his father was traveling but, after that, he now resolved he would devote himself entirely to the defense of the city after that. He would train until he could wield weapons as well as any knight in Assisi. There was honor in war, and perhaps a title. He turned his horse and went back into town.

During his father's absence, Francis divided his time between work, military drills, and late-night parties. He was fast earning a reputation as a profligate.

"Utterly undisciplined," Dona Pica heard someone say when she walked by a cluster of women outside her neighbor's door. "Frivolous," was another word that drifted past. She was returning a borrowed platter that she had filled with fresh fruit for her neighbor. When the women noticed Dona Pica, they fell silent.

"Pica! We were just talking about your Francis," one of the women, the baker's wife, hailed her. "*I* think it is hilarious the way he leads his band of young friends around town. They hang on him as if he were the god Bacchus himself."

"Or a world-renowned troubadour, like the Great Divini," added another. It was Landa, the wife of the haberdasher. "Last week he and his friends were making so much noise after curfew that my husband threatened to report Francis to the town officials. Do you know what they were doing? They were serenading every house along the street—every house with a daughter, that is. I told my Eleanor to keep her head inside, you may be sure!"

"My son, Roberto, is one of his good friends, you know," Nofra put in loyally. "He was probably with Francis that night," she admitted. "He usually is. All the young men admire Francis because he is so talented. And Roberto says he is as chivalrous as any knight!"

One of the women gave Nofra a skeptical look. The others giggled. Dona Pica smiled to cover the hurt. She knew better than anyone that her son was undisciplined, but she knew, too, that he had a compassionate heart. "He is unsettled," she acknowledged, "but you will see, one day my Francesco will be a son of God. There is much that is good in him and I know for certain that God has a great plan for him."

The ladies exchanged looks of benign tolerance. Nofra, who did not want to be part of the gossiping group, took Pica's platter of fruit to her house and then walked with Pica back to her front door.

"I am worried," Pica confided. "Have you heard that Perugia has determined to move against Assisi? Pietro told me last night when he returned from the town council meeting."

"I am not surprised. Pasquale and I have been expecting it every day," Nofra said. "Roberto and Francesco are impatient for their day of glory," she smiled sadly.

"They are not yet twenty and full of bold dreams,' Pica said. "Francesco is eager to prove himself in a real battle. He doesn't realize what a gentle soul he really has. What can we do, Nofra, we who fear the worst?" She searched her friend's sympathetic eyes. "Nothing," Pica said, answering her own question, "except pray."

Just then the hunting hounds in the Bernardone stable yard began to bark a joyful greeting. Turning toward the street, Pica saw Francis approaching on his steed. *How handsome he has become*, she thought. His chest and shoulders had filled in, his arms had grown firm and strong, his swarthy complexion had toughened, and he carried himself with refinement.

"Have you heard, Mother?" Francis asked, kissing her forehead lightly, "Perugia has finally decided to move against us. We will meet tomorrow at Collestrada. The timing could not be better since our government has just made an alliance with Foligno. Reinforcements are already arriving from Nocera, Fabriano, Bevagna, and Spello, not to mention Foligno. The battle is practically won already! Assisi's independence will soon be secure."

Dona Pica tried to smile, but tears sprang to her eyes instead. Francis gave his mother an affectionate squeeze. She did not speak but clung to his arm. Francis looked thoughtfully out at the horizon. "I am so tired of waiting for something to happen," he muttered.

The October sun did its part to make the day of battle a glorious one. It glanced off the armor and spear heads of the soldiers as the Assisi army made its way along the city's thoroughfare toward Porto San Giacomo. Banners flapped in the restless breeze and trumpets heralded the occasion.

Pietro, Pica and Angelo stood amid the cheering crowd that lined the road alongside Nofra and Pasquale. The tailor, Benetto, who had sewn flags in Assisi's colors, now distributed them proudly. Bishop Guido was there cheering alongside some of the Benedictine monks from San Paolo monastery.

Hundreds of parents, sisters, brothers, grandparents, and friends of the departing soldiers came to see their loved ones off. How the day would end, no one knew, but the people of Assisi clung to hope. If their defenders failed, it would set back their new-found liberty. On the other hand, if the day was won, Assisi would claim victory as an independent commune.

Francis rode with the light cavalry.

"They will take you for nobility, most certainly!" his friend Roberto assured him as he rode alongside Francis.

"They will not be far wrong!" Francis declared. "Today we are merely merchants' sons, Roberto, but by tomorrow we will have won honor enough for knighthood!"

Roberto laughed. His spirits were high. How could they be otherwise riding beside Francis who was so full of confidence and good cheer?

Francis noticed for the first time the poor quality of Roberto's armor and his inferior mount. He wore no chain splints, or mail. *I should have helped Roberto obtain better equipment*, he mused. But that thought vanished within the instant, when the horde of Perugian soldiers appeared on the distant hillside.

"This is our day, Roberto!" he said as the lancers picked up their pace at the command of the colonel. With energy they crossed the Chiascio River, hearts soaring. They charged before the proud Castle Collestrada, a possession of Perugia that, with luck, would soon be theirs; the spoils of war.

The approaching enemy by this time had descended to the same level as the Assisian army and was crossing the Tiber River. Its gray clad infantry spilled off the bridge and into the field of Collestrada like an ocean wave. Seeing the array of archers, Francis suddenly remembered his friend Lapo. Had he escaped the massacre at the Rocca? If so, he might be among the foot archers in the Perugian infantry. While in Assisi, Lapaccio's father had trained him so well with the crossbow that none of the boys could match him in precision or distance.

Soon the tumult of battle filled the valley. Francis unhorsed his opponent with the first charge, then followed him to the ground. Standing up to draw his sword, he caught sight of a body being trampled, unheeded, under the feet of the horses. It was Benetto, his old friend. Why was he doing nothing to protect himself? *He should be shielded—he should get out of there. What is wrong with him?* Francis wondered.

Francis moved to help Benetto, until he saw it was too late. Benetto had an arrow in his head, his eyes were blank, his battered body was lifeless. Amid the confusion of horses and soldiers, Francis tried to think what to do, but there was no time to do anything. A knight in Perugian colors was charging. Francis met the man skillfully, and easily sent him to the ground. Then he caught sight of Roberto who had worked his way up to the bridge of San Giovanni. A large Perugian knight had him by the chin and forced his head back over the edge of the bridge, exposing Roberto's poorly clad breast. In horror, Francis saw the man raise his spear.

"Nooo!" Francis wailed, but the sound of his voice was lost in a roaring chaos of rushing river, guttural war cries, and clashing metal. Fury such as Francis had never known swelled up within him. He raced to the bridge in his heavy armor, fully intent on destroying the much older, stronger, Perugian. Blinded by rage, Francis raised his sword to drive the man through before it was too late. At that moment, a second Perugian foot soldier stepped in front of him to block his attack. Forgetting all his training, Francis struck out his sword wildly, aimlessly, and ineffectually. The next moment, there was a deafening crash. Intense pain spread over his skull; he reeled in a throbbing silence. The scene around him danced in and out of focus until everything went black.

Chapter Four

"THE PATH TO PARADISE BEGINS IN HELL"

Francis opened his eyes. All around him it was as black as pitch. His whole body throbbed with pain. He lay still, listening for some sound above the ringing in his ears.

He heard dripping. The air was dank. The smell was nauseating. He heard a rustling like the scurrying of rodents. He flinched when he noticed the sound of breathing close to him. Where was he? His heart beat so loudly now that he could not hear anything else. After a long interval, he fell back to sleep.

He woke again later. A strip of pale light shone through a slit in the thick wall about eight feet above. Bodies of many men lay on the ground beside him with rats milling around them. When he shooed one of the creatures away from his face, the sudden movement sent pain shooting through his head and body.

"What is this place?" Francis wondered aloud.

"Hell," was the answer that came from somewhere in the room.

Francis turned his neck stiffly in the direction of the voice. Sitting up in a corner with his back against the stone wall was a disheveled looking knight at least ten years his senior. His doublet was stained with blood, rats scurried over his immobile legs.

"I see the similarity," Francis admitted.

The place stank of sweat, vomit, and putrefying flesh. The knight grunted, "And you look like the devil himself, now that you are conscious. I thought you were dead."

"Who are you, Sir Knight?" Francis asked.

"None of your business," was his response.

Blood and pus oozed from the man's eye and large gashes marked his face and neck. Francis pitied the man, despite his gruffness. He turned his eyes away from the grotesque sight.

"I'm Sir Montalvo di Treve," said another voice. Again, Francis turned slowly; every inch of his body ached. He noticed a man about his father's age standing in another corner of the room. His hauberk on the floor beside him was of the best workmanship. "We are in a stinking pit of Perugia. No doubt we are being held for ransom since we are all nobility here. The less valuable prisoners have probably been executed, or they are rotting in some other pit."

"I begin to understand," said Francis. "We lost the battle?"

The question needed no answer. The battle . . . Francis recalled it now. He closed his eyes as the horror of it replayed in his mind. He knew that Benetto was dead, and that Roberto must be dead, too. Who else? Had any of his friends survived? He scanned the room, but he recognized no one. In his cell there were only ten men, but he soon learned that this was just one room among many. They were in a long underground corridor of storerooms, empty vaults, and latrines beneath the streets of Perugia.

"We never stood a chance," said the first knight bitterly. "Perugia outnumbered us and outranked us from the start. Who were the idiots who thought we could win? I was only in it for the pay, but now even that is lost, thanks to the inept Assisi leadership and milksops who called themselves warriors."

"Shut up," snapped a man lying on the floor with his short cloak spread lengthwise over him like a blanket. Francis could tell from its intricate weave that it was a Burgundian wool. "We're all in the same wretched boat." This man was Baron Carmeni. Francis had never met him, but his reputation as a prosperous overlord was well known in Assisi.

A young man on the ground next to Francis awoke. He sat up stiffly in his padded armor and looked at Francis. "You must have been hit hard. You have been lying there like a corpse since we arrived. My name is Marco." He added, "Here, I saved you a scabbard full of water to slake your thirst. I knew you would be parched if you ever awakened."

Francis swallowed the water greedily from the knight's dirty scabbard. "How long have we been here?" he asked. "Does anyone care for us?"

"It must be three days at least since the battle," said the young man, "and we have had only one barrel of stagnant water between us."

"Along with a platter of putrid vegetables at which the

Perugian pigs must have turned up their snouts," Carmeni added. "Our jailers aren't wasting any money on slops for the hostages."

"If we are being held for ransom," Francis said hopefully, "we will eventually be free."

The Perugians must have mistaken him for nobility because of his charger and the superior armor his father had procured for him. That thought made him smile. How often he had tried to pass for nobility on the streets of Assisi! Then he wondered, *Does my family even know I am alive?* How great was the ransom the Perugians would demand? Would his father have access to enough money? He did not mention his fears aloud, however, but only said, "God must have some great plan for us yet. Why else were we spared?"

"No doubt so we can dream of a glorious future while we rot away slowly in this hole," said the rancorous knight in the corner.

"Is it a dream to believe that God Almighty has a purpose for every one of us? If so, then I am the greatest of dreamers!" said Francis.

It was not very long before the Perugians turned their attention to these valuable hostages. The men were given food and water, and a doctor was sent in to tend to them. Their spirits revived at these signs that negotiations for their release were underway. Progress was slow, however, subject to the volatile political relationship between the Perugians, the deposed nobility, and the new popular government of Assisi. Time moved at a snail's pace for the men in the cell. They had just one wind hole in the thick wall by which to judge night and day, rain, snow, or tantalizing sunlight. At first, they grumbled and snapped at one another, but with the passing of weeks and months, they began to form a bond.

Sometimes Francis entertained the group with songs and poems. Occasionally others joined in while the rest of the prisoners sat quietly, each with his own thoughts.

"Merry it is while summer lasts, with birdsong
But now, close by, the winds blast.
Oh, oh, but this night is long,
And I with very great wrong
Sorrow and mourn and starve."

"When you go home, Francis," Marco asked after his song ended, "will you return to the cloth trade?"

"I suppose I must, for a time. But some day, I will find a way to leave all that behind me. I was made for greatness!" he answered. "And you know," he added confidentially, "I believe God has something great in store for me."

"Idiocy!" the irascible knight snarled, but without conviction.

One spring evening, not long after this, Count Favarone Scifi and his two small daughters, Clare and Agnes, were strolling along the streets of Perugia. They had been forced to flee from Assisi during the uprising nearly four years earlier. Although their home in the Murorupto was not destroyed, it was not yet deemed safe for the ousted nobility to return.

"Are the prisoners still in the castle dungeon, Father?" asked the nine-year-old Clare as they passed the castle tower. It was more than a year since the Battle of Ponte San Giovanni on the Plains of Collestrada.

"Yes, Chiara," said Count Favarone. "They must wait until the new consuls of Assisi can reach an agreement with the government of Perugia."

"I can't wait to go back to Assisi," said Clare, "so I can imagine how homesick the poor soldiers in that dungeon must be."

Count Favarone nodded agreement but raised his finger to his lips. He was straining to hear something. "What is that?" he asked a Perugian guard in front of the castle. "Are the prisoners below singing?"

"Yes, they are. It's the "Regina Caeli," my lord. They are chanting Vespers." He turned toward the little girls. "That's evening prayers, my ladies."

"At first there was only one voice, and a fine voice it was," the sentry told them. "Then, a few more joined him, and now the whole bunch of them sings it every night. There are nearly forty men in all the cells put together. It almost sounds like a monastery, doesn't it?" The guard seemed to take a personal pride in it. "It's as foul a place to live in as you could imagine, my lord, but you wouldn't know it to hear them."

It was several more months before an agreement was reached that satisfied the officials of both Assisi and Perugia. The ransom money for prisoners was handed over, and the nobility of Assisi were recompensed for their loss of property. Taxes had to be levied on the merchants of the commune to cover costs, and public funds were taken by the new government.

~

Finally, the day came when the prisoners were set free. The men who were going north or west said goodbye. The rest made their way back to Assisi along the Via Francigena, the same road they had traveled in battle array a year and a half before. Then there had been trumpet blasts and flying banners, but on this spring day, the tramp of their feet was their only fanfare.

Passage over the bridge of San Giovanni was painful for Francis, who made it with his face set like stone and his eyes turned away from the turbulent waters of the Tiber. Although the waves that had swirled beneath the bridge on the day of the battle had long since mingled with the Tyrrhenian Sea, Francis knew that he would never forget what took place there. The events of the Battle of Ponte San Giovanni played out again and again in his mind.

Conversation flagged among the soldiers when the gray tower of Collestrada Castle came into view. Secure in the hands of Perugia, it dominated the plains where Assisi had met its defeat. The soldiers' spirits returned only after that field was behind them. The flashing poplars beside the Chiascio River and the scent of jasmine in bloom restored them. The men breathed in deeply and relished the feel of the wind against their faces.

"We have been buried like seeds beneath the earth in the Perugian dungeon and today, at last, we have burst forth!" exclaimed Francis. "We are like seedlings breaking through the soil, full of promise. Who knows what we may yet add to this world!" His companions looked at him doubtfully.

"I just want a good leg of mutton and a real bed," said one.

"Roast venison for me," said another. "And a bath!"

The twelve miles from Perugia to Assisi seemed long to the soldiers after so many months of foul air and confinement. Their legs were unsteady and their lungs were sluggish. Francis, who had already been struggling with a fever, grew weak. By the time the last of the men passed through the gates of Assisi and had gone their separate ways, Francis could barely drag his feet. He found Via San Paolo blindly, stumbling past the cloth shop without looking in. He opened the door of his house at last and fell weakly onto the nearest chair.

"*Ça alors!*" his mother cried out as she rushed to her son's side, "My poor child!" Turning to Angelo who stared open-mouthed, she said, "Angelo, fetch your father and find the surgeon at once. Tell them Francis is home and he is very ill. Send Bishop Guido, too, if you can, Angelo. Francis may have need of the Last Sacrament."

Chapter Five

THAT THEY MAY BE ONE

Lotario de' Conti gazed out of the third story window of the Lateran Palace in Rome just before daybreak. A thin streak of gold outlined the eastern horizon. There was just enough moonlight left to illumine the Lateran Basilica that stood adjacent to the palace. By its white light, he could see the stone faces of the two central statues on the church façade, effigies of the two Johns, the apostle and the baptizer. He couldn't decide if their expressions chiseled in stone were accusing or mournful. Looking out on the thirteenth-century world, they would have just cause in either case.

Lotario, who was known to the world as Pope Innocent III, turned from the window and sighed. There seemed no limit to the crises that confronted him as shepherd of an unruly flock, an untidy kingdom, and the myriad of souls who looked to him for guidance. His gaze fell on his breviary that lay open on the floor. *"You are the shepherd of Christ's flock and the prince of the apostles; to you Christ has entrusted the keys of the kingdom of heaven.*" Those words of the Divine Office were powerful, challenging, and humbling all at once.

He knew that the burdens laid upon his shoulders were united to the cross borne on the shoulders of Christ. They were burdens he shared with more than a hundred popes of the past, beginning with Saint Peter. Like those who came before him, he must guide the world in the light of truth, love, and peace. He would not have thought it was possible to do so in these turbulent times, except for Christ's promise to his disciples that "with God, all things are possible."

He had no more time to dwell on it that morning, however; the sky was growing lighter. From his window he could see early-rising faithful entering the shadow of the Basilica doorway. He must look over the notes for his homily.

Within the half-hour, the pope was crossing the piazza to the basilica. Looking up, he saw the tall figure of Cardinal Pelagius striding toward him with a dour face. "Your Holiness," the cardinal announced when he was close enough to be heard, "there is news from the East."

Innocent stood still. "News of the crusade? What news?"

The cardinal's grim look brought to Innocent's mind the faces of the two statues on the church facade, at once accusing and mournful. "The crusaders have attacked Constantinople, Your Holiness. Alexius III Angelos has been deposed and the city is burning. Many of the crusaders deserted prior to the attack, out of deference to Your Holiness. Unfortunately, the remnant of the army is now looting the sanctuaries of Byzantium and assaulting innocent civilians." The cardinal paused to allow his words to sink in. His red cape flapping in the chill morning breeze was the only color in the somber scene.

Already pale from want of sleep, the pope's face blanched. "No! It cannot be true! I insisted they go directly to Palestine."

Not content merely to relay the terrible news, Pelagius added, "The world will attribute this fiasco in this year of Our Lord, 1204, to Christendom, Your Holiness, and to your pontificate."

Innocent III knew this was true. In a way, this disaster was symbolic of the times. It was not his doing—far from it—yet it was tied to the critical issue of his pontificate. The hearts of so many had grown cold. They had forsaken the God of truth and unity for the divisive deities of the world; for gold, for lust, and for power.

Pope Urban II's crusade, just a century before, had been a success. The unity of purpose and the fervor of those first crusaders had secured their victory. By stark contrast, Innocent's "holy war" had been fraught with conflict from the start. Ulterior motives and worldly ambition were its undercurrents. There was no unity of purpose among its leaders.

Innocent had appealed to Alexius III Angelos, the Byzantine emperor, to combine forces. With the East and the West united in this cause, he had hoped to restore the Holy Land to the Christian world and, at the same time, to restore unity within the Church. Emperor Alexius had almost conceded, and the goals seemed within reach. Until now.

Innocent walked into the Lateran Basilica looking wearier than before. The homily he had carefully prepared for that day was a discourse on the words of Christ at the Last Supper. "I pray for those who will believe in me . . . *ut unum sint*, that they may be one."

Lotario de' Conti shook his head at the irony. "Oh, dear God," he whispered, "what has happened to your people? Their hearts are made of stone. Give them a new heart, I beg you. Put a spirit of peace within them. Somehow."

Throughout the busy day that followed, Pope Innocent was reminded, time and again, of the lack of unity and peace in the Christian world that he ruled. He listened to reports of events within the borders of Italy, where neighbor rose up against neighbor, and town against town until it seemed the blood must fill the rivers. Even in the heart of Italy, Assisi had instigated a blood bath that purged the town of its nobility. And then Perugia, in league with Assisi's refugees, had taken a bloody revenge.

In the south of France, tension was escalating between faithful Christians and the Albigenses, who embraced the peculiar belief that the physical world was evil. The cult was thriving and it posed a serious threat to his flock in more ways than one.

In Toulouse, the overlord Count Raymond had secretly embraced the Albigensian heresy. He was a "Believer", as members of the sect were called, and he seemed to have no conscience. Violence, debauchery, perjury, and theft were the hallmarks of Count Raymond of Toulouse. For his Christian subjects there was no justice. When their cries for help reached Rome, the pope had sent his legate, Cardinal Giovanni de San

Paolo, to assess the situation. After a year in France, the legate was now back in Rome to make his report. He told of ceremonial suicides, intimidation, sacrilege, and violence.

"The beauty of Christianity provides a striking contrast to the dark beliefs of the Albigenses," Cardinal Giovanni noted, "but there is a great deal of ignorance among the people about the teachings of the Church, and how Christianity differs from the dualism of the Albigenses. There is also, I am sorry to say, a lack of true Christian leadership in southern France. The clergy are often a source of scandal instead of the beacon of truth they should be."

"Clearly, we need missionaries to the Midi who are well educated in the faith, and confirmed in virtue," declared Pope Innocent.

"—and courageous," Cardinal Giovanni added.

At this, Pope Innocent recalled Bishop Diego of Osma, and the Spanish canon, Dominic de Guzman, who had sought permission years before to go as missionaries to the Midi. Clearly, the time had come to grant their request. Missionaries who can explain the tenets of faith and live exemplary lives could have a tremendous effect in the Midi.

The brilliant Cistercian, Pierre de Castelnau, was another holy and courageous man who came to Innocent's mind. De Castelnau was a monk at the Abbey of Fontfroide and would be well acquainted with the politics in and around Languedoc. Cardinal Giovanni had also mentioned the Cistercian Abbot of Citeaux, Arnold Amalric, who was already training his monks to preach to the Albigenses. Perhaps the hand of Providence was at work through these men, thought Pope Innocent, to form a spiritual army of missionaries to the Midi!

The pope's council was interrupted by the arrival of a large retinue in the piazza outside the Lateran Palace. Its flags and insignia bore the mounted knight and falcon, announcing Count Walter III de Brienne. De Brienne was a French nobleman with a claim by marriage to the throne of Sicily. Pope Innocent knew that Sir Walter had come to Rome seeking papal support in his bid for the throne. Pope Innocent also knew that this could never be.

At only twelve years of age, Frederick Hohenstaufen was the legitimate heir to the throne of Sicily. As his legal guardian, Pope Innocent must uphold his claim. The pope would exercise diplomacy to divert Sir Walter's ambitions.

Innocent dismissed his cardinal advisors and stepped into the piazza to greet Sir Walter de Brienne.

Chapter Six

THE VASSAL OR THE LORD?

"Iam going out with some friends," Francis told his mother, emerging from his bedroom. "I will be home later."

"May God protect you," was all she allowed herself to say. Francis had teased the doors of death for most of a year since his return from the dungeons of Perugia, but at last the danger was past. As soon as Francis was strong enough, he returned to his former ways. He spent money even more lavishly than before. He stayed out late at night and worked little during the day. He grew more restless. The glory that gave life meaning eluded him.

Interest in something beyond himself was finally sparked by news of a war being waged in the south of Italy. At the pope's bidding, the renowned French nobleman, Sir Walter III de Brienne, had taken up arms to defend Frederick II's claim to the throne of Sicily. De Brienne was the new Lord of Tarentum and Lecce, a welcome replacement for the German tyrants Italy had so long endured. Before de Brienne took command, the German General Markwald had been overpowering the pope's armies in the south. Anxiety mounted throughout Italy with each new defeat until the great Sir Walter took command. Under de Brienne's leadership, the pope's forces rallied, winning one battle after another for the pope and for Italy. Sir Walter de Brienne was Italy's champion. Even the troubadours sang of his feats.

"I know what I must do!" Francis declared one evening over a jug of wine. "I will join Walter de Brienne's army at Apulia!" His friends were amused, but Francis was serious. "This is my chance to redeem myself. Finally, to make a great name for Francesco di Pietro di Bernardone!"

Francis told his father of his plan the next day. Pietro's reaction this time was restrained. He had learned to be skeptical where his eldest son's exploits were concerned. Nevertheless, he procured for Francis a war horse and all the accoutrements of a well-to-do knight. As always, he wanted the best that money could buy for a son of Pietro di Bernardone.

Dona Pica watched these preparations for war in near despair. She made her objections to Pietro, hoping he would discourage their son. Pietro felt that she might be right, but how else could a young man such as Francis earn respect? He was utterly frivolous and useless in the merchant trade since his return from Perugia.

Then one afternoon, Francis came home on foot from the Campo di Sementone where he had gone to drill with the militia.

"What has become of your horse? Why aren't you wearing your new hauberk?" his father asked suspiciously.

"I gave it all to a poor knight, Father," Francis explained. "He was older and far more skilled than I, yet he would not have lasted a moment in battle, outfitted as he was. I would not have been able to live with myself knowing that I was so well equipped, and he had nothing."

Pietro was speechless for a full minute while he calculated the cost of Francis's armor and horse; then he exploded, "*Idiota!* I cannot outfit every hapless knight in and around Assisi! When will you learn, you profligate fool? Will you ever do anything right? You try me beyond endurance!" He clenched his fists to keep from striking his son.

Francis shrugged with indifference. He was convinced that he had done the right thing, but he did not expect his father to understand.

That night Francis had a dream in which his home was filled from floor to ceiling with weaponry, armor, shields, and visors. Every piece was of the best quality. Across each shield and breastplate was emblazoned a bold red cross. Francis wandered from room to room in awe. *All this for me!* he thought in the dream. When he awoke, he was full of zeal for his military venture. Because the dream had been so vivid, it seemed to be an omen of glory.

By the time the small troop from Assisi departed for Apulia, Francis was fully accoutered once more. Grudgingly Pietro had procured a second destrier for Francis, a superior coat of mail, fresh weaponry, and a squire. Anything less might reflect badly on the name of Bernardone.

After a full day's ride south, the troop stopped in Spoleto for the night. His squire noticed that the further along the road they went, the more withdrawn Francis became. Outside the camp, Francis dismounted his horse. He stood uncertainly for a moment, then remounted and turned his horse toward home. When his squire gave him a questioning look, Francis dismounted again and handed over the reins. "I am not sure what I am doing here, Stephano," Francis said. Sensing his master's uncertainty, the squire waited, but since Francis did not say anything more, he led the horse away.

That night Francis was struck with a fever. He was taken to a nearby inn to rest, apart from the other soldiers. He thought he would catch up with the rest of the company in a day or two. As he tossed in his bed, drenched in sweat, he wondered why he alone, of all the soldiers, lay sick in bed and powerless to make the journey. Then, he heard a voice speak to him out of the darkness.

"Francis," it asked, "is it more profitable to serve the vassal or the Lord?"

"The Lord," Francis answered.

"Then why are you exchanging the greater for the lesser? Why do you serve the vassal?" the voice asked.

"Oh, Lord," Francis cried out, "What would you have me do?"

Two days later, Francis left Spoleto. He did not take the road south to Apulia but turned back toward Assisi. Stephano accompanied him as far as Foligno where Francis sold his horse and armor. He released the squire, placing a wallet full of silver in his hand. "I cannot serve a lesser master, Stephano, when a greater one awaits my service."

The squire accepted the payment but he did not understand, nor was Francis quite sure what it meant. He went on alone.

During the long walk back to Assisi, Francis struggled within himself. He would never be a knight, he realized now. Perhaps his dreams of grandeur had all been delusions, perhaps he was really no better than the beggars he pitied or the loathsome lepers. It appeared that he would never amount to anything.

He thought of his family. What kind of reception he would find at home? His mother would be happy to see him, that he knew. Angelo would ridicule him, but that mattered little. His father's reaction, he could not predict. His mind went blank with fear when he tried to guess what Ser Pietro di Bernardone would say and do.

When he was only two miles from home, Francis was overcome with apprehension and fatigue. He stepped into the nearby chapel of San Damiano. Inside, the church was dark and quiet. Francis asked the old priest there, Don Peter, if he could stay through the night. In exchange, he offered the bag of money he had gotten from the sale of his horse and armor. It was a disproportionate sum of money and the priest refused it, but he allowed Francis to spend the night in the church.

Weary and still weak from his fever, Francis slept fitfully on the floor beneath the faded Byzantine cross. In the morning, he was awakened by a predawn chill that penetrated his riding cloak. He glanced up at the cross imploringly, then left the church to face whatever lay ahead.

When he turned onto Via San Paolo, it was still early morning. His father was outside the house on his way to work, arms filled with bolts of cloth. His mother, too, happened to be outside tending the flower boxes. She threw her arms around Francis, exclaiming that her prayers had been answered. Angelo came to the window to see what was happening, his disdain evident.

None of this surprised Francis, but his father reacted in a way that Francis had never anticipated. With a face set like granite, Pietro turned away and said nothing. He walked down the road in the direction of his shop. Francis thought he saw his father's head shaking, but Pica deftly distracted him. She brought her son into the house and prepared a warm breakfast. Francis tried to explain why he had returned, and she tried to understand.

For the rest of the day and for many days after, Francis rarely left his bedroom. He did not want to face his father or speak to anyone. He stared hopelessly at the ceiling; sometimes he beat his fists against his pillows in anger and frustration. He lay awake through the nights trying to fathom the point of his life and the meaning of his dreams. Nothing made sense. Occasionally he glanced out the window during the long afternoons, looking for answers in the boundless sky, then he closed the shutters to block out the odious sunlight.

Over and over, he asked himself, *Why? Why am I here? Why did this happen to me? Why can I do nothing right? What am I supposed to do with my life? Why am I so wretched?* But eventually it was not enough merely to rant. He began to look for answers. He desperately wanted answers. Where could he find them? Who would know?

It was then that his thoughts turned to God. Who else could plumb the depths of his heart if not the one who created it? Who else would know why he lived if not the author of life? He began, at last, to pray in earnest to a real and personal being.

"Most high glorious God, enlighten the darkness of my heart. Show me what I am to do. How can I serve You, instead of a lesser master? I understand that it was You who spoke to me out of the darkness. Here I am, I am yours. What will You have me do?"

In the stillness of his bedroom he listened and waited.

Word had reached his friends in town that Francis was back from Apulia. When they came to the house to find him, he was reluctant to speak to them. However, to refuse would be discourteous, so he invited them in. Later that same evening, Francis emerged from his bedroom.

"Where are you going, Francesco? It is nearly time for supper," his mother said as she glanced up from the table where she was seasoning a roasted chicken.

"I am going to a banquet tonight," said Francis. His mother looked at him in surprise. He did not return her look.

He said, "The Baron and Baroness Veniero are away this month in Naples, so Antonino and his brother are hosting all our friends at their uncle's mansion. My part is to supply the funds and, of course, the entertainment." His effort to sound lighthearted was unconvincing.

Dona Pica looked askance, "You know, Francesco, that Antonino is a wastrel."

Francis faced her then, "And what am I, Mother?"

Dona Pica set down her jar of spices. Placing her hands on

his arms, she looked squarely into his eyes. "You, Francesco, are a son of God. I have always known it and when you realize this, it will go much better for you. You are no wastrel. You have a true nobleman's heart."

Francis smiled at his mother's loyalty. At least, he thought, she has a noblewoman's heart. He took his cape from its peg by the door—he was always chilly these days—and he went out.

He did not go directly to the Murorupto, where the party was to be held. Instead, he walked slowly up the hill to the ruins of the Rocca Maggiore. He sat down on the wall he had helped to build and looked out past the ruins of the fortress he had helped destroy. The sun was setting over the valley with breathtaking splendor, but Francis was numb. Nothing moved him.

He attended the banquet that night, eating, drinking, and laughing loudly at every joke. He took up his mandolin and played whatever songs the guests requested. He knew them all. He had been reluctant to come out that evening, yet when the hour grew late, he was loath to go home.

"Let's serenade the ladies!" he cried. "Bring your favorite wine and your finest verses. Assisi will welcome us back!" he laughed. The crowd followed Francis down the street, singing and cheering. Francis's fine voice could be heard above all the others crooning love songs interspersed with ridiculous drinking songs. His friends who were in various stages of inebriation joined in, laughing riotously at their own buffoonery.

As they passed the house of the haberdasher, Francis overheard a man's irritated voice, "Eleanor, don't go near that window. It is Pietro di Bernardone's son, up to his old tricks."

"Who? Francesco?" an older woman's voice could be heard. It was Eleanor's mother. "I thought that foolish boy was dead."

The shutter closed and it was just as well. Francis did not want to hear any more. He slipped back into the crowd and eventually fell behind. Without his inspiration, the party died down until only Francis and a couple of friends were left.

"What is troubling you?" one of them asked. It was Giordano, a taciturn man of about his own age who was new in Assisi. Francis had not taken much notice of him before this.

Since Francis did not answer at once, Antonino Veniero spoke for him, "He is in love! Isn't it obvious? At one moment he is brimming with joy, at the next his eyes are filled with longing. What could it be but love?"

"You are right, my friend," Francis said, "it is love. I am consumed with love, but the one I love you do not know." His thoughts seemed to be far away. Antonino tried to look interested but could not muster it, so he said a laughing goodnight and stumbled away.

Giordano and Francis moved on through the Murorupto together. When they passed an empty fountain, Francis recognized the place, and told Giordano about the little girl Chiara di Favarone, who had once placed her pebbles there. Francis smiled, "I wonder if all those prayers and sacrifices had any effect. There is still a great deal of sin in Assisi," he said.

The next morning Francis heard his father preparing to leave. He was going on a business trip to the Champagne Fairs with Angelo. Pasquale and Nofra were to tend the shop in his absence. In the weeks of preparation, no one had suggested that

Francis accompany his father, nor that he run the shop. Why should they? Since his return from Spoleto, he had not so much as stepped inside the shop, even though his mother told him that his father needed help. Once, his father had directly commanded Francis to come to work but since Francis disobeyed, the subject was never broached again.

The family shared an early breakfast together before the long journey that would separate them for many months. Francis stayed in bed. He did not leave his room until he could hear the horse and cart rattling far down the road and the dogs in the stable had ceased to bark.

Despite how it must have seemed to Pica and Pietro, Francis was not angry or defiant. Behind the closed door of his bedroom a gradual change was taking place within him. After turning to God in his distress, and persisting in his prayers for many days more, he had experienced a powerful sense of God's presence. The feeling had swept over him and filled him with a longing for God. At the same time, a light seemed to turn inward on his own soul, illumining its darkest corners.

Francis left the house that morning after everyone else was gone, slipping through town and out Porta San Giacomo, avoiding anyone who might hail him. He went deep into the woods, heedless of how long he wandered or what path he took.

He saw now that he had wasted his life. He had misled his friends and acquaintances; he had disappointed his parents time and again. How selfish, how willful he had been! While he had aspired to knighthood, he had lived only for himself, scoffing at virtue and self-sacrifice—the hallmarks of a true knight. Worst of all, he had called himself a Christian. He was a hypocrite, an actor who utters lines by rote, accompanying them with empty gestures.

The contrast between his sinfulness and his sense of God's goodness nearly destroyed him. He sank to the ground on a riverbank deep in the woods and buried his head in his arms. A warbler cocked its eye at Francis and shifted curiously from shrub to shrub. The river lapped against the rocks, and gnats swirled above him. He was oblivious to everything except his own misery.

When he heard a rustling sound from the brush, Francis looked up to see Giordano, the young man he had met the night before at Antonino's party.

"What are you doing here?" each said to the other.

Giordano answered first. "I came here at dawn to fish in the Topino River, but nothing is biting today. So, if you have come to fish, you may as well give up right now, especially since you have forgotten your pole!"

Francis could not even make himself smile. Giordano laid down his fishing pole and sat on the riverbank. Francis had never spoken to anyone about all that he had been through but, at that moment, he opened up his heart and the words spilled out. Giordano listened and seemed to understand. That was all that Francis needed.

He described his whole life with brutal honesty: all the mistakes that he had made, his arrogance, his grandiose dreams, and all the bitter pain of failure, loss, and sin. There was so much emotion pent up inside that he choked back his tears until finally sobs overpowered him; he cried hard and for a long time. When he could cry no more, he was quiet and Giordano was quiet, too. In the silence and the emptiness, Francis began to understand something he had not realized before.

By laying his life out in the open, Francis saw a thread of meaning running through it; perhaps all his trials and misadventures actually had a purpose. They had taken him far afield of his goals, but they had set him down directly before God. By failing at every attempt at glory, he opened himself to the one light of true glory. God is the only real good—he saw that now—and God had not abandoned him, but seemed to be drawing Francis toward Him.

During the next few weeks, Francis and Giordano often walked in the woods and hiked the mountain trails near Assisi. Speaking his thoughts aloud to Giordano clarified them for Francis and he soon realized that the time had come to change his life.

Dona Pica was stirring the kitchen fire into flame early one morning when, glancing through his bedroom door, she noticed Francis mulling over some clothing he'd spread out on his bed. There were several pairs of shoes on the floor. He was holding open the large leather sack that he used for travel. She asked what he was doing.

"I am making a pilgrimage to the tomb of Saint Peter in Rome," he said, much to her surprise. "It was Bishop Guido's idea. I want to atone for my sins in some way."

Then, speaking more to himself than to her, he added,

"Saint Peter knew what it was like to fail, and to be rescued by the hand of God."

His thoughts returned to his packing, "I will go to the cobblers this morning to have a pair of sandals made with thick leather soles," he told her, "and I will ask the tailor to add a second lining to my cape; it may be chilly at night. Do you think the wide brimmed hat is more useful? Or this Phrygian cap? Perhaps I should pack the wool one and wear the leather one. I ought to bring another tunic but I don't think two extra outfits will fit into one sack."

Dona Pica was mildly amused. Every adventure her son undertook seemed to involve elaborate preparations and a carefully chosen wardrobe, even a penitential pilgrimage such as this. It was a worthy undertaking, however, and she offered to prepare food for the journey. Two days later, Francis stood in the doorway with a pilgrim's staff in hand. A new water gourd hung from the staff and he carried two leather packs on his back. Dona Pica watched him walk away.

Three days later, Francis kneeled before the tomb of Saint Peter in the ancient basilica built to honor the martyred first pope. He prayed for the intercession of this man who had thrice denied Christ, but who repented of his sin and finally gave up his life rather than deny Him again. He thought of Peter, the fisherman, who leapt out of his boat onto the Sea of Galilee to meet Jesus, but faltered and almost sank. He thought of the sure hand that pulled him out of the sea to keep him from drowning.

I am like Peter, Francis thought, *sinking in the vanities of the world and my own sins. Please dear Lord,* he begged, *come to my rescue as you did to Saint Peter's.*

Francis watched other pilgrims line up to approach the saint's tomb. They seemed to be playing their parts without real devotion, just as he himself had often done. *Penitents should be on their knees,* he thought, *weeping over their sins, begging for forgiveness, making restitution with all their hearts!* Instead, they filed past the tomb mechanically, one after another, genuflecting and moving on. Some pilgrims placed a small offering of a coin or two on the tomb that held the bones of the martyred saint.

Francis was chagrined. *You gave us everything, oh Lord, and, in return, you receive little more than a pious nod from your people.* Francis stood up indignantly and strode to the tomb with his money pouch open. In front of everyone, he cast the entire contents of it through the protective grill. Coins clanged as they hit the metal bars and fell against the walls surrounding the tomb. They tumbled over the marble floor, rolling in all directions. Satisfied that everyone present could take a lesson from his gesture, he turned and left.

Outside the basilica, beggars called out to passing pilgrims for alms. Amid the flowers and fountains of the open-air atrium, women in rags, children with wide, hungry eyes, sweaty men whose ratted hair had not been washed in years stretched out their hands to passers-by. Francis reached for a coin before he remembered that his money pouch was now empty. He was dismayed until his eyes rested on an old man who sat on the ground with open hands. *He has nothing either, and no expectations. What must it feel like to be so free?* He approached this man. "Sir," Francis asked, "may I make a bargain with you?"

The man put out his hands to show that he had nothing with which to bargain. Francis nodded and took him by the elbow to a secluded spot in the corner of the garden. There Francis removed his cloak and held it out to the man who accepted it greedily, stroking the soft lining.

Francis said, "For this one day, let us trade places. Take my things and wear them, if I may borrow yours. At the end of the day, we will feast together on the alms bread I have gathered."

The man could not believe what he was hearing. He readily agreed, "Aye, as Your Lordship wishes." Moments later, the beggar wandered into the piazza, self-conscious in his grand attire; Francis followed, dressed in rags.

Francis took the spot near the doors where the old man had been. "*Aumone! Aumone!* Alms! Alms!" he called out in French, loud enough to be heard above the splashing fountains "*Au nom de Dieu!* In the name of God!"

Few people took pity on this new beggar who appeared to be well-fed and groomed, but that did not matter to Francis. Bad luck made his experiment more authentic. For Francis that morning, to be poor and dejected was exhilarating. At the end of the day he shared his moldy crusts and a few coins with the beggar. They drank deeply from the clear cool water of one of the fountains and laughed at the success of their venture. No meal had ever tasted so good to Francis.

Francis left Rome the next day with only one travel bag.

He had given the other bag and half of his clothing to the old beggar. His own soft garments irked him.

Chapter Seven

SWEETNESS AND EXCEEDING JOY

Giordano was nowhere to be found in Assisi. Up till now, Francis had been too absorbed in his own inner turmoil to inquire where his new friend lived or who his family was. Soon after his return from Rome, Francis rode his horse outside the walls of town, hoping to catch sight of Giordano in the countryside where they had often walked together.

These late summer days were hot; sweat dripped down his face and neck. It was mid-afternoon but, in a spirit of penance, he had eaten nothing that day. When a powerful stench met him, he realized he was approaching the leper hospital of San Salvatore delle Pareti. Since everything ugly repelled him—above all, sickness and deformity—this was a place he always avoided. As the stench grew stronger, he crossed to the far side of the road, instinctively covering his nose with his hand. A wave of nausea washed over him. He began to gag and then to vomit into the ditch. Disgusted with himself and weary of his fruitless search, he turned his horse around.

What am I doing? he wondered as he rode back toward Assisi.

He had accomplished nothing that day and had no real goal in mind. Francis began again to reflect on his life, *What have I ever done with myself that was worthwhile?*

"Francis!" the words came to him as if uttered aloud, although there was no sound. "Everything which you have loved and desired in the flesh it is your duty to despise and hate, if you wish to know my will. And when you have begun thus, all that which now seems to you sweet and lovely will become intolerable and bitter, but all which you used to avoid will turn itself to great sweetness and exceeding joy."

Francis did not question the words or where they came from; he knew they were spoken directly to his heart by God. He was overjoyed, though he felt unworthy. He resolved to try to please God more, to deny himself more, and to despise what was not pleasing to God.

Suddenly his horse stopped in its tracks and whinnied. Looking ahead, Francis saw in the pathway the kind of person he loathed most in the world: a wretched, disfigured leper.

His horse shied and Francis recoiled, paralyzed by his revulsion at everything about the man. He considered how to get around him without getting too close and reached for a corner of his cloak to cover his nose and mouth. Then he stopped. Remembering the words he had just been given, he thought, *Shall I turn my back and flee from what I most despise?* He knew the answer and instantly dismounted.

Taking a gold coin in his hand, he approached the beggar whose wounds were wrapped in rags. Putrid flesh oozed from beneath his eyes and what remained of his nose. His lips, too, were half eaten away by disease. Struggling to control his revulsion, Francis lifted the man's hand to place the coin in it. Then, impulsively, he kissed his bloody palm and embraced him. The leper began to weep like a child, shaking from his sobs. All at once, Francis saw beyond his disgust, and realized that here was a suffering human being. He felt a surge of sympathy and love.

When he turned to go, a sweetness such as Francis had never known filled his soul. He mounted his horse and looked back toward the sick man but, to his surprise, the pathway was empty. There was no one to be seen.

"Was that you, Lord?" Francis said under his breath. No answer came, but Francis saw at once that while he had been searching for glory among the great, the most-high God was to be found among the least.

The next day, Francis took a leather pouch bulging with coins to the hospital San Salvatore. He distributed his gold into the outstretched hands of the lepers there, kissing the bloody stumps where their fingers had once been, and helping to bind their wounds in clean bandages. His smile and his gentleness drew them to him. He stayed at the hospital through the day, talking, listening, and embracing each one.

Nearly every day after that Francis visited the suffering men, women and children at the three leper hospitals outside the town, San Salvatore, San Rufino dell'Arce, and San Lazzaro. The priests of the Order of the Holy Cross, "The Crucigers," who ran these hospitals were grateful for his help. He sometimes stayed through the night to offer comfort in the darkest hours.

In his care for the lepers, Francis discovered joy for the first time. He knew that this mercy sprang not from himself but from God. It was an undeserved gift that drew him toward Divine goodness and away from his former self. His longing for God intensified, but so did his self-loathing. Between visits with the lepers, he took long walks alone in the woods, retreating into caves to plead with God for guidance. He never found his friend, Giordano, again, so he opened up his heart to God alone.

One morning, Francis was passing the chapel of San Damiano where he had spent the night of his return from Foligno without a squire, or horse, or honor. He decided to go inside the empty church again to pray. Its heavy door scraped the uneven floor behind him as it shut out the bright light of day. He walked slowly toward the front where one small lamp burned beside the altar. Since he was alone, he fell to his knees in front of the faded old cross that hung from the ceiling. He sighed and then groaned aloud. The sound echoed off the bare walls.

How his heart ached. It was nearly two years since he had left the dungeons of Perugia. His health had returned and his visible wounds had healed. Even the scars were fading. He knew now that God had not abandoned him, God had led him to the lepers. Nevertheless, deep within him there were still wounds that would not heal. He was unclean, like the lepers, but his disease was in his soul. He wondered what was wrong with him. His soul was restless, consumed with longing, but he did not know what he longed for. He clenched his fists and tears smarted in his eyes.

Once he had been certain that he was meant for great things; achievements that would make everyone in Assisi stand up and admire Francesco di Pietro di Bernardone. How meaningless that seemed now.

He remembered his strange dream about the armor; he had thought then that it confirmed his ambitions, but he'd ignored the bold red crosses that were so prominent. The cross is a symbol of suffering—why had he not considered that? He remembered, too, his peculiar sickness at Spoleto that prevented him from going to the war in Apulia. And what about the voice he had heard through his fever? "Follow the master, not the vassal," it had said. Even this he had thought, in his vanity, was a portent of glory. How blind he had been. He had continued to serve the vassal, and not the Lord!

"*Idiota!*" his father would say, and he would be right.

Perhaps God had wanted something of him once but had forsaken him because he was too much of an "*idiota.*" God must love the lepers more than He could love Francis. They had learned humility through their suffering, whereas he was nothing but a wastrel. To serve the Lord and to be loved by Him was all Francis wanted now, but it seemed impossible.

On the verge of despair, Francis threw himself flat on the floor of the empty church, his face against the ground. He felt as worthless as the dirt beneath him. He looked up pleadingly at the image of Christ on the crucifix.

"Great and glorious God, my Lord Jesus Christ!" Francis whispered, "I implore you to enlighten me. Disperse the darkness of my soul! Grant me, Lord, to know you so well that in all things I may act by your light, and in accordance with your holy will!"

Raising himself onto his knees, he searched the eyes of the painted Christ for help.

He saw a light in those eyes that he had not noticed before. It was something like the reflection of a distant candle, but the only candle in the church burned behind the cross. While he wondered at this, it seemed that the light grew, the eyes became clearer and brighter. The figure nailed to the cross took on full human size and shape. It was no longer a flat, dull image, but a vivid, suffering, human being. Blood ran down the face of Christ in streaks from the thorns that pierced his forehead. Although torment marked his features, his eyes did not convey bitterness or betrayal, but peace. The flesh and blood Christ, in the midst of his agony, looked at Francis and Francis knew that his soul lay bare before God Almighty. Nonetheless, the Lord looked at him with love. Francis returned that look of love with love.

"Francis," the Lord spoke to him, "Go and build up My house, which, as you can see, is falling into ruin." In spite of his agony, the voice of Christ was kind and commanding. It was irresistible. Three times the Lord spoke these words to Francis, whose own eyes streamed with tears.

Francis knew now beyond any doubt that Jesus loved him. He would do whatever the Lord asked of him. He would live for him! He would willingly die for him! And yes, he would build up this church, and every other church he could find that needed repair, if that was what the Lord commanded. He would do it joyfully and he would act at once.

A draft of wind made Francis shiver. The image was gone, the cross was flat and dull once more. Francis turned and looked about him as if for the first time. He noticed cracks in the wall where the aging mortar had crumbled, yellow stains on the paint, and a thick layer of dirt on the window sills. It was like his own soul, he thought, soiled and broken. But the merciful Lord had deigned to look down upon him from the cross and ask his service. His soul was flooded with joy.

He would set to work immediately to rebuild this church. It appalled him, now that he thought of it, that the house built to honor the Lord was in such a state of neglect. It looked as though it might collapse at any moment. Here Jesus was ever present, waiting for souls to come to Him. Such a gracious God and King ought to have a suitable dwelling place. Francis would do whatever he could to restore it.

Rising at last, Francis ran out into the churchyard. Don Peter, the chaplain of San Damiano, had just settled onto a bench with his breviary in the morning sunshine. Francis pressed a pile of coins into the old priest's hand.

"Don Peter," Francis spoke urgently, "please, place a lamp before the cross that hangs inside, and use this offering to buy oil." Without waiting for an answer, Francis hurried back to Assisi. Old Don Peter shook his head at the wild Assisi youth who always seemed to be in a hurry to do everything.

For the first time in most of a year, Francis entered his father's shop. He knew Pietro was still away on a business trip, so he did not bother to explain himself to anyone and no one questioned him. He gathered up as much as he could carry of the costly silk damasks, Egyptian cottons, and brightly dyed brocades. He heaped them onto his father's pack horse that stood sheltered behind the shop. Then Francis hurried off to Foligno. He knew exactly which shopkeepers would be interested in his merchandise. Within a couple of hours, all the fabric was sold. He even found a buyer for his father's sturdy pack horse.

By the end of that same day, Francis was back at San Damiano. Don Peter was surprised to see him again so soon. He was even more startled when Francis held out to him a leather purse bursting with gold coins.

"I won't accept that," the old priest said firmly.

Francis was taken aback. "But it is for the repair of the church," he explained, "which, as you can see, is falling into ruin!"

"I won't take your money. I don't know where it comes from, and I don't know what your father would say . . . I'm quite sure he would not like it."

"Don Peter," Francis explained, "I just sold a horse, and some cloth. My father can easily spare them. The money will be put to good use here."

"Keep your money, I will have nothing to do with it," Don Peter said. He stood up and walked toward the church. Pausing in the doorway he said, "If you want to repair the church, try a little old-fashioned toil and sweat. It might do you good."

Francis laughed aloud. Tossing the pouch full of gold on a windowsill, he shook Don Peter's hand, smiling at the old priest like a child who has been given a gift. He said he would set to work at once.

He began to clean the interior of the church and to assess the extent of its decay. He worked until dark, removing debris, dusting, sweeping, and patching what he could. Then he knelt down before the cross, repeating aloud a prayer that sprang from his heart. "I adore you, Lord Jesus Christ, here and in all your churches in the whole world, and I bless you, because by your holy cross you have redeemed the world." He did not move for a long time.

Finally, Don Peter left a blanket on the floor beside Francis and went to bed. The next morning, he found the young man at work again.

After a couple of weeks, the church was clean inside and out. Francis knew that he would have to obtain masonry supplies and rocks to repair the structure, but he was hesitant to go back into Assisi. His father would surely be back from his business trip by this time and Francis had a growing apprehension that he might be angry about the sale of the cloth and horse.

Francis tried to reassure himself that his father had always allowed him the use of anything he wanted. True, he had taken the very best cloth from the shop, and he had sold his father's favorite pack horse. Francis recalled now how proud his father had been of that horse; he would surely miss it. Francis had taken the cloth and horse for a good reason; the house of the

Lord must be rebuilt. Jesus himself had commanded it! At the same time, he doubted that his father would see it that way.

When Don Peter reported to Francis that his father was organizing a search party, Francis asked to clear out a pit in a dark corner of the cellar beneath the priest's house. There he hid, not daring to come out. Don Peter had heard rumors about Pietro's temper, and did what he could to help. He brought food and warm blankets to Francis and promised to reveal nothing of his whereabouts should anyone inquire.

For a month Francis lived in the cellar in fear, begging God for help. All the while, the thought of the crumbling church nagged him. Gradually he realized that if God had asked him to do something, he should behave like a faithful servant and do it. It was cowardly to hide. He decided to leave the cellar and go back into Assisi to gather building supplies, but he would go discreetly.

He first went to his home during the middle of the night to get his money and another tunic. Then, as soon as the shops opened for the day, he purchased what building supplies he could afford. His money was quickly spent, so he had to ask the stone mason's apprentice to give him some cast-off stones out of charity, for the repair of the church.

Before the morning was far advanced, Francis hurried back to San Damiano and set to work. Don Peter's respect for Francis grew from that day on. He welcomed him to his table and made a place for him to sleep in the corner of the church. Over the next few weeks, Francis returned to Assisi when he had to, but avoided drawing attention to himself while he did errands in exchange for goods or begged for good-will donations from the vendors in town.

Chapter Eight

HERALD OF THE GREAT KING

Pietro sat brooding by the fireplace, shifting with annoyance whenever Pica moved past him to skirt the table or remove a pot from the fire. Once their meal was ready, Pietro turned to the table. Angelo took his seat along one side; Dona Pica sat directly across from Pietro at the opposite end. Silence followed the customary mealtime prayer of thanks. Silence was better than angry words. Dona Pica hoped it would last. Angelo quickly ate and skulked out the door. Pietro hardly noticed.

"Where is Francis?" Pietro asked finally.

That was the question that burned within her. Where was her poor son? He had come home only one time in recent weeks, late at night. By the next morning, he was already gone. Gone before sunrise! Where *was* Francis? She wished she knew.

"I don't know," Dona Pica answered frankly. Pietro seemed as if he were ready to explode. She braced herself. When he noticed a tear slip down her cheek, he was irritated further. He shoved his dish aside, got up from the table, and walked out, leaving her alone with her thoughts.

Pietro's emotions were turbulent. His handsome, clever son had trampled the family honor, wounding Pietro's pride and, if truth be told, his heart. Of one thing Pietro was sure, the scoundrel must be stopped.

In this frame of mind Pietro went back to his shop. The brisk business of the cloth trade gave his taut nerves a respite. He was shaking hands with a customer at the conclusion of a transaction when a commotion arose in the Piazza del Mercato outside. Pietro ignored the hubbub until he thought he heard his name shouted two or three times from someone in the crowd. He went to the shop door to listen. It was not "Pietro" he had heard, it was "di Pietro." The son of Pietro di Bernardone! Scanning the fray apprehensively, his eyes lighted on an unkempt beggar who was the object of the crowd's contempt. Surely that was not Francis? When a rock, pelted from somewhere, struck the beggar, Pietro recognized by his gesture that this "*pazzo*," this crazy man, was his son, his own Francesco.

A wave of shame swept over Pietro. Shame! When he had worked all his life to earn respect. It was insupportable! He stormed into the throng, shoving and swinging at everyone in his path until he reached Francis. What now? Pietro did not take long to reflect. Francis turned to face his father and, incredibly, the emaciated young man—the object of all this scorn and derision—smiled at him. It was more than Pietro could endure. Without pausing to think, Pietro swung out and struck his son full in the face. Francis reeled, his nose spurting blood. The smile was gone but the expression of patient suffering that replaced it was even harder for Pietro to tolerate, after all Francis had put him through.

The burly father grabbed his son by the back of the neck, shook him like a limp puppet and dragged him past the subdued townspeople. No one laughed anymore. The crowd broke up. Only a chastened murmur could be heard in the Piazza del Mercato.

Pica gasped when Pietro threw open the door. Without any explanation her husband slammed his victim up against the dining table, kicking him soundly in the shins. Then, not knowing what else to do and unwilling to let go of his captive, he picked him up by the collar and slapped him repeatedly across the face. "*Idiota! Idiota! Idiota!*" he screamed. Pietro dragged Francis beyond the room and shoved him down a small flight of steps that led to the cellar where food and wine were kept cool and locked.

"The keys!" Pietro shouted. Within an instant, the steward was at his side with the keys to the cellar. Pietro locked the iron gate of the pantry. "What were you thinking?" he shouted as though his son were hard of hearing. "What did you hope to accomplish by stealing my cloth and taking my horse? Where have you been hiding? And what in God's name have you done to yourself? You look like a raving lunatic!"

Pietro did not stop shouting long enough to hear an answer to his questions; he was beside himself. The iron bars served to protect Francis from his father's fists as much as they did to confine him. At last, Pietro marched to the top of the steps. Looking back at his son, he slammed his large hand against the wall and, through his teeth he snarled, "I am too angry to reason with you. We will talk later—much later—after you have learned your lesson."

Dona Pica wept. "You are not to approach the boy," Pietro admonished his wife. "I will teach him a lesson he will never forget, as we should have done long ago."

Days passed in which the Bernardone household functioned as if nothing were out of the ordinary. Neither Pietro nor Angelo paid a visit to Francis in his captivity; they did not even mention his name. The steward had been instructed to sustain the prisoner on bread and water, nothing more.

Pica's maternal heart might have been destroyed by this fiasco, but for one small detail that had not escaped her. While Francis was enduring blow after outraged blow from his father, Pica noticed a look in his eyes that took her by surprise. There was no anger, nor did he have the look of a madman. What she saw was a look of peace—impossible though it seemed—and of strength that went deeper than Pietro's brute force could reach. Although everything was terribly wrong on the outside, she believed that deep inside her son, they were not so amiss. In that belief, she took comfort, and she clung to it as to a life-saving rope.

After almost a week of acting as jail keeper to his son, Pietro grew restless. He welcomed the excuse to leave home for a few days to conclude a business deal in Perugia. Several hours lapsed on the morning of his departure before Dona Pica felt it was safe to enter the cellar. Angelo was managing the shop that day; the sympathetic servants turned a blind eye.

Dona Pica spoke briefly with Francis. He apologized for causing her distress and he assured her that he was more well than he had ever been before. Satisfied that her son was sane and in fact at peace, she pressed some money into his hand along with a small package of food and released him from his prison. He hugged her for the last time and was gone.

When Pietro returned the next week and found the cellar empty, Dona Pica received the brunt of his wrath. She accepted his abusive words with dignity, and the bruises she received would soon heal, even if they left deep scars on her heart. She found strength in the knowledge that her son had discovered a source of true peace.

Pietro was irate. He had turned himself against his errant son, so his heart no longer ached, but he feared another danger from the madman he believed Francis had become. There was a risk of losing his livelihood to Francis. By law, Pica's entire dowry would necessarily pass to her sons in the event of her death. As her husband, Pietro, had only a lifetime interest in the money that formed the basis of his wealth. His successful cloth business and his array of properties were tied up in that dowry. Francis, in his present irrational state, would surely squander his inheritance, or worse, give it to the lepers and beggars among whom he now lived. Pietro's business would be destroyed; the fruit of all his labors, wiped out. Refusing to let that happen, Pietro decided to disinherit Francis at once.

He discovered that Francis was staying with Don Peter at the old San Damiano Church. He went directly there, accompanied by his lawyers, to try to reason with his Francis. Father and son stood face-to-face in front of the church with only a few yards of earth between them, but they might as well have been on opposite sides of an ocean. They could not understand one another.

"If it is money you are anxious about, Father," Francis offered, "every penny from the sale of the cloth and horse are here." Francis indicated the windowsill where the pouch full of gold remained untouched.

Pietro stepped forward and snatched the purse. Attaching it to his belt, he explained, "My primary concern is not this paltry sum, but the entire livelihood of our family. I want to keep it from falling into inept hands. Can't you understand?"

Francis said, "I no longer want any of your money. Bishop Guido has explained to me that I was wrong to take the cloth and horse. I am sorry. I intended it for a sacred purpose, but I know now that I was wrong."

Pietro's frustration boiled. "I care little about the proceeds of one transaction, Francesco. It is the inheritance that concerns me. It will one day be in your hands according to the law, and I have no confidence that you will manage it wisely. We must come to an agreement."

"I know, Father, I am an idiot. I have no desire to manage any money."

"You misunderstand the point, Francis." His father's voice shook with rage.

Rather than lose his temper again, Pietro turned and strode away, accompanied by his lawyers. Francis stood alone in the churchyard. Don Peter, watching from inside the garden wall, saw silent tears stream down the young man's face as his father's figure disappeared. After some minutes, Francis retreated to his customary refuge inside the church. The old priest set out for the bishop's palace in Assisi to apprise Bishop Guido of the situation.

A few days later, a bailiff appeared at San Damiano with a small armed guard. Francis was ordered to appear before the tribunal of the city of Assisi. His father intended to have him disinherited, the bailiff announced, on the grounds of mental incompetence. Francis received the summons with unexpected calm.

"I will not come with you," Francis declared. Glancing at Don Peter, who nodded encouragement, he explained, "I have been advised that the civil law of Assisi has no ecclesiastical jurisdiction over me. I have taken religious orders under my Lord Bishop Guido, and am now a servant of the most-high God alone. I am under the protection of His holy Church."

According to the law, the bailiff could do nothing but acquiesce. He returned empty handed to Pietro, who was waiting with the town magistrates at City Hall. Since his livelihood was at stake, Pietro went directly to the Bishop's palace on the Piazza del Vescovado. Bishop Guido was an ecclesiastical judge and Pietro's last legal recourse.

Later in the week, Don Peter beckoned to Francis to come down from the church roof where he was replacing broken tiles.

"Francis," Don Peter said, looking worried, "Bishop Guido has summoned you to appear before him to answer your father formally."

Francis wiped the sweat from his forehead and stared at Don Peter. "Bishop Guido is a true father of souls and he has been like a father to me. He would not summon me without good purpose. It will be a relief to put this matter to rest so that I may begin my service in earnest to God Almighty." Don Peter wondered at the young man's calm demeanor as he accompanied him to the Piazza del Vescovado. What took place that day, he would never forget.

A crowd of friends, neighbors, and curious onlookers had gathered outside the palace. Inside the walls, Bishop Guido sat in full regalia on a dais. Dona Pica stood nearby, expressionless and pale, with Angelo at her side. Nofra and Pasquale stood next to her in support. A few other men and women were in attendance in the room whom Don Peter did not know; perhaps they were relatives or concerned friends. Pietro himself stood importantly on the bishop's right side with a knot of lawyers behind him.

When Francis stepped onto the dais, he carried a look of dignity despite his smallness. His face showed no trace of fear or hesitation. He knelt before Bishop Guido to kiss his episcopal ring, then he took a place on the bishop's left side.

Pietro stated his case briefly. There was nothing new in what he said. Bishop Guido listened, then turned to Francis. "My son, I advise you to renounce any claim on your family's monetary holdings. You would then be free to serve God alone."

Francis removed his velvet cape, his tunic and, finally, his breeches. Clad only in a rough penitential hair shirt of his own making, Francis placed the pile of clothing and a small leather purse at his father's feet. He gave his father a look of forgiveness so genuine that it unsettled Pietro. Then Francis turned to Bishop Guido and said, "Until now I have called Pietro di Bernardone my father. But, because I have proposed to serve God, I return to him the money on account of which he was so upset, and also all the clothing which is his, so that I can truly say, from now on, 'Our Father who art in heaven,' and not, 'My father, Pietro di Bernardone.'"

Pietro turned scarlet. Bishop Guido arose and placed his own white mantle ceremoniously across Francis's bare narrow shoulders to attest that Francis was a penitential son of Holy Mother Church from that day forward. The bishop then took Francis under his arm and blessed him with a sign of the cross.

Without saying a word, Pietro picked up the coins and costly garments at his feet and walked out. Dona Pica looked tenderly at her son for the last time before leaving to join her husband. Angelo trailed behind his parents, his eyes firmly fixed on the ground in humiliation.

Bishop Guido whispered to his secretary, who had been recording the exchange. The man went out and soon returned with a small bundle which the bishop held out to Francis. "Here, take this, Francis. It is a spare tunic that the gardener left behind some years ago. Put it on before you go."

Once he had put on the tunic, Francis knelt again before Bishop Guido. His heart beat wildly, jubilantly, as Bishop Guido blessed him.

"Go forth now, my son. For you are free to serve God alone through His holy Church as a penitent, and by your life to be a herald of the Gospel, unfettered by any worldly attachment."

When evening closed on that momentous day, the home of his youth shrank from view as the new penitent made his way into the forest behind Assisi. He sang French songs and danced in lighthearted relief. He was a true son of God now, a "herald of the Gospel." That is what Bishop Guido had called him. He was, in truth, a herald for the Great High King, the Lord God. Francis had no place to go, and no plan, but he had never before known such happiness.

"What the hell are you doing?" Francis was startled by a gruff voice. Two men had appeared and blocked his path. Thieves and murderers were not uncommon in the forests of Mount Subasio. He knew he should be afraid, but he was not.

"I am a herald of the Great King!" he exclaimed, directing their attention to a rustic cross that he had traced with a piece of chalk on the back of his gardener's tunic.

"Oh! Excuse me!" mocked one of the men, bowing.

Laughing, the two men seized Francis, stripped off his tunic to search for money, then ripped the homemade hair shirt from his body, tearing it to shreds and grinding it into the dirt. They punched their unresisting victim over and over, until, swinging him by his arms and feet, they dumped him into a ravine, thick with icy mud.

"Next time bring the 'great king's' purse with you, herald," one of the men advised between curses. The men disappeared back into a thicket of trees.

With difficulty Francis struggled out of the ravine. His limbs were badly bruised, he tasted blood on his lip, the night wind chilled his wet body to the bone, and he had no clothing left to protect him from it. He stumbled on fearlessly through the dark forest. He could no longer dance because of the pain in his legs, but he resumed his singing through chattering teeth.

At last, beyond a copse of beech trees he noticed a light on a low hill. As he drew closer, he recognized the cultivated lands and high stone wall of Vallingegno Abbey. He knew he was only a few miles south of Gubbio now. Two torches on either side of the arched doorway burned in welcome to travelers, and he recalled the Benedictine rule of hospitality, that every stranger should be treated as Christ. He took courage and approached the door, bleeding, shaking with cold, and completely naked.

"Who are you? What do you want?" Francis was surprised by the abrupt tone of the almoner who squinted into the darkness. "We don't want your kind here. Go back into the forest! Begone!"

"Please, servant of Christ," Francis begged, "I am cold and very hungry. I have had nothing to eat today. I was beset by robbers outside of Assisi who beat me and left me for dead. Could I come in to warm myself by the fire and perhaps have something to eat?"

The monk let him in reluctantly and allowed him to sleep in a corner on the floor. Francis remained at the abbey for several days while his body healed, doing menial jobs to earn his bread, a rough tunic, and the niche in the scullery to sleep. It was clear to him, though, that he was not wanted there. He soon took his leave to live among the lepers at the hospital of Gubbio. He did not remain there long either, however, because he could not forget the command that Christ had given him. Within a few weeks, he was back on the road to Assisi, to rebuild the church of San Damiano.

"Back again?" Don Peter stepped out of his small living quarters adjacent to the church. He had grown fond of Francis during his stay at San Damiano, but he was a little apprehensive after his dramatic departure.

"Dear Father, I must rebuild the church," Francis explained simply.

"Oh, yes. Of course." Don Peter gave a shrug. The old priest took out his keys and let Francis in the church. Francis fell to his knees in front of the faded old crucifix once more. He felt he was home at last.

He turned to the tabernacle and whispered as to a friend, "In your great mercy, you led me to the lepers and I had mercy on them. You spoke to me from the crucifix and you changed my life forever. You are present now, dear Lord, in this church and in every church throughout the world, awaiting every willing soul, to sanctify it, to change it forever, to transform it with your love. What infinite love! What divine mercy!"

Don Peter walked out of the church, ashamed of the coolness of his own heart.

Chapter Nine

REBUILD MY HOUSE

"**A**lms! Give alms in the name of God!"

Francis wasted no time once he was back in Assisi. When the first shops opened their shutters the next day, he was standing in the center of the Piazza del Mercato. Although he was poorly dressed and thin from fasting, Francis called out in a cheerful voice, "The Church of San Damiano is in need of repair! People of Assisi, do not rest comfortably in your own houses when the house of God has fallen into ruin!"

He offered his hearers a deal. "If you give me a stone, God will give you a reward! If you give me two stones, God will reward you twice!"

A few people stopped what they were doing to listen.

"Whoever gives me three stones will have three times the reward! For you know that God will not be outdone in generosity!"

Most of the townspeople ignored him, convinced that this disinherited son of the cloth merchant had lost his mind. Some kept their distance out of fear of his father, whose temper was notorious by this time. But a few heard his pleas and came forward with money, lime, tools, or stones to help restore the old church. Beggars with nothing to lose offered to help Francis haul the supplies back to San Damiano.

On the way, they passed a yard filled with stones for sale. Francis decided to ask the owner for a donation, in the name of God. The owner, he soon discovered, was Father Sylvester, the old don from San Giorgio school. Father Sylvester did not smile when he recognized his former pupil.

"Don Sylvester!" Francis approached him with his hand extended but the older man ignored the outstretched hand. Unabashed, Francis made his request, "I have need of many stones for the repair of the Church of San Damiano, which has been sadly neglected these many years."

Father Sylvester squinted. "What is that to me?"

"You seem to be blessed with an abundance of stones!" Francis answered. "Would you share them—for the good of your soul and for love of our Lord, who humbles himself to dwell in houses made by human hands?"

"Don't preach to me, you simpleton!" was the elderly priest's reply. Then, on second thought, he asked, "How much can you pay for my stones?"

"I have nothing, but God will surely reward you!" Francis said.

"He who has nothing, gets nothing!" the old don retorted. He turned away.

"Wait, Father!" Francis persisted, "I will gladly pay you with alms as I earn them. Please, accept my word and my hand."

Old Father Sylvester spat very near to Francis's open hand. "If I let you take them on credit, I will have to charge double their worth to compensate for the risk."

"May God reward you, Father Sylvester," Francis answered lightly. He gathered as many stones as he could haul in a makeshift cart while the priest recorded in his ledger the exact quantity and size of the stones. Francis said he would come back for more once he was able to pay for these.

After a few months, the old church of San Damiano looked like a new church. Outside, the stones formed even rows outlined with fresh mortar. Inside, the red, brown, and deep blue paint in the vaulted ceiling was vivid once more. Light streamed in through the rose window above the door, illuminating the byzantine crucifix and the polished tabernacle in the sanctuary.

Don Peter was impressed by the quality of the workmanship and even more by Francis's ability to recruit helpers and to acquire needed supplies. The young man's zeal never flagged.

"There is only one thing more to be done before my task here is finished," Francis told Don Peter after dinner one evening. "The lamp that hangs in front of the crucifix is nearly empty and must be filled. I am going into town to beg for more oil."

"It is almost sunset, Francis. You have worked all day and I doubt you slept more than a couple of hours last night. You need rest. Go in the morning instead," the old priest suggested.

"I'm sure I couldn't sleep, Don Peter. Do you remember

when Our Lord asked his disciples to watch with Him just one hour? He said, 'My soul is sorrowful even to death.' Think of that sorrow, Don Peter! And think of His terrible loneliness in that hour."

Remembering his vision of Christ on the cross, Francis told Don Peter, "With a little oil in the lamp, I will be able to watch at least one hour with Him."

Darkness had settled by the time Francis reached the town. Just inside the gates, the prominent Bacani mansion was ablaze with lights; music poured out its windows. Obviously, a banquet was being held there. Hopeful that lamp oil would be abundant on such an occasion, Francis walked toward the house.

He stopped short when he realized that the laughter he heard was not coming from inside the house, but from some men who were playing a game of chance outside. The group was directly between himself and the door. As his eyes adjusted to the torchlight, Francis began to recognize faces. The eldest Bacani son stood alongside the two nephews of Baron Veniero, Antonino, and Collino. Standing a little apart with a cup of wine in his hand was Bernardo, whom he had not seen since the terrible uprising in 1198. Francis's heart leapt when he saw his old friend still alive and well.

Francis stood fixed to the ground, grateful for the darkness that hid him. What was he to do? His old acquaintances would undoubtedly ridicule him. In his mind he saw how he would appear to them: ragged, skinny, and absurd in his rough tunic marked on the back with a chalk cross. *They will say I am crazy*, he thought.

Francis turned to walk away quietly. Before he had taken two steps, a voice spoke in his heart, "Francis, is it pride that makes you run away?" The answer, he realized instantly, was yes. And he knew that he must not give in to his selfish pride. Francis took a deep breath, turned and walked straight up to the boisterous group.

"*Bonsoir, mes amis,*" said Francis in French, trying to sound convincingly lighthearted. "For the love of God, would you gentlemen have some oil to spare so that the lamp may continue to burn brightly before our Lord in the Church of San Damiano?"

"Well, well, well," exclaimed one of the young men, "look who has come to us this evening, *mes amis*. It is Assisi's own crazy man!" To Francis he said, "Hey, *pazzo*, what brings you here? Will you entertain us with a chanson or a story in exchange for alms?" A few of the men chuckled.

Francis did not flinch. As if they were sharing a private joke, he placed a genial hand on the young man's shoulder. "Yes," he said, "I will entertain you with not one but two stories of love and glory."

The music stopped and the door of the manor opened. Francis noticed people listening in the doorway. He began, "The first story is about a fool from Assisi, who sought glory for himself and a lady worthy of his love. His quest took him far from the mark into darkness and near despair. When he thought there was no hope left, a noble Lady showed him a new path to travel. She lighted the way and led him along it. In her service, he found glory at last and love without end and, '*Sagement e bien s'entr'amerent,*' 'Wisely and well they loved.'" He finished with a line from a popular French poem.

"The second story is about the Lord, who loved without limit and sacrificed his own glory to make a path for anyone to travel who seeks love and glory. The second story, I think you have all heard before. This man, although he was God, sacrificed his glory to become one of us, in poverty he lived and in humility he died so that each of us might share in his love without end. There is no love greater than this, and no greater glory."

"Francis," said Bernardo seriously, "who is your Lady?"

"Ah, Bernardo, you recognize the fool in my first story because you knew me well!" Francis smiled. "The Lady I serve now is Holy Poverty, maid servant of the Most-High King! By letting go of everything that I called my own in this world, my heart has been made free to love God alone and I have found peace, Bernardo, such as I have never known before."

Lord Bacani, who had been listening at the open door, invited Francis in. The group from the courtyard followed him into the banquet hall. Standing at the front of the room filled with curious guests, Francis asked simply, "Can you spare some oil for the lamp that burns before Our Lord at the Church of San Damiano?"

"Give the man some oil," the gracious host ordered. One of the servants went out and returned with a vessel full of oil. Francis took it gratefully.

"Here is a small offering, Francesco di Bernardone," came the voice of a woman in the back of the room. "I know what fine work you have done to repair San Damiano." She passed a few coins toward him in a leather pouch. Soon other guests added to it until it could hold no more. His old friend, Antonino, placed a loaf of bread under his arm.

"God bless you!" Francis said to the host and his guests. "Thank you for your generosity to Almighty God. A few moments ago, I stood outside the house afraid to speak to you about Our Father in heaven," he admitted. "Out of pride, I was afraid that you would ridicule me. But God is gracious and has rewarded me with your kindness. By emptying yourselves for His sake, your own emptiness will surely be filled!"

Late into that night, the lamp in the sanctuary of San Damiano was reflected in the dark eyes of the fool from Assisi who watched more than one hour with his Lord kneeling beneath the cross with hands outstretched and face uplifted in thanksgiving.

The next morning Francis was back in Assisi. Now that San Damiano was restored, he intended to seek work as a journeyman, offering manual labor in exchange not for money, but for altar bread and wine, new linens for the church, fitting vestments for Don Peter, and food to eat so that Don Peter would not have to provide for him.

Before beginning his search for work, Francis attended the first Mass of the day at the Church of San Nicolò di Piazza, near his family's home. After Mass, while still kneeling in the church, Francis became aware of someone snickering behind him. He turned around and a smile of recognition lit up his features. His own brother, Angelo, stood inside the doorway, pointing him out to someone. Francis got up to greet him, but when he was closer, he heard what Angelo was saying.

"There is Francis! Why don't you ask him if he will take a penny for an ounce of his sweat?"

The smile faded from Francis's face. "Angelo," he returned in a low voice, "I am afraid you are too late. I have already sold it at a much higher price than that to the Great High King, the Lord God!"

Angelo rolled his eyes and stepped aside to let his brother pass through the doorway. Outside the church, Francis saw his father a few paces ahead, waiting for Angelo. When Pietro's glance fell on his two sons, side by side, the contrast between the well-fed, self-satisfied younger son and his shabby, emaciated, firstborn son filled him with new shame. His wounded pride and a host of bitter memories surged up within him. Angelo shrank from sight when he saw his father's look.

"How dare you show yourself here," Pietro snarled at Francis. "Curses on you! Curses! Curses! Curses!" Losing control of himself, Pietro began to shout. He pointed at Francis as if he were a demon from hell.

For a moment, Francis lost his composure. "Oh please, Father, please do not curse me," he begged.

Pietro was too angry to hear; foul words spilled from his mouth while Francis cringed and people began to gather near the spectacle. Francis noticed the old beggar, Albert, amid the crowd.

"Albert," Francis called to him. "Please bless me."

Pietro stared when Francis knelt down on the ground. Albert came forward uncertainly and made a sign of the cross over Francis. "Thank you, Albert," Francis said as he got up.

Pietro spoke through clenched teeth. "May you be damned forever for what you have done."

Francis turned white. "No, Father, don't say that," he pleaded, but Pietro did not subside.

"Look at you! You have become a buffoon, an idiot, a *pazzo* to shame your family name. I curse you!"

"Albert?" Francis knelt down again.

Albert stepped forward. "I bless you, Francesco," he said, and made a sign of the cross over his head again.

"There, you see," Francis said to Pietro when he stood up, "God has given me a father to bless me in place of you, who curse me."

Pietro was rendered mute by his fury. Angelo stepped out from around a corner to join his father and the two walked away to the shop together. Oblivious to the laughter and back slapping going on around him, Francis watched them walk away. The old beggar gave Francis a look of sympathy.

"Albert," said Francis, "Will you remain with me for a few days so that whenever my father looks like he is going to curse me, you may bless me as you did today? I will see that you have plenty of food and a place to sleep in exchange."

Albert agreed. He stayed close at hand all that day and for many days after while Francis worked at menial tasks around town. The two were constantly together. At first, Pietro could not meet his son on the streets of Assisi without cursing him.

Eventually, however, it became so ludicrous to see the old beggar appear each time and bless Francis, that Pietro found it less embarrassing to simply avoid his son.

Not long after this, Francis had the idea to restore another church. If the Lord had wanted one church repaired, surely He would be pleased to have more. San Damiano, in its immaculate condition, was attracting visitors so that Don Peter was kept quite busy saying more masses, hearing confessions, and celebrating baptisms and weddings in the picturesque chapel.

San Pietro della Spina, another small country church, had fallen into disuse. It was located near some of Pietro's land holdings northwest of town. Francis had often visited it with his father when he was a child.

Once Francis began the work of restoring San Pietro, anyone passing by in the daytime could hear him singing ballads from the roof top while he replaced broken tiles and supporting beams. Between songs, he called out orders to his crew of volunteers, or invited passers-by to lend a hand in the name of God. When he needed more stones, he went with Albert into town to work or beg for money to exchange for stones from Father Sylvester.

The novelty of the profligate-turned-penitent began to wear off in Assisi, so that Francis ceased to attract attention. He continued to visit the lepers every morning after first attending Mass. From the hospital he went into Assisi to work in exchange for his meals and building supplies. He devoted the rest of each day to restoring the little country church. When darkness fell, he returned to San Damiano to spend an hour or more on his knees with the Lord.

Impressed by his life of voluntary poverty and humility, people began to listen to his simple pious reflections as he worked beside them, or knocked on doors to ask for alms. He did not seem to preach, exactly, but simply to share the joy he had found in his new life dedicated to Christ. And something about this intrigued them.

Chapter Ten

THIS IS WHAT I SEEK

Within a few months, the church of San Pietro was restored and local priests began offering Mass there. Francis turned his attention next to the ruins of a church he found buried in the woods near the leprosarium of San Salvatore.

He discovered that this church, called Saint Mary of the Angels, had been built a thousand years before by penitents on a pilgrimage. Centuries later, it was given as a gift to Saint Benedict along with the small surrounding plot of land, and now it was the property of the nearby Benedictines of Mount Subasio. They referred to it simply as "the Portiuncula," the little portion of land.

Francis spent most of the year 1207 repairing the church of Saint Mary of the Angels. He moved into an abandoned shepherd's hut on the property, and gradually restored the crumbling walls inside and out. The steeple on the rooftop assumed a new dignity when the sunlight glanced off the shining cross at its pinnacle.

At the end of February, 1208, Don Peter came to the Portiuncula to offer the first Mass. Francis almost danced with joy as he accompanied Father Peter from San Damiano. It was a laborious three miles for the elderly priest in the dead of winter, but Don Peter made it gladly because, as always, Francis's enthusiasm was infectious.

They arrived to find a small congregation already gathered. There were beggars and day laborers who had been helping Francis restore the church, along with a few curious patrons. Francis led them in and everyone knelt on the ground. All was hushed and reverent in the little church.

When Don Peter read the tenth chapter of the Gospel of Saint Matthew for the Feast of Saint Matthias, Francis felt his heart suddenly burn within him. It seemed the words of Saint Matthew's Gospel addressed him directly. He could almost hear the voice of Christ as He spoke, saying, "'Go then, preach, saying: The kingdom of heaven is at hand. Freely have you received, freely give. Do not possess gold, nor silver, nor money in your purse; nor scrip for you journey, nor two coats, nor shoes, nor a staff; for the workman is worthy of his meat. And into whatsoever city you shall enter, inquire who in it is worthy, and there abide . . . And when you come into the house, salute it, saying: Peace be to this house. And if that house be worthy, your peace shall come upon it; but if it be not worthy, your peace shall return to you.'"

Don Peter noticed that Francis's eyes were shining while he listened. As soon as Mass was over and the others had gone out,

Francis asked Don Peter to read the Gospel one more time. In the empty church, the priest read the words aloud again.

"What does it mean?" Francis asked when he finished. "Help me understand those words that sound so beautiful."

Don Peter explained that with these words Jesus sent out his twelve apostles to teach the whole world about the kingdom of God. "He tells them not to be concerned about their material needs or to fear that they might not know what to say. God will provide what they need, as long as they are doing the Father's work."

"Yes," Francis said, "yes, that is right!" He became excited. "This is what I wish, this is what I seek! This is what I want with all my heart!"

Francis believed that God spoke to him that morning through the Gospel, lifting the veil from the words He had spoken three years before at San Damiano. The house that Jesus wanted Francis to help rebuild was not merely the physical buildings, but the kingdom of God on earth, His Church!

Francis threw off his cloak and shoes. He cut his rough tunic into the form of a cross as a symbol of the cross Christ carried on his shoulders. Discarding his leather belt, he tied a length of cord around his waist to indicate to the world his new role of missionary. Francis was prepared to continue the mission of the apostles, to share the joy of following Christ.

Before many days had passed, Francis was standing in the pulpit of San Giorgio, the church adjoined to his former school. Bishop Guido had asked him to preach there, but Francis wondered if anyone would come to hear the worst student the school had ever taught. As it turned out, many did come—if only to see what had become of Francesco di Bernardone, the unruly son of the cloth merchant—and many stayed to listen.

"God give you peace," Francis began. "The Lord taught me this greeting because it is peace God wants for each of us—deep and lasting peace. I who greet you am nothing, and God is everything. You knew me when I was an arrogant fool living among you. When I was in my sin, God had pity on me," Francis told them. "In his mercy He showed me how to be merciful and then he called me to be his servant."

Francis explained what had happened to him, and that he now lived only for the glory of God. When he finished speaking, he noticed a woman slip out the back door of the church; he thought it was his mother. Every other eye remained fixed on him. Was this not the fool who had wasted his wealth on parties? The braggart who had never won a battle? Assisi's own *pazzo*? Yet, there was something irresistible in his words, something compelling in his manner. He appeared to be transformed, like a man deeply in love, or a child with a delightful secret to share.

Nearly every weekend after that Francis was asked to speak at one of the churches in or near Assisi. His message did not vary much; his heart overflowed with love for God and gratitude for His mercy. He wanted to share the path to God that he had found in penance and detachment from worldly things, and the joy he had come to know.

"Francis?" Someone approached as he walked back to San

Damiano late one evening after preaching in town. Francis quickly recognized his old friend, Bernardo Quintavalle.

"I want to talk to you," Bernardo said. "You must be tired and hungry. Can you come to my home?"

Francis agreed to return with his old friend to the Quintavalle mansion near the Bishop's Palace. Once they were seated at the dining table, Bernardo confided in Francis. "I have many possessions, Francis, but my heart longs for something else." The servants bustled about offering delicacies, but neither of the men ate much. A fire in the fireplace spread a warm glow over the repeating patterns of lapis and gold on the tiled floor. The tapestries gave the room a feeling of grandeur.

"Months ago, when you spoke outside of Lord Bacani's manor about holy poverty, your words stirred something in me. There is no peace and no love to be found in wealth, Francis. I have everything I could want and yet, I am not happy."

This is how God speaks in the heart of a good man, Francis thought, remembering the turbulent years of struggling within his own soul. *Bernardo was never blinded by selfishness and pride as I was.*

Aloud he said, "We must pray, Bernardo, that God will give you peace."

It was late, so Francis stayed at Bernardo's home that night. Bernardo found that he could not sleep; his mind was agitated. *What makes Francis so joyful?* he wondered. *He used to chase after every whim and was never satisfied. Now, he has nothing, and he seems to want nothing. If his joy is genuine, I want to know its cause.*

While Bernardo lay motionless in his bed thinking, he heard Francis stir in the bed across the room. Pretending to be asleep, Bernardo watched his guest through half closed lids.

Believing that Bernardo was asleep, Francis slipped to the floor beside his bed. He turned toward an ivory crucifix that hung on the wall of the bedroom. He began to pray. He was careful at first to muffle his sounds, but soon the grip on his heart was too strong and words began to escape. "My Lord and my God!" he whispered. Then he exclaimed, under his breath. "You alone are great, King of heaven and earth. You are love, wisdom, endurance, and rest." After a long pause, he said, "You alone are peace."

I do not know how it is, but there can be no question that this man is of God, Bernard concluded. Early in the morning, Bernardo roused Francis from his bed.

"Francis," Bernardo said, "I have a question. If a man has been entrusted with property by his master, and after many years he no longer wants the use of it, what should he do in such a case?"

"Give the property back to the master," Francis replied.

"But you see, Francis, the real case is this: Everything I have of earthly property—and there is much—I have received from the hand of Our Lord God. I long with all my heart to return it now. How should I do this?"

Francis said, "We must ask for counsel from the source of all wisdom! Let us go to the church and read in the Book of the Gospels what Our Lord would direct you to do."

When the two stepped out of Bernardo's front door, a man was waiting for them. He looked as though he had been standing outside all night. His hair was disheveled and his cloak was wet with dew, but his face was peaceful. "Peter Catanei?" Francis and Bernardo said together in surprise.

Peter was a canon at the cathedral of San Rufino. He had been present when Francis declared himself a son of God before the bishop. He had seen Francis rebuild the local churches with a zeal that seemed to bring new life to Assisi. He had attended every one of Francis's sermons in the churches of Assisi.

"I want to join you, Francis," he said. "I want to leave the world behind and serve God alone."

Francis showed no surprise, only delight. He invited Peter Catanei to come with them. The three men arrived at the church of San Nicolò an hour before the first Mass of the day. The long-time pastor, Father Rosone, peered around the corner of the sacristy into the dimly lit nave. It was not unusual for one or two pious old women to kneel in the shadows before dawn, unburdening their hearts to God after their night's fretting. Goodness knows, they had much to pray about. If the world is to be saved from its own folly, Father Rosone often mused, it will be through the prayers of those faithful women.

This morning, however, he found the three young men standing in his church. They did not look like ruffians, he decided. At least one was decidedly well dressed. Nobility of some sort, he thought. Since he detected nothing alarming in their manner, he ventured out into the sanctuary. When one of the men cleared his throat, Father Rosone shuffled up to the communion railing.

"I'm a little hard of hearing," he told them in a loud whisper. He leaned closer and, in the candlelight, recognized Francis. "My lad, it is good to see you!" he exclaimed. Francis smiled and introduced his two companions.

Father Rosone greeted the young men, then turned back to Francis. "Ah, your poor mother, Francesco! The good woman has suffered much on your account. You know your father does not bear adversity well."

Francis felt ashamed of his past and, with a new humility that surprised the old priest, he answered, "I know, Father. I have been a miserable son. May God pardon my wickedness and bring consolation to my parents." Then Francis told Father Rosone why they had come.

Francis explained that he had embraced a life of poverty. Now Bernardo and Peter wanted to follow in the same path, but they were unsure how to proceed. "We have no one to instruct us," Francis said. "We want to know what God wants of us and how we are meant to serve Him. Would you help us with the Sacred Scriptures?"

Father Rosone understood. It was a custom among the faithful to consult the Scriptures for counsel or consolation, by opening the missal to random passages and then reflect on their meaning as it bore on their own lives. He led the three men in prayer to beg for the guidance of the Holy Spirit, and then they gathered around the lectern that held the large altar missal. The old priest opened the book arbitrarily and looked at the page.

"The Gospel of Saint Mark, chapter ten, verse twenty-one," he said. He read to them first in Latin, and then in Italian so that they could easily understand it.

"'Go, sell what you have, and give to the poor, and you will have treasure in heaven; and come, follow me.'"

Again, Father Rosone opened the missal arbitrarily. "This is from the Gospel of Saint Luke, chapter nine, verse three," he noted. "It says, 'Take nothing for your journey, no staff, nor bag, nor bread, nor money; and do not have two tunics.'"

A third time Father Rosone opened the book of Sacred Scripture and read aloud. "From the Gospel of Saint Matthew, chapter sixteen, verse twenty-four: 'If anyone would come after me, let him deny himself and take up his cross and follow me.'"

Francis was amazed to hear reiterated in these diverse passages, the same exhortation that he had heard described by Saint Matthew on the Feast of Saint Matthias.

"That is exactly what we shall do!" Francis exclaimed. "We three, and any who come after us. God has made His Will clear. From this day on, these three passages will form our Rule of Life!"

Francis knelt at the feet of this priest who had baptized him twenty-six years earlier and had served most of the spiritual needs of his family. Bernardo and Peter knelt beside Francis. After giving them his blessing, Father Rosone, too, knelt to give thanks to God who had so clearly spoken through the Gospels.

"God give you His peace, Father Rosone," Francis said before he and his companions stepped out into the gray morning. The only sound was the whispered prayers of the pious women at the back of the church.

Chapter Eleven

GOD GAVE ME FOLLOWERS

Peter Catanei went directly to Bishop Guido to resign his post as canon of the cathedral and to announce his intention to join Francis in his life of poverty. "I understand," the bishop said.

When Peter rejoined Bernardo and Francis, they were standing on the steps of the church of San Giorgio in the midst of an excited crowd. He heard someone explain that Bernardo Quintavalle had fallen under the spell of Francesco di Bernardone and was giving away all his money and possessions.

"All the better for me!" an old woman tittered as she pushed her way to the front of the crowd. Peter saw her a few minutes later with coins spilling through her fingers. Children scoured the ground around her, pocketing the stray coins. When word of this extravagance reached the ears of Father Sylvester, he strode up to the front of the church. Francis smiled at him in greeting.

"You paid a paltry sum for all those stones I sold you,"

Father Sylvester accused. "Had I known you had such wealth at your disposal, I would have charged far more."

Francis looked surprised at first, thinking he must have misunderstood the priest's meaning. Then his expression changed to one of disappointment and sadness. He asked Bernardo for his cloak and, digging into its pockets, withdrew a heap of coins. "Does this satisfy you, Sir Priest?" he asked when he had dropped the coins into the old don's hands.

Father Sylvester took the money away, congratulating himself on such a profitable morning. But in the days that followed he could not forget that look of disappointment on Francis's face, or the way he said, "Sir Priest," as if the name held more dignity than he who bore it. In the middle of the night, he reflected, *That young man, Francis, despises all wealth for the love of God, while I eschew love for the sake of money. What a miserable old man I have become.*

Father Sylvester begged God for forgiveness and resolved to give every coin he had received from Francis to the poor. He closed his profitable stone business and devoted himself entirely to his role as spiritual father. The change in Father Sylvester did not go unnoticed.

"What will happen next?" an Assisi farmer commented to his family one evening. "Father Sylvester seems like a different man these days," the man said.

His wife agreed, "I like this one better!" They all laughed.

"They say the change came over him because of that Francesco di Bernardone. Just like it did for Bernardo Quintavalle and that canon, Catanei. I have not heard Francesco preaching, but I am told he is filled with the love of God. At any rate, it takes real courage to stand up and preach penance to folks who watched you grow up in luxury and who witnessed your family troubles besides. What will happen next?" he said again.

"I have heard him preach," said the couple's eldest son, Giles. "He speaks simply but beautifully, Father, as if he were opening a window to the mind of God. When you hear him, you know that the only thing worth doing is to serve God."

Both parents looked at their son. His dark eyes were thoughtful.

Before sunrise Giles left home, as he often did, to attend morning Mass at San Giorgio. Afterward, instead of returning to the farm, he went for a walk. His heart was filled with longing. He felt he needed to speak to Francesco di Bernardone. "Dear Lord," Giles prayed, "take me to the holy man."

It seemed that God heard his prayer. Coming through the gate of San Salvatore hospital, Giles saw Francis walking alone on his way into town. Giles knelt down beside the road.

"Master Bernardone," he said when Francis was close enough to hear. "Ever since I heard you speak in the church, my heart will not leave me alone. Yesterday, I learned that other men have joined you, abandoning all they have in the world to live for God alone. This is all I want in the whole world. May I also join your company of penitents?"

"God has shown great favor to you," Francis answered. "When a king chooses a knight to serve him, everyone rejoices. How much more should you rejoice that the King of Kings has chosen you as his true knight and servant!" Then Francis said,

"Come, Knight of the Round Table, I will take you to meet the others."

Giles joined Bernardo and Peter in the life of poverty with Francis, who continued to do the work God had given him, and to allow God to accomplish His will in the hearts of others. At first, his small group of penitents was met with hostility by the Assisi residents. Some people thought they must be demented, others disapproved of the young men, saying they should earn an honest living like others. Even Bishop Guido began to have doubts. He called the small group to his residence.

"It seems to me that your way of life is very hard, Francis, perhaps too hard," said the bishop. "You must consider these other men now, and no longer just yourself. It is difficult for people to understand how you can live, possessing absolutely nothing. If you persist in your life of poverty, people will think you are all crazy."

"My Lord Bishop," Francis answered for all four, "if we had any possessions, we should also be forced to have arms to protect them since possessions are a cause of strife, and in many ways, we should be hindered from loving God and our neighbor. We wish to have no temporal possessions."

Bishop Guido remained silent. He was a wealthy man with a great deal of property and endless legal disputes.

"My Lord Bishop," Francis went on, "Jesus said to the rich young man, 'Go, sell what you have, give to the poor and you will have treasure in heaven, and come, follow me.' Our Lord did not say next, 'but give up if people think you are crazy.' The rich young man went away sad, for he had many possessions.

We want to follow the Lord joyfully all the way to Calvary." The bishop commended their zeal but warned that they might not be able to persevere.

In truth, the next few months were difficult for the young men. They often ran out of food at the Portiuncula. Francis believed that it was better to work for food than to rely on others for help, but in time of need, it required humility to go door to door, to admit to failure, weakness, and dependence.

At last, he told his three companions, "Brothers, you must now make up your minds to go out begging because you have chosen the way of perfect poverty and humility. Only ask for charity, for the love of God, and in exchange for whatever is given to you, your benefactors will receive incomparable blessings. You will provide for them and for you the riches of the kingdom of heaven, a hundredfold for one!"

The next day, they went into town, taking turns at begging until their bowl was full. After observing them for some time from a distance, a man came forward and introduced himself as Sabbatino, a fisherman from the Lake of Perugia. He was in Assisi to contract business, he said, but he was curious about them. He asked many questions before leaving.

The next afternoon, when the men returned to Assisi, they found Sabbatino waiting for them with a bowl in his hands. He told them, "I, too, long for the riches of God's kingdom."

Soon after this, three more men joined the penitents: Philip, John de Capella, and Masseo. Philip had been a merchant like Francis's father, John worked as a farm laborer, and Masseo was a knight of Perugia. Looking around at the group of penitents that had doubled in size in only a few months, Francis said, "Dear brothers, let us consider how God, in his great mercy, called us not only for our salvation but for that of many. We are to go through the world exhorting all men and women by our example as well as by our words to do penance for their sins, and to live keeping in mind the commandments of God."

Some of the men objected, saying they were not ready to go out alone to preach, but Francis assured them, "Do not be afraid to preach penance even though we appear ignorant and of no account. Put your trust in God who overcame the world!"

Then Francis confided to them his conviction. "Before long many noble and wise men will join us, and very many people will be converted to the Lord and He will multiply and increase His family in the whole world."

Francis divided the small band of men into pairs and sent them off in different directions with instructions to preach peace and the remission of sin. He then set out toward the Valley of Rieti with Masseo, the knight of Perugia.

Masseo was more noble by birth than Francis, but he took orders willingly. Francis found himself wondering at this and at the devotion of all his companions. *Why did God choose me to lead such good men?* he puzzled. *Each one of these men is far better than I.*

The two men left the Portiuncula side by side in bare feet, trusting in God's providence for whatever they might need. For a week and a half, they walked south along the Via Francigena and then followed the course of the River Velino from Terni through the towns of Cantalice and Greccio. Finally, they stood on a cliff above the Valley of Rieti.

"Look! There is a castle on the crest of the hill. We will go there!" Flags flew from the turrets, horses and men moved about in front, guards stood in the battlements. Masseo looked at Francis in surprise. "What will we do there?"

"It is teeming with men, women, and children with immortal souls, Masseo, each one precious to God!" replied Francis. "We can tell them about our Father in heaven and the life of penance that gives peace!" Francis charged ahead as if he could not get there fast enough. Masseo followed. They reached the castle gates just as a procession of knights on horseback issued from the crenellated inner gate with lances in hand and banners flying. A tournament was soon to begin; people filled the courtyard and spilled out into the field beyond.

Francis stepped in front of the line of knights so that they were forced to stop abruptly. Masseo stood awkwardly beside him.

"Knights and champions," Francis's voice rang out, "Is it better to serve the Master or the Servant? That is the question God once asked of me. Of course, it is better to serve the Master. But who is the Master? Buried deep within every heart lies the answer to this question, as it was buried in mine. The one true God is the master of all! To serve him means giving up everything you cling to as to rotting timber that crumbles at the touch. Renounce your sins, your lusts, your pride, so that God can fill your heart with His peace."

Trumpets from the battlements sounded, calling the combatants to the jousting field. Francis and Masseo stood aside for the procession to pass. The commotion of a tournament day commenced and it was as if Francis had never spoken.

"Who are you?" A knight, mounted on a destrier, approached. The crest on his helmet reflected the sunlight when he moved his head. His horse's caparison displayed his coat of arms.

"We are penitents from Assisi," Masseo volunteered.

"And we are heralds of the Great High King," added Francis.

"The King you serve," said the knight, "is the true Master. I do not doubt it."

"Who are you?" Francis asked.

"My name is Angelo of Tancredi."

Despite the shadow cast over the knight's face by his visor, Francis read and understood his thoughts. "Sir Angelo, you have worn the belt, the sword, and the spurs of the world long enough. Change your belt for a rope, your sword for the cross of Christ, and your spurs for the dust of the road. Come with me and I will arm you as Christ's knight."

Masseo was astonished when the knight replied, "I will come, with all my heart."

From then on, Francis, Masseo, and Angelo traveled around the Valley of Rieti from town to town, praying, working, and preaching. Like Masseo, Francis was awed by the action of God in the hearts of those who were moved by his words. When people looked to him for guidance, however, the memory of his sinful past began to haunt him again. The more he loved God, the more he despised himself.

Masseo and Angelo noticed his growing sadness. They were dismayed, but not really surprised, when Francis told them that he wanted to be alone with God for a time. He went into a cave near the town of Poggio Bustone, in the cliffs above the Valley of Rieti. When hours grew into days, the two former knights went back into the town without Francis.

At first, they tried to live as they had with Francis, but were ridiculed by the townspeople. When Masseo offered a poor man his cloak, the man struck him in the face and took his tunic. When Angelo spoke of the love of God, a woman slammed her door in his face saying, "What do you know about love, you fool?" Children began to wait in the market square with cakes of mud to throw at them. Parents cheered on the children, and shouted at Masseo and Angelo, "Why don't you do something useful instead of living off of our hard work?"

Discouraged and hungry, they resigned themselves to eating nuts that fell from the trees, or slops that had been thrown out as refuse. When a group of men threatened to tie them to a horse and drag them out of town, they returned to the wooded hillside near the cave where Francis had gone to pray. There they waited.

In the solitude of the dark cave no sound but the wind met his ears. Contemplating his sinful past Francis wept. "Oh God, be merciful to me, a sinner."

Then, at last, out of the silence God spoke to him. "Do not be afraid, dear little Francis, your sins are forgiven." That was all, and it was everything! The tremendous weight of anxiety was lifted from his breast. He was freed at last from the sins of his past. God, in his infinite mercy, had forgiven him.

When Francis emerged from the cave his joy was visible to Masseo and Angelo in every line of his face and bearing. Their own troubles faded away at the sight of him. Francis exclaimed, "God's peace be with you, my brothers. His mercy endures forever!"

Bolstered with fresh zeal, the three men returned to the town of Poggio Bustone. No one tried to stop them this time. When some children laughed at them, Francis laughed too, and the little ones came to play with him. The same woman who had shunned Angelo, approached Francis to ask for his blessing. After they spent a few more days in the town, a priest asked if he would consider preaching at his church. Francis gladly agreed. On the appointed day, the church was filled.

The contrast was too much for Masseo. He stepped outside the church and brooded. Masseo came from a noble family and had earned great honor as a knight. He had been admired in his hometown of Perugia. *What,* he wondered, *makes people respond this way to Francis, when they show only contempt for Angelo and me?*

"Hold fast to your thoughts, Masseo." Francis was standing beside him. He had seen Masseo walk out and followed. "It is true, what you are thinking. For you are noble and good, and I am only the son of a merchant, and a sinner. I believe God has not found among any a more imperfect, or a greater sinner than I am, to accomplish the wonderful work which He intends to do."

Masseo looked at Francis. In his dark eyes he could see

kindness, sympathy, and good humor. Already Masseo regretted the doubts which Francis had so accurately perceived.

"Do you wish to know why God has given me this work, Masseo?" Francis asked. "I believe He has chosen me to confound force, beauty, greatness, nobility of birth, and all the science of the world. So that we may learn with a certainty that every virtue and every good gift comes from Him; that none may glory before Him. If anyone glory, let him glory in the Lord, to whom alone belongs all glory."

Angelo interrupted, reminding Francis that people were waiting to hear him speak. The three companions returned to the church where Francis spoke with conviction about God's infinite mercy.

The next day, Francis, Masseo, and Angelo began their return journey to Assisi. On the way, Francis prayed that all his followers would quickly be reunited. When they arrived at the Portiuncula, they found Philip, Peter, and Brother John de Capella already there. Two days later, Bernardo and Giles arrived with a new companion, a young nobleman from Assisi named Rufino Scifi.

"Before our houses were built on sand, Brother Rufino, but now you will be building a house on a foundation of stone!" Francis said when Rufino asked to join him.

"Of all houses built on sand, however," quipped Bernardo, "your uncle's house in the Murorupto is one of the most magnificent!"

Francis laughed as he recalled how much he had once longed

for a home like the Scifi mansion. "But now, Brother Rufino Scifi," Francis waved his hand to the open air and uncultivated grounds of the Portiuncula, "I welcome you to *our* home."

Sabbatino interrupted them with a message that Friar Morico, a Cruciger who had worked with Francis at the leper hospital, had recovered from a grave illness and now begged to be allowed to join them.

The brothers were delighted to welcome Morico, whose recovery seemed like a miracle. But it was a small miracle in comparison to what happened next: Old Father Sylvester walked into the Portiuncula smiling. He was wearing a penitent's robe in place of the costly cape he usually wore, and his feet were bare. For the first time since Francis had known him, Don Sylvester looked happy.

"I want to join you men, if you will have me," the priest announced. He looked around at the faces of the brothers who stared back in disbelief, and he grinned sheepishly.

"Truly God can do anything!" Peter Catanei said to Bernardo, forgetting to whisper.

"May God give you peace, Sir Priest," Francis said, stretching out his hand to the old man in welcome. Father Sylvester shook the offered hand with a smile and replied, "He has."

Twelve men now lived at the Portiuncula where Francis had first come as a solitary penitent. He rejoiced that at last he had a family united in purpose and love.

"Strangers and pilgrims, for that is what we are. God has prepared a heavenly city for us and we must live in a way befitting sojourners. We must be *friars minor*, lesser brothers, imitating our Lord Jesus Christ in humility and poverty. And because it is clear that God means to increase our company, let us go now to our holy Mother the Roman Church and lay before the Supreme Pontiff what our Lord has begun to work through us, so that with his consent and direction we may continue what we have undertaken, pledging our loyalty to him and to the holy Catholic church established at such great cost to our savior."

He told the brothers, "In a few words I have written down our Rule of Life, including, above all, the three Gospel passages shown to us by God when we sought his guidance through the Holy Scriptures at the beginning. You, Bernardo, will lead us to Pope Innocent in Rome!"

Bernardo's eyes grew wide, "I?" he asked.

"Yes!" Francis said happily. "You are well spoken and of noble birth. It is right that you should speak for us before the Lord Pope. We will all submit ourselves to you as lesser brothers."

Chapter Twelve

CHILDREN OF THE GREAT KING

Dominic de Guzman was in Rome in the spring of 1209 to report to the Curia on the situation in the Midi. Friar Dominic and his bishop, Diego of Osma, had been preaching among the Albigenses for most of three years. After Bishop Diego's sudden death, Friar Dominic continued his work there with a handful of Cistercian monks, debating the Albigensian leaders, teaching the Faith, and securing protection for Christians.

Pope Innocent was convinced that this missionary work was crucial to the cause of peace. Others in the pope's Curia insisted that military force was needed to protect the people of Toulouse and Provence from the cruelty of their overlord, Count Raymond.

While the cardinals of the Curia wrangled over the issue, Innocent was thoughtful. Through the partly open door of the room, the Holy Father noticed a cluster of men outside the Lateran Palace. Distracted for a moment, he surmised that they were penitents on pilgrimage to Rome. At the center of the group stood a slightly built man with an unusually serene countenance whose laugh rang pleasantly across the piazza.

Pope Innocent's attention was called back to the room by the arrival of Arnold Amalric, Abbot of Citeaux and head of the Cistercian order. Abbot Arnold had been overseeing the missionary efforts in Southern France. When he walked in, his face was white.

"The papal legate to the Midi, Peter of Castelnau, is dead," he announced bluntly. "Murdered in cold blood by Count Raymond's henchmen."

The room was tense. Every one of the cardinals, bishops, and priests looked at Pope Innocent. "The time has finally come," Innocent said regretfully but decisively. "I will issue a proclamation of a crusade to the Midi."

After everyone had left, Pope Innocent III walked alone through the halls of the Lateran and out the door, deep in thought. The decision to protect the people of the Midi by force of arms was not a light one. Where would he find sufficient military support for such a crusade? How would it end? Would there ever be unity and peace? "God help us!" he begged under his breath.

"Your Holiness?" Innocent was roused from his thoughts by a tall man in penitent's garb who was twisting a crumpled piece of paper nervously in his hands. A short distance behind him stood a group of similarly attired men. Only one among them looked at ease; it was the serene looking penitent he had noticed through the door of the Lateran Palace.

The tall man in his path bent over to kiss the Fisherman's

Ring on Innocent's hand. He said, "I am sorry to interrupt, Your Holiness. I am Bernardo Quintavalle, a penitent from Assisi. My brothers and I," he indicated Francis and the others behind him, "have come to seek your blessing on our work, and to pledge our obedience to Your Lordship."

Innocent, in his preoccupied state of mind, was abrupt. "Not now," he waved Bernardo out of the way. The Pope had encountered religious zealots of many kinds during his pontificate and was not readily impressed. "I do not have time for this just now."

The pope's gaze fell on Francis. Addressing himself directly to Francis, he added, "Come back at a more convenient time."

The penitents left the Lateran feeling disappointed. "Let us seek the intercession of the head of the apostles," Francis suggested, "that his successor may be moved to bless the work the Lord has given to us." They followed Francis to the tomb of Saint Peter where Francis had once cast down his coins in pious indignation. Empty handed now, and with more humility, Francis and his followers offered prayers of supplication. When they stepped out into the busy atrium, they were surprised to see their own Bishop Guido.

"What are you doing here, Francesco?" the bishop of Assisi exclaimed in greeting. "You did not tell me that you were going to Rome." Then, without waiting for an answer, he expressed alarm. "I hope you are not planning to leave Assisi? We need you there. And who are all these men with you? I recognize some. . ." he said, indicating with a nod Peter, Bernardo, and Father Sylvester, "but who are the rest?"

Francis introduced the bishop to Giles, Sabbatino, Philip Longo, Masseo, John de Cappella, Morico, Rufino, and Angelo Tancredi. "You have garnered quite a following, Francis! We must form a coherent plan for your group."

"I have our plan right here!" Francis's face lit up as he took the crumpled piece of paper from Bernardo's hand. "It is our Rule of Life in a few simple words. We have come to Rome to present it before the pope, to seek his blessing on our life of penance, and to profess our fealty."

Bishop Guido looked over the note and shook his head at such naiveté. He explained that the pope and his Curia have many concerns and cannot be so easily approached. "There are established procedures one must follow that require legal counsel and perhaps legal representation."

The men looked so bewildered, that the bishop had to laugh. "Come with me," he said kindly. "I will introduce you to someone who may be able to help us. Cardinal Giovanni di San Paolo is a trusted advisor to Pope Innocent and a trustworthy prelate. He also happens to be a good friend of mine."

That afternoon, Francis sat with Bernardo at a marble table beneath the elaborately decorated ceiling of Cardinal Giovanni's dining hall. The other brothers waited outside in the cool shade of his well-manicured garden. Despite the grandeur in which he lived, the cardinal was an unpretentious man. As a Benedictine, he owned nothing. He lived simply, wherever duty placed him, like a man on a journey. He was present in, but not part of, his surroundings.

"Tell me about your way of life, Francesco," said the fatherly cardinal.

"It is our firm determination to own nothing," Francis explained, "in order to preserve charity toward God and our fellow man. In everything we remain simple and subject to all. We care for the poor, the lame, the sick, and the troubled. We speak of the love of Christ and obedience to His holy Church to any who want to hear. We will want for nothing because we are carrying out God's will for us."

Cardinal Giovanni listened to Francis in silence.

"What are we anyway but poor servants?" Francis continued after showing the cardinal the Rule of Life he had written. "Just as a servant is not above his master, neither are we above Our Heavenly Master, who said, 'Foxes have holes and birds of the air have nests; but the Son of man has nowhere to lay his head.' Why then should we worry about providing anything for ourselves?"

After a thoughtful moment, Cardinal Giovanni said, "I will speak to the Holy Father as soon as it is possible to do so. He is preoccupied with troubling affairs, yet I think such genuine faith as yours will be a breath of fresh air to him. Many of the people in his charge are suffocating under the weight of confusion, grave heresy, unbelief, and sin. In fact, it seems to me that the entire world would benefit from the example of such faith!"

At his first opportunity, Cardinal Giovanni took Pope Innocent aside. The holy father was struck by the cardinal's earnest appeal. "I have found a most excellent man who desires to live according to the form of the Gospel and in everything to observe evangelical perfection. I am convinced that through this man our Lord wills to renew the faith of the Holy Church in the whole world." With that, Cardinal Giovanni handed Pope Innocent a neatly transcribed copy of Francis's proposed Rule.

The Holy Father was astonished. "You are not given to hyperbole, Giovanni. I would like to meet this man who can single-handedly restore the Church." Cardinal Giovanni detected a note of skepticism in Innocent's reply, but it did not matter. He would soon see for himself.

The next day, Francis and his troop of barefoot followers were called before Pope Innocent III and his consistory of cardinals. When the humble little man approached the dais, the pope and several cardinals looked questioningly at Cardinal Giovanni, who returned their look with a comfortable smile.

"Lord Pope," Francis began, "God has called us to the help of His holy faith and of the Roman Church's priests and prelates."

Pope Innocent's eyebrow went up dubiously. Cardinal Giovanni sat back, prepared to enjoy himself. Francis described to the Holy Father how he and his brothers lived, united in love for Christ. He told the stories of how many lives had been transformed. He spoke of his confidence that they were doing God's will and that God would increase their numbers. His brotherhood, he said, was like a fisherman's net cast into the sea that would one day be filled with "fishes of every kind."

How much like Christ this man speaks, he thought. *And how much am I like the fisherman who cast his net all through the night taking nothing.*

"I have read your proposed Rule, Francis," he said, "and I fear that your plan of life may be too severe. We are convinced of your fervor, but we have to consider those who will follow you and who may find this path too harsh."

Francis listened to the Holy Father respectfully. He understood that every decision made by the head of the Church must be carefully weighed. At the same time, he had no doubt that the Holy Spirit had led him to stand before Pope Innocent with his request.

"Go, my son," said Pope Innocent, "go and pray to God that he may reveal whether what you ask proceeds indeed from His most holy will in order that we may be assured that, in granting your desire, we shall be following the will of God."

Francis and his followers left the Lateran palace. "We must now pray, brothers, that God will show the Lord Pope His will," he said.

Most of the cardinals considered Francis's proposal impractical. "He should not start another religious order when he can join an order that already exists, with a built-in source of financial support," said one. "That is far more practical."

"His Rule is too vague and idealistic," put in another. "He should follow the Rule of Saint Benedict instead. It has been proven to work—why begin something new?"

"In my opinion," said another sternly, "he is doomed to fail. No one can maintain such zeal for long and even if the man were a saint, his followers could not be expected to live up to an unrealistic standard."

At this point, Cardinal Giovanni intervened, "It has been

known to work, my brother cardinals, in one other instance at least that I know of." They all turned to look at him. "I speak of the case of Our Lord and his twelve apostles."

The cardinals shifted in their seats, and someone coughed. Cardinal Giovanni's tone became grave. "He only begs for the confirmation of the evangelical way of life. If we refuse this poor man's petition as a novelty too hard to be observed, well, let us take heed that we not offend the Gospel of Christ. For, if any man says that the observance and the vow of evangelical perfection contain anything impossible to be observed, he is condemning Christ, the author of the Gospel."

When Innocent returned to his chambers that evening, he knelt before the crucifix to ask God for guidance. His heart led him one way, his pragmatic inclinations, another. That night the pope had a vivid dream. In it, he stood outside alone in a wasteland, clutching the papal scepter. The edifice of the Lateran Basilica towered before him. While he looked on, a crack began to form and spread over its outer wall. With horror he saw another crack form, and another, until he knew the whole church must fall. He tried to cry out, but no sound would come from his lips. He tried to raise his arms to stop it, to run to support it, but he stood paralyzed. Then, just as the wall of the Lateran began to sway, out of the darkness stepped a small man dressed in a robe tied at the waist with a rope. In bare feet he strode calmly up to the tottering Lateran and rested his back against it. The building immediately stood upright and was restored. It looked strong, beautiful, and noble once more. When the man turned around,

Innocent knew that it was Francis, the penitent from Assisi. His eyes had that singular look of serenity, even in the dream.

When the pope awoke, he knew what must be done He had known it all along. After a whispered prayer that his cardinals would not oppose him, he summoned Francis to return to the consistory that very morning. When the pope and his Curia had assembled, Francis came forward.

With uncharacteristic warmth, Pope Innocent stood up and proclaimed, "Truly this is the pious and holy man by whom the Church of God will be restored!"

Not one cardinal objected. The pope stepped down from the dais and embraced Francis, saying to him and to his followers who looked on, "Go with God, brothers, and announce salvation for all, as the Lord reveals it to you. And when the Almighty has multiplied your numbers, come back to me, and you will find me ready to charge you with a greater inheritance."

Francis knelt at the pope's feet to profess obedience and to receive his blessing. All the brothers then knelt at Francis's feet to profess obedience to the pope through him.

Cardinal Giovanni took the penitents under his direction. Francis was ordained to the diaconate and all of them received the tonsure as a sign to the world that the Holy Father had approved their work and way of life. When they left the Holy City, they were true "Friars Minor,"—Lesser Brothers—emptied of self will, subject to all men and to God through his vicar on earth. They were poor, homeless, and at peace.

With light hearts, the band of Friars Minor traveled north

along the Via Francigena, pausing in front of every church they passed or steeple that pierced the horizon, to pray as Francis taught them. "We adore thee, Christ, here and in all thy churches over the whole world, and we praise thee because by thy holy cross thou hast redeemed the world." To gawkers, they smiled and said, "God's peace be with you."

Soon they came to the Valley of Spoleto, where they walked from town to town, praying, doing penance, performing works of charity in the hospitals and in the streets, and begging for their food. Wherever they stopped, Francis preached with conviction and an understanding of the human heart that drew men and women. The Valley of Spoleto seemed to come to life as they moved through it. Followers trailed the brothers from town to town, gathering in crowds to hear Francis speak. Conversations in the shops and fields and at the family dinner tables inevitably turned to these new penitents, who really seemed to live what they preached, and who had discovered a source of joy that was possible for everyone.

Several weeks after leaving Rome, the Friars Minor arrived within sight of Assisi. Night was falling, but the town was still two miles off. Francis stepped off the Via Francigena into the densely wooded roadside. The rest of the men plunged trustingly into the brush behind him, batting mosquitoes away from their bare ankles. The ground felt cool and soft under their feet at first, but it became hard and rocky as it sloped upward. When he got to the top of the slope, Francis pulled back some branches to reveal an abandoned shed on the bank of a small stream.

"The Lord has provided shelter for us, just as he did for the Holy Family on that most holy night when God first came among us!" Francis said triumphantly. "I often visited this abandoned shed on the way to my father's landholdings as a child. It has been at least ten years since I was here last, but it still stands!" He laughed as he recalled the memories. "My brother, Angelo, and I used to play in the Rivo Torto here. The old shed was our palace, our jousting tent, our castle, and our cathedral, depending on the game. Tonight, it will serve as our stable of Bethlehem!"

The twelve men settled at once into an orderly life of prayer and work in the drafty shed on Rivo Torto. Each day they offered morning prayers together and then went into Assisi to attend Mass. They worked at whatever jobs they could find in exchange for food or good will. They visited the sick and shared their faith in God by their example of charity more than by words. At dusk they returned to the shed beside the river to pray together, giving thanks to God for the opportunity to serve Him that day.

They gave little heed to the concerns of the world around them. When news reached Assisi that the German king, Otto IV of Brunswick, would be passing through on his way to Rome to be crowned Holy Roman Emperor, Francis advised the brothers not to be distracted by petty politics and earthly kings. "Blessed is he whose hope is in the Lord alone," he said, quoting Jeremiah.

On the day King Otto was expected to arrive, however, the celebration was impossible to ignore. Church bells rang throughout the countryside and a holiday was declared so that the people could line the Via Francigena to cheer. King Otto was to pass within a few yards of the shed at Rivo Torto. Heralds announced his approach with trumpets and loud cries.

"Brother Phillip," Francis said, "you are tall and your voice is strong. When the emperor passes by, stand on the side of the road and quote the Psalms aloud so that he will hear you. That way we will fulfill our duty to uphold the light of the Gospel before all, not making any distinction of persons. The rest of us will remain inside, praying and praising God."

When His Majesty was within earshot, Philip proclaimed in a loud voice:

"'Praise the Lord, oh my soul, in my life I will praise the Lord! Put not your trust in princes nor in the children of men, in whom there is no salvation. Blessed is he whose hope is in the Lord, whose reign shall last forever and ever.'"

Amid the pomp, King Otto paid no attention to the preaching friar. He merely waved ceremoniously as he passed. Other people, however, took notice. Some who welcomed the German ruler as a source of security for the country grumbled, "Why can't those religious zealots keep quiet? 'God give you peace,' they always say. Well, King Otto may be our only chance for peace in these times!"

A peasant, standing with his donkey, added ominously, "Their numbers are growing. At first it was just that crazy cloth merchant, Francesco di Bernardone. Now there are at least a dozen of them! They are a nuisance on every street corner, begging and praying as if they were holier than everyone else. If the winter doesn't finish them off in that shed on Rivo Torto, I will personally see to it that they leave!"

Yet the number of Friars Minor continued to increase over the next several months. Brother Leo, a priest from Assisi, joined them, then Brother Illuminato, Brother John the Simple, Brother William of England, and Brother Juniper, whose jokes and pranks earned him the title of "God's Jester."

One evening in early spring, the friars were gathered in the shed chanting vespers when a commotion outside interrupted them. Everyone looked toward the door. In came a man, back first, leading a donkey by its bridle. The donkey balked but the man insisted in a firm voice, "This place is for donkeys, not men, my pet. There ye go." He prodded the animal into the middle of the shed, forcing the brothers' backs against the walls to make room.

"What is your intention, *bonhomme*? Why do you bring your donkey in here? There are so many of us here already!" queried Brother Juniper, who found the situation hilarious.

"Ha!" sneered the peasant, "this shed is more suited to a donkey than a band of itinerant preachers. Next thing you know, you'll be building a monastery and inviting more of your kind to stay. Well, me and my donkey are here to ensure that you do no such thing. And if you want something to occupy yourselves—seeing as ye've got no jobs—you can just tend my donkey. We are staying, and no mistake about it."

The man looked defiantly at Francis, who looked back at him thoughtfully. But he did not reply. Instead, he turned to the brothers and said, with a twinkle in his eye, "I know for certain that God has not called me to entertain a donkey, but to show men the way of salvation by preaching and wise counsel."

He beckoned to the brothers to follow him around the donkey's flanks and out into the brisk evening. "God's peace be with you," he said to the peasant before leading the brothers away. The budding branches around the shed rattled in the wind as the men knelt on the ground to finish praying vespers.

Beneath a brilliant moon they trudged along the banks of Rivo Torto until they found a clearing in the trees to spend the night. With rocks for pillows and leaves for warmth, the brothers rested while Francis slipped deeper into the woods to praise God for this new poverty.

In the morning, he emerged smiling. "Like the Son of Man, we have nowhere to lay our heads! What a privilege it is to endure cold, uncertainty, and true poverty like the Holy Family once endured!"

His joy was irresistible; no one was troubled. The poor friars continued their daily routine of prayer, penance, and service to others, confident that all would be well as long as they did the will of the Father.

Several weeks later, the sound of footsteps on the fallen leaves of the forest floor signaled someone was approaching.

"My brothers!" rang out the cheerful voice of Abbot Larione from the Benedictine Monastery of Mount Subasio. "Word has reached us on the Mount that your shed is now an ass's stable! Cozy as that sounds," he said, laughing, "I have a change of locality to propose."

The friars gathered around him.

"Our Portiuncula close to here is not being used. There is land enough for three or four times your number at least! The church, Saint Mary of the Angels, that Francesco repaired, could be the seat of the growing Order of Friars Minor. Would you consider accepting it as a gift?"

The brothers were enthusiastic. Here was a solution to their problem and it was freely given! Francis alone looked troubled.

"What is the problem, Francis?" asked the Abbot, noting his reserve.

"As Friars Minor, we may own nothing," Francis explained. "If we were to take possession of a parcel of land and a chapel, we would have to build a wall around it to protect it. We would have to hire guards to fend off robbers, and we would lay awake nights worrying that it might be trespassed, or stolen from us."

Abbot Larione laughed, "Dear Brother Francis, I will save you all that worry and bother. I will not give you the Portiuncula, after all."

The other friars looked doubtful about this turn of events.

"I will *loan* you the land at a rent of one basket of fish per annum," he said, "The monks of Mount Subasio are fond of fish. They will agree that I have struck a good bargain."

By the end of that day, the Friars Minors were praising God in the chapel of Saint Mary of the Angels. Since they owned nothing, moving into the Portiuncula simply meant crossing the threshold. The old hut that Francis had patched and occupied before was still standing and soon each of the brothers had built a wattle and daub hut for himself on the surrounding land. The

Portiuncula was not their home, they did not own the earth it stood upon, but it was a center from which their charity could radiate.

Chapter Thirteen

PERFECT JOY

Every morning at sunrise, the Church of Saint Mary of the Angels echoed with the sound of morning prayer. After Mass, the Friars went out to work or remained behind in prayer.

Brother Masseo and Brother Sabbatino often went to the leper hospital to care for the sick. One morning, Francis went with them. Walking from bed to bed, he noticed a miserable man sitting in a corner by himself. His bedding and clothes were extraordinarily filthy, his hair was matted, and there were worms crawling on his sores.

"He refuses to let anyone near him," the hospital attendant explained.

Masseo added, "We have tried to clean his wounds and comfort him, Father Francis, just as we do every other patient. He kicks and scratches and even tries to bite. His curses are so horrible that I have almost given up."

Francis approached the man who lay with his back to the room. The stench of his wounds, combined with the smell of human excrement and sweat, surrounded him. "May God give thee peace, my brother," said Francis.

The man turned in his bed and spat at Francis's bare feet. "What peace can I look for from God who has taken it away from me and made me into a putrid and disgusting object?"

Francis felt a surge of pity. "My son, be patient. The infirmities of the body are allowed by God in this world for the salvation of the soul who bears them patiently."

"In that case, I am damned!" he retorted. "It is impossible to bear patiently the pain that afflicts me day and night. And those brothers who care for me are useless. They do nothing to help."

Francis said, "My son, I will serve you as well as I can since you are not satisfied with the care the brothers have given you. What would you have me do?"

The man spoke as if to challenge Francis. "Wash me all over. I am so disgusting that I cannot bear myself."

"I will do so willingly," Francis said.

Francis heated some water in the hospital's kitchen, stirring in a pungent mixture of medicinal herbs. He gathered a stack of the softest cloths he could find and returned to the bedside. The patient put up no resistance while Francis washed the wounds all over his body. Brother Masseo knelt beside him to pour the warm water on the cloths. Brother Sabbatino stood by to dispose of the dirty ones. A small crowd of patients and staff gathered to watch. It seemed miraculous that this man had finally accepted help.

After a while some of them noticed quiet tears streaming down Brother Masseo's face, while Francis kept gently washing the wounds. The patient's taut muscles relaxed, he whispered something that looked like thanks, and placed a hand gratefully on Francis's arm. At last, his whole body was clean. Francis covered him with a warm blanket and stepped away. The man was asleep. The onlookers marveled as each returned to his own place.

Sabbatino and Masseo walked back to the shed at Rivo Torto alone. Francis went into the woods to pray.

"It was the most beautiful thing I have ever seen," Sabbatino said to Masseo, "when the festering wounds and wasted flesh of that poor man become whole again under Francis's touch! His skin was as sound and fresh as any baby's skin when we left. It was a true miracle. And no less miraculous was it to see his rancor melt away with the sores. The joy almost seemed to radiate from Francis's face! What do you suppose it means?"

"It means," said Masseo, "that our fealty is well placed in this man, Francis, who can work miracles, and make nothing of it. He thinks of himself merely as a humble instrument through which God can work."

By this time, the Friars Minor were becoming known in some of the neighboring regions beyond Assisi. Weeks later, Francis and Brother Masseo went to Alviano, near Terni to preach and were met by a small crowd in the town square. The two friars decided to recite the Liturgy of Hours loud enough so that more people would notice and gather to listen. At first, swallows dove in and out from their nests in the gray towers around the square, chirping and warbling so that no one could hear the Friars.

Francis stopped reciting the prayers and said, "Sister Swallows, it seems to me that the time has come when I should have a chance to speak; now you have said enough!"

To the crowd's delight, the birds began to gather around the two friars. More men and women came to see what was going on. One swallow perched on a windowsill and twisted its head as if trying to listen. Francis laughed. "Hear therefore God's word and keep still while I preach," he said to the birds.

The swallows ceased their twittering and did not stir as long as the two friars were praying. When the chanted prayers were finished, the crowd around them was large and Francis began to preach. The swallows remained respectfully silent. When Francis finished his sermon with the words, "God's peace be with you," the swallows resumed their noisy chatter.

The miracle of the swallows in Alviano established Francis's credibility with the people of that region. Word traveled, and more people wanted to hear from the Friar of Assisi who could tame the birds. Soon, whenever he and his companions entered a town, the church bells would begin to ring to alert the residents, who swarmed out to hear Francis preach.

Before long, whole communities of lay people formed to devote themselves to living the Gospel as Francis directed them. They dressed in poor tunics like the Friars Minor and cared for the sick and the poor. They prayed in common and used only what material goods they absolutely needed. "To keep anything more would be to steal from others in need," Francis said.

The brothers who had been with Francis from the beginning

did not enjoy the adulation; they preferred the mockery and the rejection of the early days. Francis, too, would have preferred humiliation to admiration, but he accepted it as a means to reach people with God's Word.

"When I look at a holy picture in church I am reminded of God," he told them. "I do not worship the paint and canvas—I hardly give them a thought except as instruments. In the same way, by our lives of penance and our holy example, we direct people's minds and hearts to God, not to ourselves. We are nothing except God's troubadours who seek to draw hearts upward and to fill them with spiritual joy."

Aware of the growing following that Francis was attracting, the bishop of nearby Terni was skeptical. Francis took Brother Leo and went to the bishop at his residence one day to ask for permission to address the crowd in front of the cathedral, but the bishop refused. "I will preach to my own people, young man," he said, "I do not need your help."

Francis knelt for his blessing and went out where Leo waited for him. A few minutes later, the bishop heard a knock on his door. When he found Francis back again, he was angry and asked him what he meant by such impertinence. Francis explained, "My Lord Bishop, when a father sends his son out the door, what choice does that son have but to return to his father by another door."

The bishop agreed to let Francis preach after all—just once—outside the cathedral church. He listened to every word, and after Francis finished, the bishop stood and addressed the crowd. "From the beginning, our Lord has enlightened the church through holy men who have fostered it by word and example. But now, in these latter days He has enlightened it through this poor, undistinguished and unlearned man, Francis. Therefore, love and honor our Lord, and beware of sin."

Francis followed the bishop back into the cathedral and threw himself on the floor at his feet. "I assure you that no man in this world has ever done me such honor as you have done me this day. Other men say, 'This is a holy man,' and they attribute glory and holiness to me, rather than the Creator. But you have distinguished between the precious and the worthless." Much surprised, the bishop smiled and gave Francis his blessing before he left.

On their way back to Assisi, a cloud settled over Umbria and an icy wind arose.

"Brother Leo!" Francis shouted above the wind, "if it were to please God that the Brothers Minor should give, in all lands, a great example of holiness and edification, take note and carefully observe that this would not be a cause for perfect joy!" Brother Leo made a mental note of this.

"Brother Leo," Francis called again to his companion who was a few paces ahead, "if the Brothers Minor were to make the lame walk, chase away demons, restore sight to the blind, and raise the dead after four days, take note that this would not be cause for perfect joy."

Brother Leo nodded his head and took note.

"Brother Leo," Francis called out a third time, "if the Brothers Minor could speak all languages, if they were versed in all science, if they could explain all Scriptures, even if they had the gift of prophecy, take note that this would not be a cause for perfect joy."

A freezing rain began to fall. Brother Leo slackened his pace, and called back to Francis, "Father, teach me then where to find the cause for perfect joy."

Francis answered, "If, after we finally reach the Portiuncula, hungry, exhausted, and nearly frozen to death; if, when we knock at the gate, the porter should come out angrily and ask us who we are; if, after we have told him that we are two of his brothers, he should answer angrily, 'You are liars, you are two impostors going about to deceive the world. Begone, I say!' If the porter leaves us outside to suffer from cold and hunger—then, if we accept such injustice and contempt with patience, believing with humility and charity that the porter really knows us and that it is God who makes him speak against us, Brother Leo, make note and carefully observe that *this* is a cause for perfect joy!

"And if we knock again, and the porter comes out in anger, with oaths and blows saying, 'Begone miserable robbers!'—and we accept it all with patience, joy, and charity, Brother Leo, take note that *this* is indeed cause for perfect joy. If we bear all wrongs with patience and joy, thinking of the sufferings of our blessed Lord, which we would share out of love of Him, Brother Leo, note that here, finally, is cause for perfect joy.

"For, above all the graces and all the gifts of the Holy Spirit which Christ grants to His friends, is the grace of overcoming oneself, and accepting willingly, out of love of Christ, sufferings, injuries, discomfort, and contempt; for in all the other gifts of God we cannot glory, because they do not proceed from ourselves, but from God.

"But in the cross of tribulation and affliction we may glory because, as the Apostle says, 'I will not glory save in the cross of our Savior, Jesus Christ.'"

By this time, Leo and Francis had reached the Portiuncula. There was no gate in the hedge, nor a porter to throw them out, yet they did glory in the cross of Christ as each one went to his own hut, cold and hungry.

Shortly after this, Francis revealed to all the friars his new plan to go beyond the borders of Italy to bring the message of salvation to the Saracens, who did not yet know Christ. There was a chance he might even die a martyr's death there!

Taking Brother Angelo, Francis set out for the Adriatic Coast. The two friars begged their way onto a ship bound for the Far East, but they got no farther than a day's journey out into the Adriatic when a violent storm rose up. The ship was forced to the opposite coast in Dalmatia, and there it would remain until spring. Francis and Angelo were informed that there would be no more ships that year. For the time being, Francis had to give up his plan to convert the Saracens.

As he and Brother Angelo returned to Italy and made their way back to Assisi through the March of Ancona, preaching along the way, they realized that although the mission to the Far East had failed, God was using them for a different purpose. People who would never have heard them preach, came out in large numbers, and new friars joined the order almost every day.

In the village of San Severino, Francis was invited to preach at a convent. The crowd he drew was so large that the enclosure could not hold everyone. Some people were sitting on the walls, some had to be content to listen outside the door without being able to see. While he waited for men and women to gather, Francis heard the music of a troubadour playing outside. The music stopped, and Francis, who had picked up the tune, began to sing it with new words that spoke of the love of God for his creatures.

His voice was melodious and the words were well chosen. His audience cheered when he finished. Laughing, he bowed modestly. He recalled his youthful ambition of one day becoming a troubadour. How much more wonderful had been God's plan for him, yet it was not really so different. Instead of telling tales of earthly love, his prose spoke of the love that surpasses all understanding, the longing of every human heart.

Outside the convent walls, the world-renowned troubadour, Guglielmo Divini, was forced to end his performance prematurely because his audience unexpectedly dispersed. Something, he knew not what, was drawing them into the convent enclosure. As poet laureate of the court of King Frederick II, it was unheard of that the Great Divini could not hold his audience. Accompanied by a few of his most devoted fans, he followed the mass of people through the wide-open doors of the convent to see what was luring everyone away. Inside, people respectfully parted to let the celebrity work his way to the front.

Divini was amazed to find Francis at the center of all the attention, small and unimpressive in his rags. His singing voice was not bad, Divini thought, but it was not at all trained. It lacked the projection and control of a true professional. Yet admittedly there was something appealing in his manner when he spoke. What was it? Divini watched critically. At first, he thought only of Francis's delivery, but soon he began to listen to the words.

Like everyone in Europe, Francis had heard of the Great Divini. But by sight, he did not recognize this splendidly dressed gentleman. Francis spoke of how each soul is precious and immortal, created by God and for God. He spoke about the love of God and his Church, about sin and its wages of eternal death, about the urgency to convert, to confess, do penance. He told of Christ's death on the cross as a ransom for souls, and of God's infinite mercy.

The troubadour listened, and his eyes began to fill with tears. Few people noticed, since all attention was fixed on Francis. So it surprised everyone when the Great Divini suddenly sank to his knees and wept aloud. "Brother!" he exclaimed. "You have exposed my very soul. Take me away from this world of men and show me the path to God!"

Gently, Francis lifted the troubadour to his feet. "Go and ask God for the peace you are seeking, sir. If it is His plan that you find it with the Friars Minor, then tomorrow you shall become Brother Pacificus, whomsoever you may be today."

Brother Angelo, Brother Pacificus, and thirty-six new friars from Ancona, returned with Francis—who was now twenty-nine years old—to the Portiuncula before the winter of 1211.

These were the newest members of the Order of Friars

Minor. Among them were troubadours, priests, knights, lawyers, fishermen, farmers, laborers, sailors, merchants, scholars, teachers, and young men with no profession. Few would have imagined that another facet was soon to be added to this multi-faceted Order of Friars Minor, and it was, perhaps, the loveliest one of all.

Chapter Fourteen

LADY OF POVERTY

"Please, Rufino, speak to Brother Francis for me.'

Outside the church of San Giorgio on the first Sunday of Lent, Rufino's cousin, Lady Clare Scifi, took him aside to plead with him. Clare was the eighteen-year-old daughter of Count Favarone and Ortolana Offreducio. The sermon Francis gave that day had set her heart on fire and she longed to speak with him in person.

"He does not allow women at the Portiuncula, Chiara. In fact, he rarely speaks alone to women at all, unless they are seeking spiritual direction," Brother Rufino answered in a low voice.

"I *am* seeking spiritual direction, Rufino!" she insisted. "I have never before heard someone who speaks the way he does. He has given words to my thoughts and wings to my soul. He will not refuse you, Rufino, I am sure of it. With a little planning, I can meet him anywhere he likes. Please ask him."

Brother Rufino was thoughtful. Other than Francis, there was no one he admired as much as Clare, but Rufino was not sure what Brother Francis would think of such a bold request. To meet privately with a woman was unheard of. In these days when immorality among the clergy was common matter for gossip, Francis avoided any occasion of scandal. On the other hand, Rufino knew that when Clare was determined, nothing could stop her. And, in truth, Rufino decided, there really was nothing wrong with her request.

"I will try to bring it up with him," he finally promised.

That evening, as Francis and Rufino walked back to the Portiuncula in the gathering darkness, Rufino chose his moment.

"Brother Francis," he began, "one of my cousins has asked to meet with you." He paused, then added, "Ordinarily that would not be a problem, of course, but in this case . . ." he hesitated, "well you see, my cousin is a woman. It is the Lady Chiara di Favorone di Offreducio. I told her it was impossible but she begged me to ask anyway."

After a thoughtful moment, Francis answered, "I have long wanted to meet your cousin again, Brother Rufino." He recalled the little blond girl in the Murorupto with a smile. "Her reputation for holiness and generosity to the sick and the poor has singled her out, so that even I have heard of it. She is like a Friar Minor in many ways. It would be wrong to deny her wish in this matter."

Before many days had passed, Brother Rufino arranged a meeting between Francis and Clare. As soon as they were introduced, it was evident that their two hearts beat as one with the same love for Christ and the same zeal to serve Him. They were like two candles that, put together, form a single bright flame.

Nothing in the material world attracted either of them. Poverty for the sake of God alone gave them joy. Over the course of many meetings that Lent, they reinforced each other with sympathetic understanding. Clare learned from Francis, and Francis learned from Clare.

Just as she had hoped, Brother Francis sympathized with her desire to leave the world of wealth, which was becoming ever more odious to her. She wanted to live like the Friars Minor in poverty and simplicity, contemplating Christ crucified, and saving souls through prayer and penance. For his part, Francis believed that Clare had a role to play in restoring the Church. She would be a light in the world darkened by sin. Her example alone might lead others to conversion; he was certain that the power of her prayers would.

His old friend and advisor, Bishop Guido, had died a year before, but the episcopal successor in Assisi, Bishop Guido II, had known Clare Scifi since her childhood. He, too, felt that she was called to something exceptional. When Francis told him about Clare's longing to live in poverty like the Friars Minor, the bishop encouraged it.

The bishop expected opposition from Clare's family. He thought that her parents, Lady Ortolana and Count Favarone, would come to accept her decision in time but, he was quite sure that Ortolana's older brother, Monaldo, would try to stop her. Count Monaldo Fiumi of Coriano was a formidable man in the affairs of his commune, his estate, and his family. Despite that, the bishop did not discourage the work of God in Clare's heart.

Having won the bishop's approval, all that was left for Clare to do was to finally sever herself from her family and the world. Under Bishop Guido's guidance, she and Francis agreed that on Palm Sunday she would leave her home forever.

When Palm Sunday arrived, she went to Mass with her family. Sitting beside her sisters, Clare fully realized what it would mean to leave her family and she began to cry quietly. She looked up when she heard the voice of Bishop Guido beside her, "My daughter, Chiara," he said. Bishop Guido had come down from the sanctuary and was standing in front of her with a palm branch in his hand. The eyes of the congregation followed him curiously as he held out the branch and said to her, "Take this palm branch as a sign of your undivided devotion to Christ." That was all the encouragement she needed. She took the palm branch and smiled at Bishop Guido through her tears. Her resolve never again wavered.

Long after the Scifi household had settled to sleep that night, Clare was still dressed in her finest gown. Her chiffon veil fluttered softly about her head as she paced back and forth in her bedroom. When, at last, it was time to go, she woke her sister.

"Agnes," she whispered, "it is time."

Agnes got up at once to dress, taking care not to disturb their youngest sister, Beatrice, sleeping in the bed beside her. Clare took one last look at her little sister. *She will be a comfort to mother*, Clare thought.

Clare had confided her plan to Agnes after the Palm Sunday service that afternoon. The sixteen-year-old Agnes thought that if she had not already been betrothed, she would like to do exactly what Clare was about to do. They agreed it would be best not to tell their mother lest she inform their father or, worse yet, their Uncle Monaldo who would stop at nothing to prevent her from leaving.

By the dim light of a candle, the girls tiptoed into the hallway and peered around the corner at the front door. Clare said, "Come with me." She placed a finger over her lips and turned around. Agnes followed Clare to the back of the house and behind the armory, where a small door led into an empty passageway.

"The Door of Death?" Agnes asked, shivering involuntarily. "It will be boarded up."

"I removed some of the barricade this morning. Follow me."

At the end of the passageway was a plain door of solid wood, reserved for the removal of the dead from the home. It was usually barred on the inside and blocked by tightly wedged boards on the outside.

The two sisters shoved with all their strength, until the door shifted slightly. They paused and Clare said, "I have to do this. Nothing can stop me." She gave a tremendous heave and the door opened, casting the boards aside, and sending logs tumbling out into the side yard. The girls stood motionless in case the noise had aroused anyone. All was still.

At last, they were out in the cool night air under a sky flecked with stars. They walked briskly in the direction of the Portiuncula with a mild wind blowing their hair about their heads. Clare's heart beat fast as she told her sister of the irresistible urge that pulled her to a life of poverty. "I think of Christ as a kind of mirror on the wood of the cross that continually reflects two images: the glory of God, first of all, and the image of His children who look upon it. By looking in that mirror, Agnes, I can see what God wants me to be."

"What does He want you to be?" Agnes asked.

"A reflection of His Son!" Clare answered.

"But such poverty, Clare," said Agnes, "why must it be so absolute?"

"Because poverty is the ultimate humility," she said. "It is the humility of complete dependence, like Christ's total poverty on the cross."

Agnes could barely keep up with her sister's quick steps. Finally, she asked, "What would you think if I were to join you?"

Clare was not surprised at this; she knew her sister well. "I wish you could, Agnes, but you have been promised to Lord Rainerio. He would be decidedly against it." Clare smiled.

After a few minutes, she added, "Help Mother to understand, Agnes, that I am seeking a more perfect union with Christ than it would be possible to have in ordinary life. She and Papa have always taught us to love and serve God above all else. That is all I want to do with my whole heart."

Ahead of them stood the Church of Saint Mary of the Angels ablaze with candlelight. The arched doorway framed by oak trees, shone brightly in the dark forest. Clare's face became jubilant. Agnes began to cry. Both were startled when their cousin, Rufino, stepped out of the darkness.

"May God's peace be with you, Cousins," his familiar voice

was a relief to their taut nerves. "Go directly into the chapel, Clare. Brother Francis has said that you may stay to watch the ceremony, Agnes, if you like. I can escort you home afterward."

Inside the church, Brother Sabbatino announced, "She is coming!" All the brothers knelt expectantly on the bare ground. The wooden altar was lined with such a profusion of votive candles that the stone walls seemed to dance with light and shadow. Never before had the chapel been so adorned, but this was an extraordinary night. A member of the highest nobility was to embark on a life of holy poverty united with the Friars Minor in obedience to Francis. The Lady Chiara di Favarone de Offreducio was to become Sister Clare, Lady of Poverty.

Clare's silken hem brushed the stone floor as she walked down the center aisle toward Francis, who waited at the front. His gentle smile and a nod of his tonsured head reassured her. At the front of the church, she repeated the vows of poverty, chastity, and obedience to the Holy Roman Church and to Francis. She then stepped outside where Agnes helped her exchange her costly gown for a rough woolen robe. When Clare returned, Francis cut off her hair and placed a tight black veil over her head. Beside the golden heap of hair on the ground a pair of wooden sandals had been placed for her bare feet.

Finally, Francis put his hand on her veiled head and formally declared, "Because by divine inspiration you have made yourself a daughter and servant of the most high King, the heavenly Father, and have taken the Holy Spirit as your spouse choosing to live according to the perfection of the holy Gospel, I resolve and promise for myself and for my brothers to have that same loving care and special solicitude for you as I have for them."

When Clare stood up, the friars and Lady Agnes took candles and followed Francis and Clare out of the church. Chanting the *Te Deum* softly, the procession moved along the dark, empty road to the Benedictine convent of San Paolo in nearby Bastia. With candle in hand, Clare walked alone through its iron gate. Two nuns welcomed her and bolted the gate. Here she was to stay temporarily, to await her family's reaction.

She did not have to wait long. The next evening, one of the sisters tapped Clare on the shoulder while she was praying after compline. She had visitors who insisted on seeing her at once. Before she had time to react, the door of the chapel was thrown open and in marched her father, her Uncle Monaldo, her Uncle Paolo, her cousin, Boso, and a few other men whom she recognized as Uncle Monaldo's friends. They approached her directly.

"Enough of this nonsense, Chiara. Come home now," was her Uncle Monaldo's brusque greeting.

"I am a consecrated virgin, Uncle. I have taken a vow of obedience to the Holy Father and to Francesco di Bernardone. I cannot leave," she said defiantly.

"You owe obedience to your father," replied Monaldo.

"I do not think my mother or my father would insist that I violate my promise to Almighty God," Clare said, looking to her father for help.

"Your mother and I want what is best for you, Chiara," her father coaxed.

"To serve God as a consecrated virgin is best for me, Father, I am certain," she said. Then turning to her uncle, she added, "This is what God wants of me."

"What *would* be best for you is a whipping." Monaldo's voice began to rise—he never liked to be contradicted. He took Clare's arm and began to drag her toward the door. "You will come with us."

Clare slipped out of his painful grip and ran to the front of the church. She stood beneath a life-sized fresco of Christ on the cross and with one hand placed firmly on the altar, she turned to face the men.

"I belong here, Uncle Monaldo, at the foot of the cross." Brushing off her veil, she revealed her shorn head, a sign of her vow. Clearly, she had chosen her Lord and already sworn fealty.

Monaldo took a step toward her but Count Favarone put out a hand to stop him. Monaldo turned away in disgust and strode out the door with the rest of the men following close behind. Clare restored her veil with shaking hands, then fell to her knees in front of the altar and wept.

The next day Francis procured permission from the Benedictine Abbot, Larione, to move Clare from the convent of San Paolo to another convent on the opposite end of Assisi. The sisters at the more secluded convent of Sant'Angelo near Panzo took Clare in without incident. A few weeks later, they took in her sister, Agnes, too.

"I have thought of little else since you left, Chiara," said Agnes in response to Clare's look of surprise when she entered her sister's cell. "My heart spoke to me long before this, but I did not listen. After you took your vows, I knew I would find no peace until I followed the same path. Francis has agreed to let me take vows right away."

Clare threw her arms around her sister. "I am so happy, Agnes! What do Mother and Papa think of it?" she asked. "And what have you done with Lord Rainerio?" After a pause, she added apprehensively, "And what about Uncle Monaldo?"

Agnes looked down at her hands, "I haven't actually told them yet," she confessed. "At first, Mother was terribly upset by what you had done, but I think she began to understand when I told her that you wanted to give your life to God alone. She has great respect for Brother Francis and the Friars Minor. I hope she will understand when she finds out that I have joined you," Agnes added, a little doubtfully.

Clare wondered how long it would take for the men to arrive and try to take Agnes home. Agnes continued, "As for Lord Rainerio, Bishop Guido has assured me that my obedience to God's call takes precedence over a promise of marriage made for me by my guardians." She smiled. "Perhaps in time, Beatrice will have him." The sisters laughed.

Agnes glanced nervously out the window and turned pale. "Oh, no."

Uncle Monaldo stood outside the gate arrayed in full armor and accompanied by at least a dozen men at arms. Their father was nowhere to be seen.

Shouts could be heard and the creaking hinges of the gate announced their entrance. Clare and Agnes knelt down beneath the cross in Clare's cell and begged the Mother of God to intercede. "*Ave Maria, gratia plena, Dominus tecum . . . ,*" they began.

A knock at the cell door interrupted them, and one of the Benedictine sisters entered. "The Count of Coriano wishes to speak with you, Lady Agnes. He said you are to come at once, and to come alone." Clare hugged Agnes and assured her that she would be praying.

"So!" Monaldo's voice boomed when Agnes stepped into the cobbled courtyard. "You *are* here! At least I have found you before you promised away your life and livelihood. Come with me this instant," he demanded.

"Uncle Monaldo, please listen," Agnes pleaded. "Long before now, I made a vow of my own to serve and live for God alone." Monaldo's face became stony. Agnes began to whisper the Psalms to herself for courage, "'He is my rock, and my salvation, my fortress. I shall not be moved.'"

"You have been bewitched by your sister and that crazy beggar-monk, Francesco di Bernardone," Monaldo said through clenched teeth. "Your parents might tolerate such nonsense, but I will not. I insist that you come back with me while Lord Rainerio and his estate can still be yours. I have brought my soldiers to see to it that you do not resist."

Two men took Agnes firmly by her arms. When she pulled back, they hesitated, but Monaldo gestured to them to continue and they dragged her toward the gate. Agnes tried desperately to hold onto the gate, the trees, anything on the way. She cried out to Clare for help. More guards moved in.

From her cell, Clare heard her sister's screams. In a loud

voice she took up the Psalm that Agnes had begun. "'My hope is in God, He only is my rock and my salvation, my fortress. On God rests my deliverance and my honor, my refuge is God.'"

She pronounced the words loudly and distinctly so that Agnes could hear, "'Trust in Him at all times. Save us, oh God!'"

Within minutes the guards' grip on Agnes began to loosen and she slipped to the ground, as if she were dead. Incredulous, Monaldo demanded that his soldiers explain what they were doing.

"She's as heavy as a millstone," one of them exclaimed.

"Lift her up, I tell you!" Monaldo insisted, but no one moved. He pushed the men aside to lift her himself, but she slipped out of his arms, too, like a sack of lead. In a fit of wrath, he raised his fist to strike his niece's head. Out of the tense stillness came Clare's voice as she continued to pray, "God have mercy. Save us, oh God."

Monaldo seemed frozen while the men looked on. Then at last, he let his arm drop. He stood up and grunted an order to his men, and they all walked away, leaving Agnes on the ground.

The next day, Agnes took the vow of obedience to the Holy Roman Church through Francis. Bishop Guido gave them the use of the church of San Damiano for their convent. When one of the Benedictine sisters asked to join them, followed soon after by another young woman from Assisi, Francis was confirmed in his conviction that these women he called the Poor Ladies of San Damiano had a God-given role to play in restoring the Church.

Leaving Clare and her companions under the protection of

the friars, Francis now turned his attention to another task: to share the Christian faith with the Almohad Saracens who were invading Spain. If God permitted, he hoped to go on to Morocco to preach directly to the leader or Miramolin—the Calif Muhammad el-Nasir himself.

Chapter Fifteen

THE HOPE OF THE CHURCH

"I will go with you!" a man of about thirty fell in step with Francis and Illuminato one day as they were making their way to the Iberian Peninsula. "If we succeed in converting the Miramolin, what glory will redound to your order! That is, to *our* order—if you will accept me. If we fail, our martyrdom will likewise serve the glory of the order!"

"Who are you, sir?" Francis asked.

"I am Elias Bombarone, a mattress maker, as was my father, but I want to be a Friar Minor and accompany you to Spain, to Morocco, and to anywhere else in the world you go! I have watched your order grow and gain respect throughout Italy!"

"Elias Bombarone," Francis answered. "Of course, you are welcome to accompany us and, if it be God's will, to remain with us as a Friar Minor. But you must realize that our order exists to bring glory to God alone." Brother Illuminato was uneasy in the company of this brash newcomer but Francis accepted anyone who approached him with sincerity.

Soon, however, Francis became ill and the mission to Spain

was delayed. Before the three companions even reached the northern border of Italy, the Almohad Saracens were defeated on Spanish soil and the Miramolin died in Morocco. Francis could not guess what plans God had for him this time, but he had learned to accept God's will.

On the way back to Assisi, Brother Elias volunteered to remain in Tuscany to establish the Friars Minor more widely. Francis agreed to this, although he never thought in terms of establishing the order. He believed God would take care of that.

Miles away in Rome, Pope Innocent III was looking for ways to put a fire into the cool hearts of men, both in Europe, where many Christians had grown tepid, and in the Holy Land, where Christianity was under attack. Calling together the political and religious leaders of the world, Pope Innocent convened the Fourth Lateran Council, "to eradicate vices and plant virtues, to correct faults and reform morals, to remove heresies and strengthen faith, to settle discords and establish peace, to get rid of oppression and foster liberty, to induce princes and Christian people to succor the Holy Land."

In that autumn of 1215, Rome was teeming with dignitaries. Dozens of archbishops, hundreds of bishops, almost one thousand abbots and priors, and countless political representatives had come to the Great Council. The Patriarchs of Constantinople and Jerusalem were there. Emperor Frederick II had sent his Archbishop. The kings of France, England, Aragon, and Hungary were represented.

Into this mix of worldly power and spiritual leadership

unwittingly ambled the barefooted Francis with a handful of his Friars Minor. They came to Rome out of obedience to the Holy Father who, six years before, had instructed him to return when the Almighty had multiplied their numbers.

His order had indeed grown. It included monasteries and hermitages scattered throughout central and southern Italy. The Poor Ladies at San Damiano, too, had increased in number and were now considered the Second Order of Francis. Through written correspondence between Clare and Pope Innocent, they had already been granted papal recognition and the privilege to live in complete poverty.

Francis intended to ask Cardinal Giovanni di San Paolo to be his mediator again in Rome, but when he arrived, he learned that the cardinal had died. Without someone in the Curia to help, Francis knew that it would be difficult to approach the Holy Father, especially during the Great Council. Another time would do just as well, he decided. "We can make use of our time in Rome instead to humbly beg and implore everyone to persevere in the true faith and in a life of penance, since there is no other way to be saved," Francis said to his brothers.

The Friars visited the sick and begged for food to share with the poor. In the streets, they noticed beggars accepting blankets and bread from a tall, simply dressed noblewoman with a small boy at her side. When she saw Francis, she approached shyly.

"Brother Francis?" she asked tentatively. "I am Jacopa de' Settesoli. I feel as if I already know you."

Francis said, "We noticed you caring for the poor."

"Oh, yes," she said, "and I will tell you why. Years ago, when you were in Rome, I overheard you speaking to one of your friars in front of the Septizodium—those ruins along the Via Appia where so many of the city's homeless take shelter. You said, 'My brother, when you see a poor man, behold in him a mirror of the Lord. In the sick, too,' you said, 'consider that He bore our sicknesses.' I have never forgotten that," Lady Jacopa said. "Since then I have tried to serve the poor and the sick in the small ways that I can, out of love of Our Lord and his Mother."

Francis exclaimed, "You are like a Friar Minor in Rome! I will call you, not Lady Jacopa, but Brother Jacoba!"

Jacopa laughed and turned to her son, a boy of about five who reached up to whisper in her ear. "My son wants me to invite you and your friars to stay at our home while you are in Rome," she said. "He is certain you will accept when you hear that we have a fresh batch of honey almond pastries," she said with a laugh. "My husband, Gratiano, would also be honored."

Francis accepted gladly since the friars had no place to stay in Rome. Jacopa's husband, Gratiano Frangipani, belonged to one of the oldest families of Roman nobility. His palatial residence stood in the center of the city next to the ancient Colosseum built in the first century. The Frangipanis had installed a small chapel in the Colosseum to honor the early Christian martyrs who died there. Despite their great wealth, Jacopa and Gratiano lived modestly. Francis found that the Friars Minor could live with them in simplicity during their stay. They would have easy access to the chapel, and to the delicious pastries!

On that first evening, Gratiano Frangipani informed Francis of a plan to restrict new religious orders. "There have been too many cases of religious zealots who gather a large following and then fall into heresy," he told Francis. "The Council will likely require all new orders to adopt either the Rule of Saint Benedict or the Rule of Saint Augustine."

Francis was thoughtful. He believed that God intended his order to be different from those other orders. His friars were to be obedient to the pope and to revere bishops and priests; but unlike those orders, the poverty of a Friar Minor must be absolute. There should be nothing that belongs to him or to his community, not even property.

Without Cardinal Giovanni di San Paolo, who could make a case for the poverty of the Friars Minor at this critical time?

One morning, Lady Jacopa hurried to Francis who was working at the hospital near the Lateran. "Cardinal Hugolino heard that you are staying with us—he has asked to meet with you!" she said. Cardinal Hugolino, Count of Anagni and Bishop of Ostia, was considered the single most influential member of the Curia and was known for his holy life and generosity to the poor. Francis was eager to meet him and perhaps to seek his counsel.

"Welcome, Brother Francis," the old cardinal rose and bowed when Francis entered his rooms near the Porta Asinaria. Though embarrassed by such deferential treatment, Francis liked the cardinal at once.

"I have wanted to meet you, Brother Francis, ever since you first stood before Pope Innocent six years ago to ask his blessing for your order. I thought that such audacity could only be the work of the Holy Spirit! When you spoke, I marveled that a man of such admirable simplicity could also comprehend what is profound and beautiful in the Faith, as you so clearly do."

Francis replied, "Of myself I know little, but all truth and goodness flows from the Cross."

"You are right! Would that the powers of the world were content to place themselves there beside you. That is where they should be; where we all should be." The cardinal was thoughtful for a moment. "It gives hope to the Church, however," he continued, "that God has not abandoned us, as perhaps we deserve, but appears instead to be working through men like you and like Friar Dominic here." The cardinal signaled to a man with reddish-brown hair who had just arrived in the doorway.

"You summoned me, Your Lordship?" the man spoke with an accent that Francis did not recognize.

Cardinal Hugolino introduced him to Francis. "This is Friar Dominic de Guzman. In France, he leads a group called the Preachers of Toulouse. Their mission is compatible with yours, Francis, to encourage virtue and to teach the true faith. He has met with tremendous success in France. He is here in Rome with the Bishop of Toulouse seeking approval of his new order."

Turning to Friar Dominic, the cardinal said, "This is Francesco di Bernardone, founder of the Friars Minor, penitents from Assisi. He is our light of hope in Italy."

Dominic's eyes lit up with recognition. "Brother Francis, I would like to see your order and mine combined and living under the same Rule in the Church!"

Friar Dominic was dressed in the same way as Francis; he wore a rough dark robe tied at the waist by a simple cord.

The men spoke at length and as they exchanged stories and ideas, they realized that they were meant to reach the hearts of men through different paths. They would not combine orders, they decided.

Although disappointed, the cardinal was more impressed than ever by their prudence and charity. *How the Church would benefit from such men in its hierarchy*, he thought. He said to them, "Since the pastors in the early Church were poor and consumed by charity, why shouldn't we choose bishops now from among your friars?" Cardinal Hugolino looked hopefully from one to the other but he saw at once that this would not do.

Dominic spoke first. "My lord, with all respect, the dignity of their state should suffice my friars and I would not permit them to seek any higher office."

Francis added, "My brothers are called Friars *Minor*, Your Lordship, so that they may never become *majors*. Their vocation teaches them to remain in a humble condition. If they are to be truly useful to the Church, I beg you, never permit them to become prelates."

Cardinal Hugolino sighed. "Then it must be by example of holiness and faithfulness—through prayer, sacrifice, and preaching," he said, "that your two orders will breathe new life into the Church."

The next afternoon, Lady Jacopa sought out Francis in the Colosseum chapel. She could hardly wait to speak to him. "Pope Innocent has made a surprise announcement!" she told him as he came out. "The Great Council has decreed that every new order must adopt the Rule of Benedict or Augustine, just as we expected, but Innocent has insisted that this measure must *not* include the Order of Friars Minor whose own preliminary Rule he had already approved!"

Francis went with Jacopa and Gratiano to hear Pope Innocent's concluding remarks to the Council. When they arrived, the Holy Father was standing in front of the Lateran Basilica, beneath the statues of the two saints, John the Baptist and John the Evangelist. With the shepherd's staff in his hand, he spoke to the assembly and to the entire world.

He urged priests to be holy above all else, to seek wisdom and knowledge of the true Faith and to teach it faithfully at all times. He reiterated the doctrine of the Real Presence of Christ in the Holy Eucharist—Body, Blood, Soul, and Divinity—as the source and the summit of the true Faith. The pontiff lamented all division among the faithful and offered his hope that the East and the West might be reunited under the successor of Peter, the rock upon which Christ built His church. He told of sacrilege and violence against Christians in Jerusalem and begged Christians to strive for peace. In conclusion, Innocent reminded the world, "Only those will obtain mercy who have mortified the flesh and conformed their life to that of the crucified Savior."

"That is the goal of my life!" Francis spoke aloud in his excitement to his friend Lady Jacopa. "That is my whole purpose!"

After the Lateran Council, Francis and his friars left Rome full of fresh zeal. When Francis reached the Portiuncula a few weeks later, a grasshopper jumped onto his hand, as if to welcome him back. "Sing, Sister Grasshopper," said Francis to the small insect. "Rejoice and praise the Lord thy Creator, who is great indeed!"

The grasshopper rubbed its legs together and began to chirp. After a short performance, Francis said, "Thank you, Sister Grasshopper." It jumped from his hand to a nearby fig tree.

Every morning for a week, when Francis emerged from his cell, the grasshopper greeted him with a song and afterward returned to its perch in the fig tree. One day it did not come. "Everything in this life is passing," observed Francis. "'The grass withers, and the flower falls, but the Word of the Lord endures forever.'"

Chapter Sixteen

FOR THE SALVATION OF OTHERS

"**P**ope Innocent lies dead at Perugia," Brother Elias announced one afternoon in July of the following summer. "Since the Great Council, he has been traveling throughout Italy promoting the new crusade. When he reached Perugia, he fell ill and died within a day."

Francis made a sign of the cross and intoned "Eternal rest, grant unto him, Lord." After a pause, he added, "And let perpetual light shine upon him." Elias, in his distracted state, had forgotten to answer the prayer.

"May he rest in peace. Amen," Elias added absently. Then he said, "It is a remarkable thing, that while the body of the deceased pope lay in state in the Cathedral, robbers broke in during the night and stripped it of its costly robes and ornaments, leaving it as exposed and unadorned as any pauper's corpse. Twenty-four hours earlier, this man had been the most influential ruler of the Christian world!"

Francis was saddened by the disrespect for Christ's vicar on earth. He summoned the friars to the chapel to pray for the soul of this pope who had been their champion in Rome.

The next day Francis went to Perugia to pay his respects to the deceased pope. While there, he met Cardinal Hugolino, who was now involved with the selection of the next pope. But he took time to go with Francis back to the Portiuncula to see for himself how the friars lived.

After observing that the friars ate their simple meals from the bare ground and slept on straw, Cardinal Hugolino said, "Brother Francis, your brothers, who are so good, live in such poverty! I fear how it will be on the day of judgment for those of us who are not as holy but who live so luxuriously day after day." Hugolino returned to Perugia, more convinced than ever of the sanctity of Francis and his Order of Friars Minor.

A few days later a new pope, Honorius III, was consecrated at Perugia. Having seen the body of his predecessor dishonored in the Cathedral of Perugia, he observed, "Not for ourselves do we live, but to bring salvation to others." The life of the Church went forward, with Honorius III at its helm.

The Fourth Lateran Council had directed religious orders to meet at least once a year, to read a chapter of the Scriptures in common, to receive instruction, and to discuss any changes within the order. The Friars Minor prepared for their first general chapter meeting to be held on Pentecost of 1217. By this time, there were nearly one thousand Friars Minor throughout the Valley of Spoleto, Tuscany, and the Marches of Ancona, even into the Kingdom of Sicily. Among them were men from nearly every kind of background. Francis delighted in the variety of "knights" at his "round table," as he called them, but he found it humbling, too.

A few days before the chapter meeting, Francis confided to Bernardo, his first follower. "The brothers have asked me to preach and so I will, just as I have always done. But what if all the brothers, when I am ready to begin, start to cry out against me saying, 'We do not want you to rule over us any longer, for you are not eloquent as you should be, and you are too small and simple! We are ashamed to have such a simple and poor-looking Superior.' They would be perfectly right, Bernardo!" he said. "I am afraid they may cast me out with scorn."

Bernardo laughed, but Francis added, "It seems to me that I would not be a true Friar Minor unless I were just as happy when they deposed me in disgrace, as when they held me in respect. If I am happy when they honor me in their devotion—which may well be a danger to my soul—I ought to rejoice and be far happier when they abuse me, for this is a sure spiritual gain.'"

The day arrived for the chapter meeting. Francis looked out at the assembled friars—among them were his first disciples, many who had joined along the way, and some whom he had not met until now.

"Rejoice, little ones of Christ!" Francis called out from the doorstep of the chapel. The friars formed a semi-circle that spread out like a fan across the little portion of land and into the surrounding trees. "On this Feast of Pentecost give glory to God the Father, the Son, and the Holy Spirit. Our Lord said, 'Everyone who acknowledges me before men, I also will acknowledge before my Father in heaven.' Our Lady first acknowledged

Christ before men when she carried him under her heart, and now we Friars Minor must carry Christ in our hearts into the world to bear witness to Christ."

Francis appointed friars to go to places where no one had yet heard of them: Lombardy and Venetia in Northern Italy, Hungary, Spain, and England beyond the Alps. He sent Brother Pacifico with a group to the Midi to preach among the Albigenses. He sent Elias to preach to the crusaders in Syria, Illuminato to Northern Africa. Sixty other friars he sent into Germany. A few were to remain behind in central Italy. He gave them his blessing and then joyfully declared, "It would not be fitting for me to send you into privation and insult without exposing myself to them also, so I have decided to go to France."

The Friars left the Portiuncula that same day without money, change of clothes, letters of authority, or provisions of any kind, to go to places they had never seen before. For his journey, Francis took Brother Masseo and Brother Sylvester with him. When the three had gone as far as Florence, they paused on a hill to view the beautiful walled city. The cathedral dome of Santa Reparata was visible above all the tiled roofs around it. The streets bustled with horses and carts, men, women, and children.

Suddenly pensive, Francis said to Masseo and Sylvester, "We must remember, brothers, that our friends are those who cause us trouble and suffering, shame or injury, pain or torture, even martyrdom and death. My little brothers, it is these we must love and love very much, because for all they do to us, we are given eternal life."

The two men were puzzled. Did he expect to die at the hands of the Florentines? Or did he have a premonition of some other trouble? There was no time to ask. Church bells began to ring across the city and a group of children ran to meet Francis, "*Il santo!*" they shouted. "The saint!" Men and women of the town followed close behind, eager to see the holy man they had all heard about.

The throng followed the friars through the gates into the heart of the city. Francis stopped in front of the cathedral. Someone called out, "Tell us how to be like you, Francis! What can we do? How can we find peace like yours?"

Francis replied, "Do not strive to be like me! I, your servant, am the worst of sinners. Imitate our dear Lord! No greater love hath any man than that he lay down his life for his friend. As Christ did, so you do. Lay down your life each day. Empty yourselves and God will fill you a thousand times over with his mercy and his peace. Do not place your trust in the uncertainty of riches but in the living God and become rich in good works. God alone is good; He alone is holy and worthy of all praise and blessing for endless ages."

While Francis was speaking, an elderly prelate stepped out of the bishop's palace next door. He noticed the reverence of the crowd and the simple eloquence of the speaker. *The sanctity of this man is plain*, he thought. When Francis finished, he realized that the prelate was his friend from Rome, Cardinal Hugolino.

Francis knelt for a blessing, and then the cardinal said, "You and your companions must be my guest in the Episcopal Palace, where I am staying while the Bishop of Florence is away."

"It will be my honor, Sir Cardinal, but first we must beg for our bread," said Francis.

"You need not beg! The Bishop of Florence has plenty for all of his guests," the cardinal protested.

"It would be wrong for me to dine in comfort on the bishop's fine food, while my brothers are risking their lives for the sake of the Gospel in foreign lands. At last our brotherhood has grown large enough to go forth and preach to all nations, as Christ commanded! I myself am taking a small group to France," Francis told him.

Cardinal Hugolino frowned. "Come with me, Francis. We must speak where it is quiet."

Once inside the bishop's residence, Cardinal Hugolino asked Francis about his plans for his expanding order, and what Form of Life he had written to guide them.

"A Friar Minor's Form of Life is to follow the Gospel," Francis answered simply.

"Not everyone understands the Gospel as you so clearly do, Brother Francis," the cardinal objected. "You must give some account, some application of the Gospel to life within your order, so others will know how to live." The cardinal wanted to know how he had ensured that the Poor Ladies of San Damiano would be cared for in his absence. And how could he ensure that all his friars preach faithfully and well, especially now that many new friars had never even met him? Had he obtained letters of papal protection for his friars in foreign lands? Without some official acknowledgment from the Church, they might well face imprisonment, or starvation. Strangers with no credentials in those countries, the cardinal said, were treated harshly.

"A Friar Minor must not fear hardship for the sake of the Gospel," Francis objected.

"A Friar Minor will not have much opportunity to share the Gospel from prison," countered the practical prelate.

Francis was distressed. He simply wanted to share his joy in the love of God. Never had he considered a need to establish rules, provide guidelines, or control the movements of his followers. He always believed that God would work in each soul just as He had worked in his.

"God has made of you a leader, Francis, in spite of yourself," Cardinal Hugolino said sympathetically. "I want to help you bring organization to your sons and new daughters. The first thing we must do is to gain the confidence of Pope Honorius and the Curia. Come to Rome at the turn of the year, Francis. If all goes well, I will obtain permission to act as your advisor."

Francis hesitated, "I must first go to France, Sir Cardinal. I have sent all my sons to dangerous places to suffer hardship and perhaps to die. It would be wrong for me to remain in Italy in safety and comfort."

"My son," said Hugolino, "you cannot leave Italy when your order is so young. You are its head and its heart. If you cross the Alps, it will scatter and fail, and the Church will be deprived of a treasure."

The next day, Francis was walking south again with Brother Sylvester and Brother Masseo, resigned to stay in Italy until his order was more firmly established, with rules and provisions to guide it. Soon he was back in Assisi where the brothers could easily reach him with questions or problems. He rarely traveled beyond Umbria, but established ministers to "serve and not be served" in each region where the Friars Minor went. They were to be "mothers" to the group, he said, and not masters.

At this time, friars who had been sent to foreign lands began to return to the Portiuncula. The group that had gone to Germany was the first to come back with stories of the troubles they encountered. At first it went quite well, they said. They had learned that *ja* was the German word for "yes," and it was a most useful word. By offering it in answer to questions they did not understand, they had been able to move unhindered through the towns. They were given food, blankets to fend off the icy cold, and a sheltered place to sleep. So far, so good.

But when someone asked a question to which *ja* was apparently the wrong answer, people started to shun them. Their *ja* became less confident. When they heard the angry word, *haretiker*, hurled at them, they finally understood. "We are not heretics!" they tried to explain, but no one could understand them. One night a crowd came after them with a noose, and the friars ran away. They were willing to die for the true Faith, they said, but not for heresy.

More friars returned from other countries with similar stories. Some were beaten, some were dragged by horses, some were stripped and chased out of towns. Hearing of these experiences, Francis recalled Cardinal Hugolino's advice to obtain letters of protection for his friars. Yet, Christ had no such letters when he came to preach, nor did he require his apostles to carry letters.

Francis returned to Rome in the winter of 1218 to discuss the organization of his order with Cardinal Hugolino. The sun was beginning to set when Francis and his small group of friars arrived. Francis first visited his friend, "Brother Jacoba."

"Your visit is timely, Francis," Lady Jacopa said as she winked at her young son. "I am just about to bake a batch of almond pastries!"

Early the next morning, Francis found Cardinal Hugolino outside the Lateran Basilica where he had been offering Mass. "You have come, Francis!" he exclaimed. "And none too soon. The Pope and his Curia will be happy for a respite from the bad news that troubles the Church."

Francis listened sympathetically while Cardinal Hugolino recounted the pope's struggles with Emperor Frederick Hohenstaufen, with the Albigensian crusade, and with a rising feud in Rome that threatened the pope's life.

"As you can imagine, Francis," Cardinal Hugolino said, "the pope and his cardinal advisors would welcome a message of hope such as only you can deliver. Besides," he added confidentially, "I am convinced that hearing you will dispose them all to support you and your order of mendicant friars."

Francis started at the cardinal's suggestion that he should preach to the Curia. "I cannot preach to the pope and his cardinal advisors! I am ignorant and unlettered," he protested. "Surely it would be better for you to address the Curia on my behalf. These are the leaders of the Church—educated and holy men. They will think I am simple and ridiculous because that is what I am. Perhaps they will hate me and tell me I have no business trying to lead the Friars Minor."

"You will speak well as you always do, Francis, about the love of God," the cardinal assured him. "Surely that is for everyone, educated or not. I remember how you once moved Innocent III to tears."

"I spoke then as a son seeking the blessing of his father," Francis objected. "I did not come to offer advice or to preach a sermon to him and his Curia. I would not know what to say."

The cardinal was bemused by the holy man's reticence. "I can help you prepare a speech, if you like. You can memorize it and simply repeat it to the Curia," he offered.

So together Cardinal Hugolino and Francis composed a homily designed to allay any qualms the cardinals might have about his order. In the days that followed, Francis repeated it over and over to himself while Cardinal Hugolino arranged a meeting with the Curia. When at last the day arrived to deliver his homily, Francis stood before them just as he had stood before hundreds of other crowds, but this time he was nervous.

"Most revered sirs, knights of the pope's round table," he began, forgetting already the proper form of address. Francis stopped. The men looked back at him curiously. His mind was blank. *There are so many of them, they are so learned*, he thought. "I know nothing," he said aloud. He noticed Cardinal Hugolino's look of surprise and begged God for help.

He remembered then, the promise Christ made to his disciples, "Do not be anxious about how or what you are to say, for the Holy Spirit will teach you in that very hour what you ought to say."

"I know nothing, and I am nothing," Francis began again. "God is all. When I was in my sins God said to me, 'Francesco di Bernardone, you must die to yourself.' He told me, 'Do not be anxious about your life, what you shall eat, nor about your body, what you shall put on. Consider the lilies, how they grow; they neither toil nor spin, yet I tell you, even Solomon in all his glory was not clothed like one of these.'

"The clothing with which He clothes me now is more beautiful than the costliest silk. It is with the cross that I and my brothers are clothed. For Christ once said, 'Where your treasure is, there will your heart be also.'"

As he spoke, Francis began to gesture with his arms and moved about the floor in his joy at God's message. His learned audience was spellbound. Cardinal Hugolino smiled. This did not even resemble the speech they had prepared, but it was far better because it issued from a heart deeply in love with God. When Francis finished, Pope Honorius gave his whole-hearted blessing, and the Curia posed no theological objection to the Friars Minor.

Later that day, the cardinal admonished Francis, "Now, you must compose a more complete Rule of Life to ensure your order remains faithful to your vision. And, it must be practicable." Francis had to admit that conflicts and questions frequently arose among the friars that were not addressed explicitly in the Gospel. They looked to Francis for a resolution, but Francis knew that he would not always be there. And though his first followers shared his understanding of absolute poverty, others looked for ways to modify it so that they could own property and dwell in houses. Some wanted papal protection from insult, some wanted their "rights" acknowledged and the authority to punish anyone who violated them. Tension was developing among his followers because of these different opinions.

Francis began having a recurring dream. "In my dream," he told the cardinal, "there is a little black hen with a large brood of small chicks who run helter-skelter, peeping, and stumbling. The hen is frantic to gather them under her wing but there are too many. I am that black hen, and it is plain that I cannot take care of all my sons."

When Cardinal Hugolino suggested that he study the Rules of other religious orders and try to incorporate them into his. Francis replied that he would write a Rule of Life, yes, but it must be faithful to the first Rule of Life, the three Gospel passages that God had shown him. That is what Pope Innocent III had approved.

"But it must be practicable," the cardinal's words haunted him.

On his return to Assisi from Rome, Francis was swarmed in the market squares by admirers; sometimes they met him with songs and called out "*Il Santo!*" He knew that it was not himself but the love of Christ that attracted them, the example of Christ that they saw in his poverty, the mind of Christ found in the Gospels that penetrated his simple speech. The more the people came to love Christ, the more his joy was restored. He preached tirelessly throughout central Italy.

One afternoon, as Francis walked with Brother Masseo and Brother Angelo in the hill country outside the town of Bevagna, their gaze fell on a meadow where shafts of sunlight broke through the shifting clouds. Drawing closer, they noticed birds on the ground whose colorful plumes dotted the meadow like wildflowers. More and more birds came so that the friars were amazed at the variety gathered together in one place—jackdaws with white-ringed eyes, jet black crows, and doves with iridescent feathers, plovers, swifts, nuthatches, swallows, and martins.

Francis walked into the field, but the birds did not startle. They gravitated to him. He bent down to touch a dove who bowed its head for him stroke. Another nudged in so that it could be petted, too, and then another. "What beautiful creatures you are, even more than King Solomon in all his splendor!" Francis crooned. "*I know all the birds of the air and with me is the beauty of the field, for the world is mine and the fullness thereof . . . offer to your God the sacrifice of praise.*"

Standing up, he spoke to the birds with a smile, "My brothers, you should praise your Creator and always love Him." The birds craned their heads toward Francis, flapping their wings and shifting their feet like an expectant congregation so that he laughed. Since they did not move, he gave them a little sermon. "God gave you feathers to clothe you, wings so that you can fly, and whatever else was necessary. God made you noble among His creatures and He gave you a home in the purity of the air. Though you neither sow nor reap, He nevertheless protects and governs you without any solicitude on your part."

Francis made a sign of the cross over the birds. At this they began to sing, each in its own language. At his command, the birds rose together from the ground, filling the sky, dipping, soaring, and flapping their wings in every direction until none were left.

"It was as if the birds had been waiting to hear God's praises," Francis remarked to Angelo and Masseo. "I should remember never to neglect even the least of God's creatures who praise God by their simple obedience to nature. Everything about them speaks of the glory of their Creator!"

For a year and a half after his visit to Rome, Francis kept within easy reach of Assisi. New friars joined the order almost every day, coming to the Portiuncula to learn from him and to receive his blessing. At the same time, Francis tried to compose a formal Rule of Life. It was a laborious work that required thought and a great deal of prayer.

All this time, Francis felt God wanted something more of him. He told a group of brothers one day, "I long to go beyond the borders of Italy, to bring to the Saracens the joy of the cross of Christ."

"But, Father Francis," one of the brothers objected, "the Saracens, who do not know Christ, will not be likely to receive your message with joy. They are more likely to kill you."

Francis smiled. "Christ came into a world that did not know Him. I, too, want to carry His message of salvation to a people that do not yet know Him. And if they take my life, I will be following even more closely in the footsteps of Christ."

However, he could not leave Italy yet. Not only his friars,

but the Poor Ladies of San Damiano still needed guidance. As more women joined the Poor Ladies, more convents had to be established in Perugia, Siena, Lucca, and Florence. Together, Clare, Francis, and Cardinal Hugolino composed a Rule of Life for the Poor Ladies that respected their "privilege of poverty," as Clare called it.

By the time of the Pentecost chapter meeting in 1219, Cardinal Hugolino had sent out letters of introduction for the friars to the bishops and priests of any place that Francis and his friars were likely to travel. Soon after, Francis received a "Letter of Commendation" from Pope Honorius that friars could carry with them as proof of their fidelity to the Church. All these measures helped to establish the order more firmly, while the Rule was still taking form in the mind of its humble architect.

Chapter Seventeen

THE SULTAN OF EGYPT

Cardinal Hugolino was now satisfied that the friars could travel with reasonable safety beyond the borders of Italy. With joy that they could now fulfill Christ's command to, "go, teach all nations," Francis sent his brothers off to foreign lands.

Some left for Tunis in Africa, some to Syria, some to Greece, some to Morocco, ready and willing to meet their deaths if necessary, to spread the message of salvation, the Gospel of Jesus Christ. Francis appointed two men to act as vicars in his absence: Brother Gregory of Naples and Brother Matthew of Narni, both capable leaders.

Finally, with Brother Peter Catanei at his side, Francis set sail from Ancona for the Nile Delta in Egypt where the Fifth Crusade was well underway. After a long journey they were met at the port by Brother Illuminato, who had been sent to Northern Africa the year before, and a new friar, Brother Caesarius of Speyer. They walked toward the crusaders' camp on the marshy lands of the Delta, and Illuminato described to Francis the tense state of the holy war.

The crusaders were entrenched in a prolonged siege of Damietta, where Sir Jean de Brienne hoped to secure a stronghold. If the crusading army took Damietta, he would attack the Egyptian capital of Cairo, crippling the enemy who held both Egypt and Palestine. From that point on, the conquest of Palestine would be easy and Jerusalem would be in Christian hands once more.

The pope's advisor, Cardinal Pelagius, had followed the crusading army to Damietta. In the absence of the emperor, he assumed control as supreme advisor. As soon as he arrived, he was in conflict with Jean de Brienne. When Pelagius was struck with malaria. de Brienne was left again in charge, for the time being. It remained to be seen whether the cardinal would survive.

The sultan of Egypt, Malek al-Kamil, with the aid of his Turkish general, resisted the Christian army skillfully. His slave soldiers had built a tremendous bastion in front of the walls of Damietta and blocked all waterways to the city with a network of heavy chains. In the sultry heat of the Mediterranean estuary, the French crusaders were erecting a floating siege tower such as the world had never seen. It was nearly as large as an island and bore an iron spike that protruded from its tower like a giant tooth. No bastion would be able to hold fast against such a powerful machine.

Francis immediately sought out the sick cardinal to ask permission to cross enemy lines and preach to the sultan before it was too late. The magnificent galley of the cardinal legate was easy to locate in the harbor; its bright red canopy and golden tassels contrasted sharply with the drab military ships. After listening to Francis, the wretched prelate immediately refused his request to cross the battle line. "You would be killed instantly," he said. "Or worse, they would take you for an emissary—albeit an odd one—and think we were suing for peace. We would be powerless to help you." He would hear nothing more about it.

The cardinal's anxious thoughts returned to the siege of Damietta. He had little confidence in the leadership of Jean de Brienne, and it frustrated him to be rendered helpless by his fever. Francis tried to make the cardinal comfortable, but the prelate's anxiety of mind and his diseased body gave him no respite.

"De Brienne is not the fearless leader that his brother, Walter, once was," Pelagius complained while Francis wiped his hot forehead with a cool cloth. "Our goal was to take Cairo but now he says that if the siege of Damietta drags on much longer our army will be exhausted. Even if the siege is successful, he says he will only use it as a bargaining piece. Preposterous! To weaken the enemy and then leave while the rest of Egypt remains in the hands of the enemy!"

"Is the conquest of Egypt necessary?" Francis asked simply. "The goal of the crusade was to reclaim the Holy Land."

"You are not a military man, Francesco di Bernardone, so of course you would not be expected to understand," said the prelate impatiently. "If we do not take Alexandria and Cairo as well as Damietta, Christian men, women, and children in Egypt will continue to suffer under their harsh oppressors and there will be no real security in the Holy Land. Most of the wealth and strength of Egypt lies in its port cities, with Cairo as its center of power. If the Egyptians are allowed to continue to thrive, nothing will prevent them from rising again. With Egypt in Christian hands, however, our hold on the Holy Land would be secure and the name of Christ will be glorified." Cardinal Pelagius dropped back on his pillow, exhausted from trying to explain this situation.

Filled with foreboding for the coming battle, Francis made his way back to the camp where he spoke to the soldiers about the urgent need of repentance. He reminded them of the great sacrifice Christ made for the salvation of every human soul.

"Crusaders of the Cross of Christ," he said to them, "avail yourself of the grace that Christ won by his death on the cross. Prepare now to meet death knowing that He accompanies you in your suffering and waits to embrace those who serve Him with faithfulness and love."

The next day, when the siege engine advanced, Francis tried to keep in mind the cardinal's glorious vision. He uttered a prayer for the brave soldiers on its deck as it crashed against the gates of the sultan's bastion, crumbling its walls with the iron tooth. He saw men jump from ram to parapet and from parapet to ram, wielding pikes, spears, lances, and sickles. Crocodiles gathered in the river below and vultures darkened the sky above as bodies began to fall into the Nile. Wails could be heard from Christian and Moslem men alike; wails of pain, anguish, and hatred.

Francis ran to the bank of the river, beckoning to his friars for help. Together, they pulled body after body out of the water. With tears in his eyes, Francis wiped away the mud and stemmed the bleeding wounds. He tied up mutilated stumps where limbs had been hacked off, and when he could, he provided comfort to the dying. Gently he closed the eyelids of hundreds of corpses. His heart ached as he buried the dead in shallow pits of sand.

Deep inside him, emotions churned as his mind returned to the night of the raid on the Rocca Maggiore above Assisi in 1197. He had been young then, sinful, proud, and confused. Because of his actions then, he knew that men just like these had suffered and died. In his mind he saw the faces of his friends at the Battle of Collestrada, too: Benetto's battered body and blank stare under the horses' hooves and Roberto, bent over backward on the bridge of San Giovanni under the point of a Perugian sword. "God forgive us!" Francis repeated under his breath. "God forgive us."

As night closed in on the delta, the crusaders knew they had won. They held the citadel and Damietta was within their grasp. Over the next few days, the camp of the crusaders was tense with expectation as Jean de Brienne, Cardinal Pelagius, and the Sultan al-Kamil began negotiations.

Unbeknownst to de Brienne and Pelagius, the sultan had received word from his father, the powerful Sultan Malik al-Adil, to expect no help from him or his brothers. His father was dying and the terrible Genghis Khan was moving westward through Asia, ever closer to the borders of Syria. All their combined forces were needed in Syria, his father said. The old sultan advised his son to offer the crusading army a compromise they could not refuse so that they would be content to leave quickly. "Then you must hurry to the aid of your brethren against the Mongol horde," he commanded his son in a written note.

The three leaders of the Holy War met outside de Brienne's tent under the burning Egyptian sun. Generals and soldiers from both sides looked on from a distance.

"You may take the Holy Land. It is yours," the sultan told de Brienne tersely. "My father has preserved the wood of the cross of Christ in Damascus. This, too, will be restored to you."

The King of Jerusalem could not believe what he was hearing. He hardly dared to breathe lest the meaning of the wonderful words somehow slip away.

"At what cost?" interrupted Cardinal Pelagius suspiciously. He was seated while the others stood, but he was no less intimidating.

"The Franks leave Damietta," was the sultan's simple answer.

De Brienne's relief was visible. He was ready to agree at once, but the final decision lay with the cardinal.

"No!" snapped Cardinal Pelagius with vehemence. "Damietta will be ours! What is more, we will not leave Egypt until we have taken Alexandria and Cairo as well. To be sure, the Holy Land will be restored to us, and the wood of the cross besides! But we will have Egypt first."

Negotiations went no further. The sultan returned to Damietta to prepare for the onslaught. Jean de Brienne reported the situation to his dispirited men. Cardinal Pelagius returned satisfied to his galley.

In the somber days that followed, Francis approached Cardinal Pelagius again with the request to cross enemy lines. He longed to tell the sultan about Christ, he explained. It was an opportunity he could not miss.

The cardinal lost patience. "Go if you are determined. It will mean certain death, of course, and no one will come to your aid. If you live to speak to the sultan, be sure he understands that you do not speak on behalf of myself, nor of the Holy Father, nor of the King of Jerusalem. You represent no one but yourself."

"I will speak only on behalf of the Great King," said Francis.

"What?" said the cardinal in alarm, and then grasped his meaning. "Oh, yes, of course," he said, waving his hand absently.

The sunlight reflected on the river so brightly that Francis and Illuminato had to squint to see. They were crossing the Nile at last. Francis could hardly believe it. He dared to hope that today he would meet the sultan. Who could tell what might follow?

The instant he and Brother Illuminato stepped onto the opposite shore of the Nile River, they were seized by soldiers who saw that they were unarmed and took their audacity as an affront. "Soldan? Soldan?" Francis repeated the word for sultan between blows.

Across the river, on the crusader's side, a handful of men watched. "The sultan awards one gold bezant to any man who brings him the head of a Christian," one man noted ominously.

"Where does that friar find such courage?" another wondered aloud.

"I can do all things in Him who gives me strength," a voice from behind answered. The kind-looking man who spoke was the Bishop of Acre, Jacques de Vitry, who had come with several other priests to witness the siege of Damietta and to offer spiritual aid. Beside the bishop stood, Father Colin and Father

Michael, whose respect for Francis was growing by bounds. It was all the bishop could do to restrain them from leaping into a boat to join Francis on the other side.

As if to confirm the source of his courage, Francis sang loudly as the soldiers led him away with Illuminato. "*Though I should walk in the midst of the shadow of death, I will fear no evil. For Thou art with me.*"

Soon the figures of Francis, Illuminato, and their captors disappeared. The small crowd on the bank dispersed, doubtful of ever seeing the friars again.

By the end of that day, Francis and Illuminato were brought before the sultan of Egypt, Malek al-Kamil. Bruised, bleeding, and disheveled, Francis had one thought on his mind when he entered the sultan's opulent quarters: the conversion of this powerful leader of a vast nation. Was he not, after all, a man with an immortal soul like everyone else, destined for eternity and in need of the message of salvation, the Word of God? Was he not the spiritual father of many people? His conversion could change the course of history and lead untold numbers to Christ.

"You trod upon the cross! You are no true Christian then?" the sultan demanded from his silk cushion seat. Slaves waved ostrich plumes above his head to cool the air of the sultry afternoon. Despite his luxurious surroundings, the sultan sat upright, his dark eyes riveted to the two friars as if analyzing them.

Francis and Illuminato looked down at the carpet. Francis laughed aloud when he noticed for the first time the pattern of gold crosses on the plush cerulean background.

"Honorable Majesty, there are many crosses besides the

cross of Christ," he explained. "Next to the Savior of the world at Calvary hung two criminals on crosses just such as these. Not every cross is the cross of Christ, but only the one true cross through which salvation comes, the cross that was endured for love of us."

"What do you mean, 'for love of us'?" The sultan was curious. "Explain your meaning."

Francis told the sultan about Jesus Christ over the course of several hours that day. He was ordered to return the next day, and the next, to stand before the sultan and explain his meaning.

In those three days, Francis told Sultan al-Kamil that Jesus came to earth at Bethlehem of Judea as a child, to endure poverty and humility; that he lived and taught throughout the region of Israel so that men might know how to live. Francis spoke of Peter, the "rock" upon which Christ built His Church. He spoke of the grace of the Holy Spirit that Christ won by sacrificing His life, and that He sent to guide His Church on earth. He talked about the sacraments that He instituted to give men strength on their earthly journey. He spoke tenderly of the Eucharist, the sacrament of love and the perpetuation of the sacrifice Christ made on Calvary. He told of the beatitudes that Jesus proclaimed from a hill by the Sea of Galilee.

The sultan listened in silence, his expression inscrutable, his piercing gaze never straying. When Francis described the passion and death of Christ, "the perfect fulfillment of the beatitudes and the ultimate act of Divine Mercy," Illuminato saw the sultan's eyes glisten. Then Francis told of the resurrection of Christ and his commission to his disciples to "teach all nations, baptizing them in the name of the Father and of the Son and of the Holy Spirit."

"You weave a wonderful tale, Friar," said the sultan at last.

"The most wonderful thing about it," said Francis, "is that it is no tale, but the truth."

"The truth," repeated the sultan enigmatically. "The truth that your Jesus was a great prophet in his time."

"Yes!" agreed Francis. "A great prophet! One who speaks the truth."

"The truth," said the sultan again. He looked as though he did not like the word.

"The truth that he was a great prophet," Francis said, "and that He defeated death once and for all. The truth that He lives even now, the eternal son of the living God. The truth that He and the Father are one and that the love between them is the infinite, living Spirit of God. The wonderful truth that He loves us, that He saved us from our sin and from death by his sacrifice."

"Where is the evidence of this truth?" al-Kamil asked.

"In your heart, oh sultan."

The sultan glanced at his men but their faces, like his, were inscrutable, their eyes downcast. After a few moments he said, "The punishment for tempting to convert one who has embraced Islam is death."

Brother Illuminato's mouth went dry but his face betrayed no emotion. Francis smiled, "My brother and I are standing here before your court because we do not fear death," he said. "Through death salvation comes."

The sultan acknowledged the force of his statement with a slight nod.

"You are a clever man," said the sultan, "and I admire your courage. At least sit at my table and eat as my guest."

He directed his slaves to prepare a meal for the two friars. Jewel-encrusted goblets and Venetian glass platters filled with exotic foods were set upon a linen tablecloth. Francis recognized the cloth as linen of Pelusium; there was none finer.

Before he let them go, the sultan gave Francis a small ivory horn, gilt about the edges and marked with the sultan's insignia. "Take this with you as a sign that you have earned my respect," he said. "Then no one may harm you."

Francis accepted the gift and said, "Wherever I sound the horn, people will gather to hear about the truth of Jesus Christ!"

The sultan looked alarmed. Taking Francis aside, he said quietly, "Be careful what you say and where you say it!" Lowering his voice further he added, "Pray for me, Friar Francis, that God may reveal to me which faith is more pleasing to Him."

At the sultan's command, Francis and Illuminato were escorted to a boat that brought them back to the camp of the crusaders. Word of their return spread quickly through the camp.

Francis and Brother Peter Catanei left Egypt when the crusading army took possession of Damietta on November fifth of that year, 1219. Many new friars remained behind in Egypt where they were given a church of their own by the Bishop of Acre. And many more men joined the Friars Minor there.

Carrying with him the sultan's ivory horn, Francis and Brother Peter went first to the ancient port city of Pelusium on the northeast corner of the Egyptian Delta where Joseph, Mary, and the child Jesus had once rested in their flight from King Herod's soldiers. Once a stronghold of Egypt, this city had been razed a hundred years before, but its importance as a shrine of the Holy Family was never lost.

From there Francis traveled along the Mediterranean coast of the Sinai Peninsula into the Kingdom of Jerusalem to visit the holy places where Jesus had lived. He prayed at the manger in Bethlehem where Christ was born in the reign of Caesar Augustus. He found the home at Nazareth where the child Jesus grew in age, grace, and wisdom. Francis envisioned Christ's agony at the Garden of Gethsemane and wept on Mount Calvary. He kissed the ground of the Holy Sepulchre where Christ was buried and from which he rose from the dead, and he gazed up to heaven from Mount Olivet where Jesus ascended to his heavenly Father.

Francis and Brother Peter finished their pilgrimage at the port city of Acre where Brother Elias and Brother Caesarius joined them for the return journey to Italy. At noon, the four friars sat together on the ground beside the bustling harbor to share a piece of mutton. A man in the drab garb of a Friar Minor approached, visibly distraught.

"Father Francis," he called, waving his hand excitedly. "I am Brother Stephen. I am so glad you are alive and that I have found you!" He did not wait for his greeting to be returned but delivered his message at once. "I joined the Friars Minor only a few months before you left. I was at the Saint Michael's Day chapter meeting two years ago with Brother Giles—I will never forget it. You said that the Gospel is our Rule of Life and that a Friar Minor must always bear the cross in his heart like the first apostles. Many of us treasured your words, but the men you left in charge, Brother Matthew and Brother Nicholas, must not have understood you."

"What do you mean, Brother Stephen?" Francis was alarmed.

"So much has gone wrong since you left, Brother Francis! There is confusion among the brotherhood."

Brother Stephen told Francis that when a rumor reached Italy that Francis had died at the hands of the sultan, his vicars, Matthew and Nicholas, did not wait to verify the rumor, but immediately instituted changes in the order. "And they do not have the spirit of true poverty, Brother Francis," Brother Stephen said. "They have been ashamed that Friars Minor have so few laws, unlike the more established religious orders. I was sure that you would not approve of the rules they made that are not found in the Gospel and do not belong to the Church. I decided to find out for myself whether you still lived and what you would think. It was important enough so I . . . ." Brother Stephen hesitated. Looking abashed, he admitted, "I did not ask permission of my minister or anyone else, Father, but took it upon myself to, ah, to borrow a copy of the new legislation." He held out a document several pages long. "I arrived by ship from Ancona only this afternoon. How fortunate that I found you right away!"

Brother Stephen noticed the mutton that the brothers were about to share. "Oh, Brother Francis, it is Monday! I must tell you that according to the new regulations, meat is forbidden on Mondays."

Francis could hardly believe what he was hearing. He quickly read over the new legislation imposed on all the Friars Minor by decree of his two vicars. He turned to Brother Peter who had once been a lawyer.

"Lord Peter," he said with mock solemnity, "according to the law as decreed in this document, it is forbidden for a Friar Minor to eat meat on Mondays, as well as Fridays and Saturdays as proscribed by the Church, nor is dairy permitted on Wednesdays or Fridays, unless it is a gift. What shall we do?"

Brother Peter answered in the same spirit. "My Lord Francis, in this case you must do whatever it pleases you to do. As founder of the Order of Friars Minor, you have the power over your vicars."

"In that case," said Francis, "let us eat what is put before us as the Gospel says."

With a clear conscience, Brother Stephen joined the men in their meager lunch. Afterward, the five friars begged passage on a ship bound for Italy. Later that night as darkness closed in, Francis stood alone on the ship's deck, deep in thought. Brother Stephen's report was troubling. Would he be able to save his order? Would it ever be the same? His head began to ache, and he felt a chill that had nothing to do with the coastal breezes.

Chapter Eighteen

THE LEAST AMONG MEN

By the time their ship reached the port in Venice that spring of 1220, Francis was suffering from a high fever and intense abdominal pain. Elias, Caesarius, Peter, and Stephen took him by mule to a hermitage to rest.

After a few days, when Francis felt better, he began to form a plan to save his order. Now that he was back in Italy, he would call a chapter meeting of all the Friars Minor throughout the world. There he would emphasize the spirit of the Gospel. Next, he would write the new and unequivocal Rule for the Friars Minor, as Cardinal Hugolino had long ago urged him to do.

He was eager to begin, so the small group of friars set out at once. Because his illness had affected his eyes, Francis was forced to move slowly, with his head bowed down to shield them from the sun. Brother Elias walked beside him guiding the mule and reported what he had learned from the friars at the hermitage.

While Francis was in the Middle East, Brother John de Capella had organized the lepers under his care into a brotherhood. Young and old, sick and poor, male and female alike, were admitted to this fraternity. Their only work was to care for the sick, institutionalizing what had formerly been a spontaneous work of mercy, so that Brother John de Capella did nothing else but manage his brotherhood. Showing a disdain for local laws and sensibilities, he had marched with his mixed congregation to Rome to seek the pope's blessing.

Francis groaned as he listened. "My chicks," he said, "My wayward chicks. How can I keep you under my wing?"

There was more. Elias reported that Brother Philip had received the authority from the pope to excommunicate anyone who dared disturb the peace of the Poor Ladies at San Damiano. Some of the brothers are distressed by this, Brother Elias said, but he himself thought it commendable.

"But a Friar Minor must not administer punishments!" Francis objected in dismay. "A Friar Minor must turn the other cheek as Our Lord did. He is not a superior who commands and expects to be obeyed, but one who serves!" Elias kept silent.

They reached the city of Bologne in the late afternoon. Hoping to find some of their brothers in the city, they asked a passing tradesman whether he had seen any Friars Minor in the area or knew where they might be staying. "Of course," the tradesman answered. "Everyone in Bologne knows. The House of Friars is in the Old City." Then, by way of pleasant conversation he added, "They have recently added a *studium* to the place. Amazing!"

Francis turned paler than he was before. After thanking the informative tradesman, Elias asked Francis if he wanted to go there to rest. "To stay in a 'House of Friars'?" he exclaimed, "No,

I will never stay in such a place. They are no true Friars Minor who have a house of their own."

The five men slept outdoors that night and prayed under a moon shrouded in mist. They rested their heads on rocks with the earth as their bed. In the morning, Francis found the House of Friars in the Old City exactly as the tradesman had described it. Brother Peter Stacia met them and proudly informed them that he was responsible for the construction and had established the school.

Francis told him firmly that such a house could not belong to any Friar Minor. Had they abandoned their vow of poverty?

Brother Peter Stacia protested. "We did not build the house so that we may live in comfort, Father. Our cells are sparsely furnished. We built it so that students may have a place to come to learn what theologians have taught about the Word of God."

"Of course, we should honor and revere all theologians and those who serve us with God's word, because they give us spirit and life," Francis said, looking at Brother Peter with gentleness, "but, Brother Peter, theologians run schools, they study, and they teach. They are treated with respect as they deserve. A Friar Minor does not seek the praise of others but to serve. A Friar Minor should be least of all. If he owns costly books, he must have a fine house to shelter them. If he runs a school, he must be revered."

Peter Stacia felt humiliated and was furious. The two men parted uneasily.

Utterly dispirited, Francis made his way back to Assisi. As he approached the Portiuncula, a large stone building came into view that had not been there when he left. When Brother Leo saw Francis, he ran to welcome him back and to inform him, with tears in his eyes, of the great divisions that had arisen among the Friars in his absence. And worse, he told him, when some of the brothers tried to protest, they were punished, some were even expelled. A few left the order of their own accord.

"Now, no one dares to speak out for fear of reprisal," Leo said. Francis was sick at heart now that he realized how deeply the order was divided. Somehow a critical misunderstanding of his mission and what it means to "take up the cross and follow Christ" had taken hold while he was gone.

Raising his aching eyes with effort, Francis pointed to the imposing building near the Portiuncula. "What is this structure built so close to us that it casts a shadow across the Portiuncula?"

Leo told Francis that it was a house built to shelter the growing number of brothers who come for chapter meetings.

A house to give shelter to the friars—could this be true? A Friar Minor must never own a house! Forgetting his sickness, Francis charged up to the new dormitory and climbed to its roof. As tears streamed from his infected eyes, he angrily tore off tile after tile, throwing them to the ground. A small group of friars stared at him from below. Some felt vindicated but others became angry.

Two knights of Assisi shouted at Francis to stop what he was doing. Francis paused, his head aching terribly, and challenged the guard to tell him why he should stop, since "the friars do not need a house."

"This house is not the property of the friars," said the guard.

"It was built by the people of the city of Assisi to house the friars. It is the property of the commune. You are trespassing."

Abashed, Francis stopped and climbed down from the rooftop. "Since this house belongs to you, sirs, I have no right to touch it."

The next morning, Francis asked Brother Angelo and Brother Leo to accompany him. Just as the apostles had looked to Peter for guidance, Francis would take his troubles to Peter's successor, the bishop of Rome.

At that time, the pope was at Viterbo, halfway between Assisi and Rome, to escape the violence that had erupted in Rome between political factions. When Francis arrived, he waited a long time outside the door of the pope's chamber. It would not be right for a Friar Minor to disturb the Holy Father at work by knocking at his door. When the Holy Father finally emerged, he was surprised to see the humble friar.

Francis bowed down at the feet of his shepherd. "God grant you peace, Holy Father!" Then getting up, he said, "My lord, the Friars Minor need guidance, but I am ashamed that you should trouble yourself with us, the least of all your sheep. I humbly ask Your Holiness to give us the Lord Bishop of Ostia, Cardinal Hugolino, as our protector and guide in your name." The pontiff helped Francis up and agreed to his proposal.

Hugolino was in Viterbo with the pope at that time. Francis found him and explained the divisions that were devastating his order. Cardinal Hugolino agreed to help in the name of holy Mother Church, and he acted quickly. He asked Pope Honorius to revoke Brother Philip's authority to punish offenders of the

Poor Ladies of San Damiano. He made sure that Brother John de Capella did not receive papal approval for his order of lepers.

Brother John left the Order of Friars Minor angrily. The two vicars, Brother Matthew and Brother Gregory, were dismissed from their positions, upsetting many of the friars who sided with them.

Cardinal Hugolino next sent letters to all the bishops under his authority assuring them that the Friars Minor were still in good standing. He encouraged other cardinals to do the same. Finally, Pope Honorius issued a letter directing all bishops to allow the Friars Minor to operate within their regions. A few months later, the pope issued another letter, this time to the ministers of the Friars Minor, insisting upon a novitiate year in which new members be trained and tested before being admitted to the order. The cardinal hoped this would weed out anyone unable to follow the rigors of the order.

All of this weighed heavily upon Francis who longed to be at peace with his brothers and a servant of all. The role of the authoritarian, issuing decrees and doling out punishments, was bitter to him. At the same time, he knew that to neglect the situation would be far worse. By autumn of that year, Francis had composed the beginnings of a Rule.

In a voice still weak from sickness, Francis read what he had written to his small group of advisors. Because his diseased eyes pained him, reading was laborious.

"The Rule and life of the friars is to live in obedience, in chastity, and without property, following the teaching and the footsteps of Our Lord Jesus Christ," he began. The new Rule reiterated the old Rule, followed by a list of sparse regulations regarding the particular events in the life of a Friar, his clothing, his life of prayer and service, and frequent and devout reception of the sacraments. It addressed their missionary role and the necessity of fidelity to Catholic teaching, and it concluded with an exhortation. As he neared the conclusion, he began to speak spontaneously and his spirit of joy returned. All around the Portiuncula, brothers stopped what they were doing to listen to the familiar and beloved voice of their master.

"In the love which is God, I entreat all my friars to put away every attachment, all care and solicitude, and serve, love, and adore our Lord God with a pure heart and mind. We should make a dwelling place within ourselves where He can stay.

"We must hold fast to the holy Gospel of our Lord Jesus Christ. Of his own goodness he prayed to his Father for us saying, 'Holy Father, keep in thy name those whom Thou has given me, that they may be one even as we are. These things I speak in the world, in order that they may have my joy made full in themselves . . . Sanctify them in truth, Thy word is truth.'

"It was the Lord who created and redeemed us, and of his mercy alone he will save us. In the name of God, I entreat the friars to grasp the meaning of all that is written in this Rule for the salvation of our souls."

After he finished, no one spoke for many minutes. Finally, Brother Elias broke the silence. "This is not really a Rule of Life, Father Francis. Not a practicable one, at least."

"How can you say such a thing?" Brother Peter said. "Our Father Francis has poured his soul into this document, laboring day and night."

"It is the fruit of hours of prayer and holy insight," added Brother Caesarius, who had helped Francis prepare the document.

"Oh, it is very moving," Brother Elias added quickly. "It is a beautiful piece of poetry."

"But poetry does not make a useful Rule of Life for a religious order of this size!" said Brother Matthew irritably. "Is it not obvious to everyone that this so-called 'Form of Life' lacks the precision of a legal document?" Brother Elias and a few others nodded in agreement.

While the men hotly debated the practicality of his proposed rule, Francis stood up quietly. "I resign as leader of the Order of Friars Minor," he said. "But here is Brother Peter Catanei." He turned to his old friend, "Let us all—you and I—obey him instead."

Everyone was shocked, except Brother Peter who had been forewarned by Francis, but he was miserable. Francis knelt at his feet to receive a blessing and then indicated that the other brothers should do the same. Obediently the friars filed past Francis to kneel at the feet of Brother Peter. Many wept silently as they did so.

Francis explained to the assembly that now he would be free to devote more time to writing a better Rule of Life for the order, a Rule that would preserve it as God had intended it to be. He left at once for the hermitage of Fonte Colombo. There he labored to produce a document that would satisfy his legal-minded friars as well as the pious disciples from the early years who more perfectly shared his vision.

I must keep in mind the advice of my cardinal protector, Hugolino, that it should be practicable or it will not meet the approval of the pope and the Curia, Francis thought. *Above all, I must remain true to the commission God gave me at the foot of the cross at San Damiano.*

For weeks he prayed for inspiration and wrote with painful effort. Meanwhile, the order suffered from his absence. When Francis did appear, it was never to take command, but to tell his superiors to command him. Some friars tried to take advantage of this leadership vacuum to impose change on the order. Brother Peter's authority was not sufficient to stop them or to maintain peace. His time as vicar came to an abrupt end when he died suddenly only three months after Francis had resigned.

After consulting with Cardinal Hugolino, Francis announced that Elias Bombarone would succeed Brother Peter as head of the Friars Minor. Here was a natural leader, both firm and practical, Francis thought. He did not always see things the way that Francis did, but he was devoted to Francis nonetheless. With time, Francis hoped Elias would come to share his vision for the order. In the meantime, Francis knew that he would manage the practical concerns of the order, so that Francis would be free to complete his work on the Rule. Elias himself felt perfectly equal to the task.

At last the time arrived for the General Chapter Meeting of Pentecost 1221. Francis had called all Friars Minor to it when he first returned from the Middle East. He hoped to clarify what it means to take up one's cross to follow Christ as a Friar Minor. He wanted to remind them that this was not a learned order of preachers, like the Dominicans who were trained to inspire love of God by teaching Scripture and theology, nor an order that concerned itself with a single all-consuming project such as caring for the sick.

A Friars Minor's primary work was to win souls by prayer and example in humble service. Above all, it was to lead souls to God through self-denial and suffering united in prayer to Christ's Passion. Francis wanted to emphasize the proper understanding of Christ-like poverty that truly owns nothing, not staff, books, or even bread. And he hoped to renew their commitment to obey Christ through His Church and through the order. All of this, infused with a passionate love of Jesus Christ, should restore unity within the order. If they would accept it.

Chapter Nineteen

GREAT THINGS TO GOD

Cardinal Capocci, deacon-cardinal of Santa Maria in Rome, arrived by horseback at Assisi's Piazza del Mercado the day before Pentecost. Although the energetic prelate had been to Perugia many times on Church business, he had never gone to Assisi. Why should he? It was one small commune among dozens scattered across Italy with nothing remarkable to set it apart. On this particular spring morning, he could see that it was a beautiful town, like many other towns of central Italy.

Cardinal Capocci was there to attend the General Chapter Meeting of Friars Minor for Cardinal Hugolino, who could not come. He was curious to see in person the vagabond friar of whom he had heard so much. A kind of craze of enthusiasm for the "Poverello from Assisi" had swept over Italy after his daring encounter with the sultan of Egypt. But what impressed Raniero Capocci was the fact that the circumspect Hugolino spoke of Francis and Clare of Assisi with an awe approaching reverence.

Cardinal Capocci was also aware that Pope Honorius III placed great hope in the new mendicant orders. One founder,

Dominic de Guzman, was a personal friend. This was an opportunity for Raniero Capocci to decide for himself what to think of Francis of Assisi.

As the highest-ranking Church official at the General Chapter meeting, Capocci traveled with noblemen, knights, a bishop, several priests, deacons, religious brothers, clerks, and numerous footmen who accompanied him as he rode into town. When he pulled up the reins of his horse outside of the Church of San Rufino, at least a dozen others arrived at the same time. Naturally, this entourage attracted the attention of the townspeople and tradesmen.

Pietro di Bernardone stepped out of his shop to survey the newcomers. Yes, he decided, there were potential customers among them. He smiled graciously as they dismounted in the Piazza del Mercado.

"Do you know where the chapter meeting of the Friars Minor is to take place?" the clerk inquired.

"Friars Minor?" said Pietro stiffly, as though the term were distasteful. "I know nothing of their doings, my lord. But if you or your companions are in need of textiles, you have come to the right place!" He brightened. "Travelers often have need of a second suit of clothing, or a fresh tunic. My friend, Benetto, the tailor next door, can work wonders with my excellent cloth in no time. Perhaps you would like to see my linens made in Pelusium? Such delicate linen is hard to come by. Or could I interest you in my oriental silks, unsurpassed in suppleness and flawlessly woven, if I do say so myself, he added with feigned humility.

A few of the men in the cardinal's entourage went into the

cloth shop to look around. While they looked, they talked to one another. Since they did not know who Pietro was, they spoke openly. And because they knew a great deal about Francis, what they said was largely accurate. Thus, Pietro learned what had become of his wayward son.

Eventually Cardinal Capocci called his company back to attend Mass at San Rufino Cathedral, after which they dispersed to find lodgings near the Bishop's Palace where Cardinal Capocci was to be an honored guest.

When Pietro went home that evening, he was absorbed in his thoughts. Dona Pica was seriously ill, perhaps at death's door. She lay quietly in her dark bedroom and noticed nothing unusual in her husband's taciturn manner. He decided not to disturb her with news of their son. The shock, he thought, might be too much for her. In truth, he did not like to speak of either of their sons, the subject made him uncomfortable.

His consideration for his wife's sensibilities was misplaced. For fifteen years she had refrained from mentioning Francis in her husband's presence, but her firstborn was continuously on her mind. She prayed for him ceaselessly. Only once had she heard him preach in all the years since he left home. It was in the church of San Giorgio the first time he spoke there, long ago.

She had since heard stories about him from gossiping townsmen; some that gave her comfort and some that disturbed her. When she heard that Francis had gone to the crusades, she remembered how much he had always wanted to travel. For months she heard nothing more of him until one day word reached her that her son had died in Egypt at the hands of the

Infidels. She wept inconsolably and waves of resentment toward her husband swept over her. Pietro wondered what was bothering his wife but decided that whatever it was, it would pass. He did not ask.

Only in recent months did she seem to be at peace again. This was because she had finally gathered all her courage to ask the Bishop of Assisi what he knew of her son's death. To her amazement, she learned that Francis was not dead, that he had returned from the East, and that the pope in Rome had blessed him and his followers. Some people even hailed him as a saint! She could hardly believe it. More than once she almost told Pietro, until she thought better of it. He would only ridicule the idea. So, Lady Pica continued to pray for Francis, but she longed for a glimpse of him. Since her recent illness, she supposed that she must die without the comfort of ever seeing her son again.

It had been a turbulent decade and a half in the Bernardone family since Francis left home. Angelo, who had been united with his father in disdain for Francis, proved to be inept at the cloth business. Pietro grew irritated with him and eventually Angelo moved away from Assisi to one of his father's land holdings near Foligno. Pica soon realized that Angelo would not be coming home. Pietro's tongue lashings in the latter years had cut too deeply. Now that she was dying, she was terribly lonely. In her dim bedroom, Pica sighed.

"What is it, Pica?" Pietro asked from his seat near the fireplace. "Are you feeling worse? Should I get the doctor?"

"No, it is nothing," she answered quietly.

To herself she thought, *There is so much suffering. We make most of our misery for ourselves. Then again, our sins are manifold; there is much to atone for. No doubt it is best.* She drifted into a long, painful sleep. When she awoke, Pietro was at her side. He looked weary, irritable, and frightened, all at the same time.

"You must be tired," she managed to whisper.

"You have been moaning and calling out in your sleep these past twelve hours," Pietro said.

"Pietro," she hesitated, "There is one thing I want. I want to see . . . Francis."

"I'm afraid that cannot be," said Pietro coldly. "Since the day he said that I am no longer his father, he is dead to us."

"Sometimes I think, Pietro, that Francis was more alive than most of us."

Pietro shook his head but said nothing.

After a few minutes, Pica ventured again, "At least I want to know how he is." She had dared not speak of Francis in all those years. Now, as she lay dying, she just wanted to see Francis one last time. "It has been lonely since Francis left," she confessed, encouraged by Pietro's silence. Her weak laugh was self-conscious. "You will think it is silly, I suppose, but after Nofra died and Pasquale moved away, there really was no one else to talk to, no one who even remembered Francis as we knew him. I miss the boy, Pietro." Her breath came and went painfully as sadness choked her. "He was troublesome to you, I know, but he had a good heart."

She continued. "I never mentioned to you what people say

about him since he left us. They have said he was out of his mind, and that he was too idealistic. But now, Pietro! Now they say that he is a saint! Think of that, Pietro."

When Pietro still said nothing, she lifted her heavy eyelids to the place where her husband had been kneeling beside her bed. He was not there. A tear rolled down her sunken cheek.

Pietro di Bernardone walked briskly along the Via Francigena beyond Porto del Sementone and out past the Campo de Sementone. He skirted around the Church of San Damiano where the Poor Ladies lived. Chiara Scifi had been just as crazy as his son, he thought. Perhaps she had been duped by him, and look where it got her! He shook his head as he passed the convent. On he walked toward the little portion of land that belonged to the Benedictines of Mount Subasio. He had heard the visitors in his shop say that they were going there to hear Francis—*my son*—preach. Pietro swallowed hard. *That idiota, preach?* Well, he would judge for himself if anything had changed in the years since the last time Francis had preached all manner of idiocy in his father's house.

Pietro hoped that he would be able to look at Francis without being noticed. Perhaps Francis would not even recognize his old father if he did catch a glimpse of him. Pietro had to admit that time had taken a toll, even on himself.

Before long, he realized that there was no danger of being recognized. He was not sure he would even be able to get close enough to see or hear Francis. The number of friars and pilgrims pouring into Assisi and filling the road to the Portiuncula was beyond anything he had imagined. *There must be at least a thousand*, he thought.

He looked out over the fields and into the forest near the church. Everywhere he turned he saw friars. When he was closer, he noticed the makeshift huts covered with mats of reeds that were scattered like seed across the field. Between these huts sat groups of friars talking seriously together in groups or praying in unison. The words that reached his ears all seemed to be spoken in praise of God; there was no idle conversation. No one paid attention to him, except to offer an occasional smile as he jostled his way forward.

Finally, Pietro found a spot where he could watch but not be noticed. He was pressed on all sides by the crowd. Some people he recognized from town, but most he had never seen before. There were far more than a thousand, he realized. *There must be at least three thousand, maybe even more. What are they all doing here? Where have they come from?* he wondered.

Looking toward the church of Saint Mary of the Angels, he noticed the cardinal he had seen the day before. Behind him stood a small friar, half-hidden by the prelate's crimson robes and flanked by two tall friars. One wore the same gray habit that most of the friars wore, one was in black robes such as the new Order of Preaching Friars wore. That man, too, had been at the Piazza del Mercado on the previous day. Pietro knew his name was Friar Dominic.

A hush fell over the crowd when the small friar stepped forward. He was more shabbily dressed than all the others and seemed frail. He kept his eyes sheltered by his bony hand as if the light of day gave them pain. Pietro braced himself. *That is Francis! Why, he is sick! He looks too weak to stand.* Pietro noticed that every eye in the place was fixed on his son.

"My children, we have promised great things to God," Francis said. His voice seemed surprisingly strong, ringing out clearly enough to be heard by the thousands. It was melodious and unmistakably full of joy. Petro listened thoughtfully to his son's eloquent speech. "And God has promised even greater things to us. If we observe what we have promised to Him, we shall certainly receive what He has promised to us. The pleasures of this world pass quickly away, but the punishment which follows them is eternal. The sufferings of this world are trifling, but the glory of the next is without bounds."

Francis went on to encourage the friars in their vows of obedience and in charity for one another. He emphasized the importance of suffering, temperance, purity, chastity, and "to be at peace with God, with men, and with our own consciences." He told them to practice holy poverty with love.

"And I command you all here present to take no thought about what you shall eat or drink, or of aught else that is necessary to the body, but only to pray, and to praise God; for He has you in His special care. Let each of you receive this command with a joyful countenance."

When Francis finished speaking, all the friars began to pray. Pietro looked awkwardly from right to left. He would tell Pica that he had seen Francis and assure her that their son was fine. When he turned to go, he rubbed shoulders against a brother who stood nearby. The friar apologized, although Pietro knew it had been his own fault.

"No matter," Pietro said. "I am Pietro, the clothier in town." He did not know why he said this, nor why he held out his hand to the friar. Perhaps he just wanted to prolong the encounter with this kind-looking man. He had remarkable eyes, almost sublime in appearance. He smiled at the elderly tradesman and placed a hand in his. "I am Anthony, just arrived with some friars from Sicily. Eventually I will be going on to live in Padua. Although I used to be an Augustinian Friar, I became a member of the Friars Minor under this holy man, the founder." He indicated Francis. "Be assured that your wife is well aware of him," he added mysteriously.

Pietro thanked the young Friar Anthony. While he walked back to town, he asked himself why he had thanked him. Laughing at himself, he thought how absurd he must have seemed, yet he detected no ridicule in that man's eyes. There was only kindness.

Pietro reached home just a few hours after he had left, but he was too late to tell Pica what he had seen. She had died without hearing news of their son.

Pietro was troubled, but then he remembered what Friar Anthony had said. Now he understood it. He had no doubt that Pica was aware by this time of how Francis was doing.

Days later at her funeral Pietro described to Angelo the look on Pica's face in death. It had been as radiant as a young mother gazing at the child in her arms for the first time.

That same year Pietro followed his wife into eternity, with

hope inspired by the memory of Pica's joyful face in death. She had understood something that he never had, and Francis understood it better than either of his parents—only God matters, and nothing else. At last he, too, realized this. When Pietro closed his eyes for the last time, he knew Francis would one day stand at the right hand of God and he hoped that—through God's infinite mercy—he, Pietro di Bernardone, might be allowed to stand with him.

Chapter Twenty

THE TABLE SET BY THE LORD

"The Portiuncula has never been more beautiful!" Brother Elias crowed that day of the Pentecost Chapter Meeting. After giving his talk, Francis sat on the bare ground at the feet of his vicar and looked out over the valley. He had to agree. The sky was crystal clear above Mount Subasio and the sun shone warmly on the cornflowers in the grass. But it was not the Umbrian landscape that impressed them; it was the droves of Friars Minor, the seemingly endless waves of poorly clad brothers from every corner of the world who had heeded Francis's call to attend the General Chapter Meeting. The forest, the scattered meadows, the roadway all the way up to the gates of Assisi, as far as the eye could see, were filled with friars.

There were pilgrims, too, who had come to the Portiuncula to share in the spiritual fruits of such a gathering. One pilgrim for whom Francis had a special regard was Dominic de Guzman, founder of the Order of Preaching Friars and missionary to the people of the Midi. At Francis's request he, too, stood in front of the Church of Saint Mary of the Angels with Francis and his vicar, Elias.

"How will you provide for so many?" Friar Dominic wondered aloud.

"I have told the brothers to take no thought of what they shall eat or drink but to trust that God will provide for His little lambs."

"But that seems injudicious, Brother Francis," said Dominic with genuine concern. "You have called them here. Don't you feel any responsibility to provide for them?"

Francis smiled at Dominic. A few moments later, Francis pulled on Dominic's sleeve and pointed toward the end of the visible road. A large procession of knights, noblemen, tradesmen, and peasants approached with cartloads of food. They had come from Assisi, Spoleto, Perugia, Spello, and all the surrounding country, carrying sturdy tables and barrels full of fruit, meat, bread, and cheese; vessels of wine, and fresh, clear water.

While he unloaded the carts, one knight from Gubbio told Friar Dominic that when they saw the size of the General Chapter Meeting, his townsmen joined with the monks at Vallingegno Abbey and all the neighboring towns to provide food and drink for the travelers. It was remarkable, he said, to see the entire region united, for once, in the cause of hospitality.

Friar Dominic went back to Francis and apologized for his hasty criticism. "The Lord truly has special care of these holy servants of poverty," he told Francis. "I did not fully understand this before, but from now on, I will observe evangelical poverty in my Order of Preachers as I have witnessed it this day."

Looking out over his "garden of friars," Francis recalled the day Christ spoke to him from the cross at San Damiano. "Rebuild my house," the Lord had said. Francis smiled to think how slow he had been to understand. Now that his eyes were dimmed by time and illness, he saw it all so clearly. Here, in this little portion of land on the Feast of Pentecost, 1221, were the living stones that, through the grace of God, would rebuild the Church of Christ.

"The 'stones' will not hold together, however," Elias reminded Francis, "if we do not have an adequate Rule of Life as the cement."

Francis sighed. He had long ago written the form of life that God had taught him, and Pope Innocent had given it his blessing. Since then, Francis had reiterated it clearly enough to lead tens of thousands of people to change their hearts.

But it was not enough; it was never enough. Brother Elias said so, Cardinal Hugolino said so, Friar Dominic must also think so, since he had adopted the Rule of Saint Augustine for his own new order.

Francis asked permission to take Brother Leo and Brother Bonizio, a canon lawyer, with him to work on the Rule at a hermitage near Rieti. Brother Elias could hardly deny Francis his choice of companions, but he was apprehensive about what kind of Rule such a group might produce.

On the road outside of Rieti, Francis became too weak to finish the journey on foot. Leo and Bonizio asked a farmer to lend them his mule for the use of their sick friend. The farmer agreed but would not take the chance of losing his mule to strangers, so he insisted on going with them.

The three men walked along beside the mule while Francis rode, keeping his sore eyes covered with a cloth until the sun was down. He slumped over the mule, exhausted and lost in prayer.

"Where exactly are we going?" the farmer asked the brothers.

"To the hermitage at Fonte Colombo," Brother Bonizio answered.

"There is no hermitage near Rieti that I ever heard of," the farmer said suspiciously.

"Oh, yes, the Friars Minor come there often," Brother Leo assured him.

"In truth!" the farmer exclaimed. "Are you Friars Minor? Do you know of the holy man called Francis?" he asked.

Francis raised his head. "I am Francis," he said.

"Well, let me tell you something," the farmer said, stopping in his tracks. "A great many people put their trust in you, Friar Francis. Please be as good as you are said to be and never be anything other than you are expected to be."

Francis halted the mule and dismounted. Prostrating himself on the ground, he kissed the farmer's feet, saying, "Thank you, good man, for this admonition. I will always try to live up to it, for truly, a man is only what he is before God, and no more."

A little flustered, the farmer helped Francis back onto the mule. The group continued past a monastery deep in the woods, and then a church a mile beyond that. When they came to a tiny, rustic chapel, they stopped. Francis dismounted and thanked the farmer for the use of Brother Mule. He did not go in to the chapel but disappeared among the oaks.

"Where is he going?" the bewildered man asked the brothers.

"Francis has turned a cave into a private chapel where he can be alone with the Lord," Brother Leo explained. "There are other caves where Brother Bonizo and I can pray in solitude. We will meet for common prayer in the chapel that you see here."

"So," the farmer observed, "the world is your hermitage!" He chuckled and told the friars to let him know when they were ready to descend the hill again. He promised that "Brother Mule" would be available.

Francis remained inside his cave for days, only coming out to hear Mass and to say prayers with the other two friars. He fasted and he prayed, begging for the right words to come to him. After many weeks, he announced that he was ready to compose a Rule of Life as God saw fit to illuminate him. Brother Bonizio and Brother Leo knelt outside the cave while Francis remained inside, on his knees, before a cross he had scratched into the rock.

He called out, "Brothers, please write and say that the life of the Friar Minor is this: to observe the Holy Gospel of Our Lord Jesus Christ by living in obedience, without any property, and in chastity." Brother Bonizio repeated what Francis said so that Brother Leo could write it down.

After a silence Francis added, "Say that Brother Francis promises obedience and reverence to his holiness Pope Honorius and his successors and to the Church of Rome. The other friars are bound to obey Brother Francis and his successors." Brother Bonizio repeated it, and Brother Leo wrote it down.

A few minutes later he called, "Please write that if anyone wants to profess this Rule he must sell all that he has and give it to the poor. The minister must not interfere so that new friars may dispose of their goods freely. And please write: Take nothing for your journey, neither staff, nor scrip, nor bread, nor money." For an instant Brother Bonizio hesitated. He knew this was a sore point for many of the brothers because it did not seem "practicable." Nevertheless, he repeated it, and Brother Leo wrote it down.

"And add: They shall not resist the evildoer, letting themselves be despoiled without resistance." The friars added it.

"Write this: Obey the minister appointed to you in all things. But if a minister should not allow you to follow the Gospel literally, then you are no longer bound to obey him." Straight through the night, they repeated and wrote all that Francis dictated.

By morning Francis was finished. The three men separated to pray and rest. After a few more days, they returned to the Portiuncula. Francis presented the lengthy document to Brother Elias.

Brother Elias greeted Francis with a strange coolness. Francis was surprised when Elias took the document and set it down without looking at it. The next day, Brother Elias still said nothing to him about the Rule, nor the next day. It was a week before the vicar finally came to Francis to announce that he had somehow misplaced the new Rule. It was nowhere to be found, he declared. He was sorry, he said, but it could not be helped.

Francis wailed aloud. "It was the Rule God gave to me! Do you really mean that you lost it?" he asked in disbelief

"I am afraid so," said Brother Elias.

Francis returned to the hermitage of Fonte Colombo and began all over again to dictate a Rule of Life to Brother Bonizio, who repeated it to Brother Leo, who dutifully wrote down every word.

The trio were making slow progress when, one afternoon, the quiet of the hermitage was broken by the sound of men approaching through the brush. Brother Elias Bombarone soon came into view a short distance away. With him stood a group of friars. "Father Francis!" he called out. His voice echoed and fell silent.

Brother Leo and Brother Bonizio watched apprehensively as Francis emerged from the cave, wincing in the bright daylight. He peered out at the crowd of friars standing behind the vicar. "Why have all these brothers come?" he asked Brother Elias.

Brother Elias told him, "These are almost all the ministers of Italy, Francis. They heard that you are writing a new Rule of Life for the Order and they are afraid that it will be too hard. They asked me to say that if it is too difficult to obey, and even if the Holy Father approves it, they will not bind themselves by it."

In despair, Francis cried out, "Oh Lord God, answer for me. What am I to do?" He raised his arms toward heaven, waiting for God's answer. No one moved. Francis stood as if transfixed.

Finally, he turned to the ministers and said, "My Brother Ministers, the rule that I have written is not mine, but God's. It is to be obeyed without alteration, *without alteration!*"

Brother Elias did not know what to say. He looked at the ministers and eventually they turned around and left the hermitage.

Francis spent several more weeks at Fonte Colombo in prayer and reflection. The division among his friars caused him great suffering. These were the children God had entrusted to him, the chicks that he was unable to keep under his wing. He wept so much that his eyes became swollen and inflamed. This agony brought him still closer to Christ on the cross.

When he returned to the Portiuncula, with his new Rule in hand, he let Brother Elias know that he was taking it to Rome. He would present it to Cardinal Hugolino for his consideration. Brother Elias nodded enigmatically.

On the day Francis was to set out for Rome, a young friar came to Francis to ask his permission to own a book. He read the Divine Office every day, he said, and he enjoyed poring over the Psalms in his spare time. His minister had given him permission to keep the book, but the young man feared that Francis might not approve.

"Father," he asked, "may I be permitted to own the book of the Psalms?"

Francis answered kindly, "My son, if you own an expensive book, then you must have a stand on which to keep it, and a room in which to store it with a roof over it so that it will not be damaged by the weather. Soon you will need a servant to bring it to you whenever you call out, 'Bring me my book!' No, my son, true poverty owns nothing, not even books."

"But," the young man objected, for he very much wanted to keep his book, "my minister has allowed me to keep it."

Francis lost his patience. "Oh, your minister has allowed it? Well then by all means keep your books! And build a grand library, too, and be sure to hire servants who can lift and carry for you. Now go." The friar walked away, confused and sad.

Francis sank to his knees and clutched his head in his hands. "Oh God, forgive me," he whispered.

Then he leapt to his feet and ran to the young friar before he was out of sight. Throwing himself at his feet, he said, "Forgive me my son, and may God forgive me. You must not have a book or anything else for your own. It was God who gave me this precept to live in absolute poverty, taking *nothing* with you, not sandals, nor scrip nor anything else. It is not for me to alter the rule that God has given us."

Nevertheless, the friar kept his book of the Psalms; his minister allowed it.

Francis left for Rome to place his Rule directly into the hands of Cardinal Hugolino. As protector of the order, the cardinal would inspect and prepare it for Pope Honorius to read. Cardinal Hugolino took the copy of the Rule but he was struck by the terrible state of Francis's health, and told him to rest before they would look through it together.

The next day, Cardinal Hugolino pored over the Rule that Francis had brought. He changed some of the terminology so that it would be more appropriate for a legally binding document.

And he made changes to address the controversies within the order. These, he believed, made the Rule more practicable for the rapidly expanding order, and less likely to be a source of discord among the friars.

Francis accepted all the changes without protest, until he saw a line drawn through the words, "Take nothing for your journey, neither staff, nor scrip, nor bread, nor money."

At this he balked. "These are the words of Our Lord! He gave them to me when I first left the world to follow Him. It is the command He gave to his apostles!"

Cardinal Hugolino explained to Francis that the words themselves were too often misunderstood by his own friars and led to internal disputes. He pointed to the unambiguous conclusion, ". . . live always according to the poverty, and the humility, and the Gospel of our Lord Jesus Christ."

"Francis," Hugolino said, "the spirit of those words of the Gospel are what form this document."

Francis finally agreed to the cardinal's changes but he was deeply divided within himself when that Gospel passage was struck from the Rule. It was one of the trilogy of verses that had inspired him at the very beginning. Francis felt betrayed by those friars who would not tolerate it, and he feared that he himself had betrayed those faithful friars who had embraced it.

While Francis silently agonized, Cardinal Hugolino set in motion the legal process of getting this Rule formally and canonically approved so that the Friars Minor would at last be a legally recognized religious order. In the next few weeks, Francis became easily agitated. He recognized the turbulence within himself and, in his distress, begged God for help.

"Francis," the gentle voice of the Lord spoke to him in prayer one night, "if you had faith like a grain of mustard seed, you would say to this mountain, 'Be removed,' and it would obey you."

"What mountain, Lord?" Francis asked.

"This mountain of temptation," the Lord answered.

Francis suddenly saw his anguish over the order in a different light. How had he forgotten that a Friar Minor must have *nothing* of his own? The order was not his—it was the Lord's from the beginning. Francis was only God's troubadour, bringing the joy of the Gospel to his people. He had been chosen for his simplicity, so that whatever God worked through him would be ascribed, not to him, but to its true source, divine grace. At last, his anxiety for the order was put to rest.

"Let it be done to me according to Thy word, Lord," he prayed. Then he turned his thoughts in a new direction. *I understand now that this order is not mine, but His. My concern now must be with my own salvation.*

On the twenty-ninth of November, 1223, Pope Honorius III issued an edict approving the Rule of Life of the Friars Minor. The order finally had canonical standing and the pope insisted that this Rule of Life was organically one with the original Rule that Innocent III had approved in 1209. Francis accepted the new Rule as the official Rule of his Order of Friars Minor.

The news was received with jubilation. Waves of enthusiastic men and women engulfed Francis wherever he went. Crowds met him at each new town to hear him preach, seeking to touch him and, sometimes, to be healed. The little friar from Assisi was hailed everywhere as a saint.

When he returned to the Portiuncula, Brother Elias met him with ambivalence. By this time, both men were aware of their insurmountable differences. Elias had a grand vision for the future of the order significantly different than the vision of its humble founder. At the same time, Brother Elias loved Francis. It was impossible not to.

Brother Elias agreed to let him spend Christmas at the remote hermitage high in the cliffs over Greccio. On his way there, Francis stopped to preach in the town of Greccio. It was by then only a couple of weeks before the Feast of the Nativity of the Lord. There was a chill in the air and the wind whipped through his thin tunic. Francis reminded the people of Greccio that the Holy Family also endured bitter cold in Bethlehem on that night of nights when God entered the world in the form of a helpless infant.

He confided in a friend, Giovanni Velita, a secret plan he had formed with the Holy Father's approval. In the two weeks before Christmas, Velita was kept busy running errands between the town and the hermitage where Francis stayed.

On Christmas Eve, it was announced throughout the region of Greccio that there was to be a special midnight Mass in the hills above town. The bells of all the churches rang out in the deep of the night. Friars and townspeople formed a procession with candlelight and torches that wound up the steep hillside. The sound of their Christmas hymns echoed over the countryside.

The procession went past the friars' hermitage and on up to the stony cliffs that jutted from the hillside. There beside a cave stood a makeshift stable, illuminated by candles with an ox, an ass, and a lamb sheltered beside it. Hay had been placed in a small cleft in the rock to represent the empty manger as it must have been in Bethlehem, awaiting the arrival of the newborn savior of the world.

One of the friars offered the Mass of the Nativity on a stone altar. Wearing the white robes of a deacon, Francis sang the Gospel in his rich tenor and preached the homily. He spoke with tenderness of the humility of Christ and was filled with such an intense love for Jesus that he could not utter his name without being overcome by emotion. He managed to say only, "the Babe of Bethlehem," each time he tried.

As he spoke, he turned to the empty manger. The people who stood near the front turned, too. A ripple of excitement swept across the congregation when they saw that the manger was no longer empty. A beautiful baby was sleeping there. Francis left his make-shift pulpit and approached the child. The baby opened his eyes and reached out to Francis, who took him in his arms, and cradled him close to his heart.

With tears streaming down his face, Francis tenderly laid the little one back into the manger. After Mass, men and women pressed forward to kneel at the creche where the Christ Child had appeared, and to touch the hay He had rested on. Francis disappeared into the far reaches of his cave.

A few months later Francis returned to the Portiuncula to attend the Pentecost chapter meeting and to meet the first priests ordained within the Order of Friars Minor. These men had studied theology and completed a novitiate year but many of them had never met Francis. Indeed the Order of Friars Minor no longer depended on its founder for its life. It was like a thriving plant that has taken root and put out shoots while the seed that first nourished it withers away. Only, in this case, the seed continued to enrich it with his example, his prayers, and especially with the suffering that God was soon to share with him.

Chapter Twenty-One

TO BEAR THE CROSS OF CHRIST

Near the end of July, 1224, Francis took a few friars with him to their hermitage on Mount Alverna in Tuscany. Brother Leo, Brother Masseo, Brother Angelo, Brother Rufino, and Brother Illuminato had all been with him from the earliest years and they accompanied him now. They would celebrate the Feast of the Assumption of Mary followed by a time of prayer and fasting—a "Lent"—that would last four weeks until the Feast of Michael the Archangel. Francis sensed that his sickly body would never recover, and he wanted to spend time with God in this hermitage that was the most isolated of all

When they arrived at the small chapel and few mud huts that comprised the hermitage, Francis found a shallow cave in which to spend the night alone in prayer. Concern about the animosity among his friars began to trouble his thoughts again. He begged God for a sign that he was doing His will.

The next morning, he stepped out of his cave into the mist that covered the plateau above the Casentino Valley. Except for the crunch of pebbles beneath his feet, no human sound broke the silence. From out of the shadows a dove suddenly flew in front of him. He looked up as it fluttered its wings and hovered over his head for an instant. It broke into song and flew into the sky. Francis smiled. Then another dove darted out, flapping and spinning with joy. It, too, flew off cooing noisily, and a third dove came along singing its morning song. It hovered longer than the other two, then landed on his shoulder. More doves came to perch on his arms and outstretched hands, and to rest near his feet. Then, rising together, the flock of snow-white doves dipped and soared and disappeared into the morning mist. Francis laughed and said, "Thank you, Lord, for such a sign."

After celebrating the Feast of the Assumption, Francis told the brothers, "I know that my death is approaching. I wish to be alone with God and lament my sins. Brother Leo can bring me a little bread and water, as seems good to him, but if anyone else comes here, please answer for me and let no one come to me."

Francis remained alone, joining the others only for Mass and common prayer. Then, one day he told the friars, "I long to know God's will for me now. I believe He will speak to me through the Gospel as He has done before. Brother Leo, will you open the book of the Gospels with your consecrated hands three times so that I can learn what God wants of me?"

Each time Brother Leo opened the book, it fell to a passage describing the Passion of Christ. "Clearly it is the Lord's will that just as I have spent my life trying to imitate Christ in my actions, so now as I approach death, I must be conformed to Him in the sufferings and pains of his bitter passion," Francis said.

He withdrew to a more remote place. He and Brother Leo

crossed a ravine by means of a fallen tree trunk. He made a hut for himself on the other side and asked Brother Leo to come to him twice a day; once in the morning to bring bread and water, and once after midnight to join him in praying Matins.

"When you step onto the bridge, call out the first line of the Psalm which says, '*Domine, labia mea, aperies*—Lord, open my lips,'" Francis instructed him. "If I answer you with the response '*Et os meum annuntiabit laudem tuam*—that my mouth may declare your praise'—then approach so that we may pray together. If you do not hear me, then do not come."

For days Francis remained in this secluded spot. Brother Leo came and went, sometimes joining Francis for prayer, sometimes returning alone to his cell, having received no invitation.

One night, just before the Feast of the Exaltation of the Holy Cross, an angel visited Francis when he was alone. It played a single note on a violin. The sound was so beautiful that Francis thought his soul might leave his body. The angel said to him, "I have come to give you strength, so that you can receive what God is going to give you with patience and humility."

Early the next morning, before sunrise, Francis knelt outside his cell with his head uplifted. "Oh Lord, Jesus Christ," he whispered, "two graces I ask of you before I die. The first is that in my lifetime I may feel, as far as it is possible, in my body and in my soul, the pain that you felt in the hour of your bitter Passion. The second is that I may feel in my heart the love with which your own heart was inflamed when you endured your cruel Passion for us sinners."

Francis knew that God had heard his prayer, and he prepared

to accept whatever God would send him. Then, from out of the sky, a fiery light came rapidly toward him. It was so bright that it filled the whole mountain and valley below with a light like the midday sun. When it was close to Francis, it stood still. He peered directly into the dazzling light but it did not hurt his usually sensitive eyes.

At first, he didn't understand the vision before him but then, all at once, he saw it plainly—it was a brilliant seraph with six wings. When it opened its wings, Francis could see in the center of the light a figure of a man that seemed to be fixed to a cross with arms outstretched and feet together.

Francis was frightened until he looked into the eyes of the figure. They were filled with such tender love that Francis knew at once this was Jesus Christ in the hour of his Passion. His fear left and he felt only gratitude and peace. But when he considered that the Son of God, who was so gentle and so powerful, was pierced by nails and fixed to a cross, he was overcome with sadness.

While Francis knelt on the ground, rapt in this vision, he began to understand that he was being asked to endure a martyrdom—not of bodily death—but a martyrdom of suffering. From this time on he would experience a consuming fire of love like that which burned within the human heart of Christ during his Passion, and his body was to endure tremendous pain.

Later that day, Francis asked all the friars to come to him. He explained that something had happened to him that was from God. After initial hesitation, he described the vision, and told the brothers that Christ had spoken to him. He did not tell them what the Lord had said, nor what had happened next. They were mystified when they saw that Francis could barely walk, and that he kept his hands covered by the sleeves of his tunic.

When Brother Leo noticed blood on Francis's tunic, Francis pulled him aside to confide in him alone. "God gave me the wounds of his crucifixion," he said, "so that I might share in his suffering and, oh, Little Lamb of God, he has filled my heart with such charity that it burns within me."

Francis covered his feet and hands with bandages. Only Brother Leo was permitted to see the wounds, since he took care of Francis as his body grew weaker. The wounds in his hands looked like dark lumps in the shape of the head of a nail. On the backs of his hands were fleshy points bent backward like nails that had struck a hard surface when they were pounded in.

Visible on the top of his feet were more dark lumps and out of his soles protruded fleshy points, bent backward. His hands and feet did not bleed but they were painful. In his side was a deep wound such as a lance would make. This wound would not heal but bled intermittently like a fresh wound and caused Francis searing pain.

Brother Leo grew shy around Francis. "Brother Little Lamb of God, if the One who gave me these wounds should remove them, all that would be left is my body and soul, the same as any other man," said Francis trying to reassure him. "Every good that we have is from God, and He alone deserves to be honored. In truth, I am less worthy of these gifts than the worst sinner."

It occurred to Leo that he would like to have something from Francis that he could always keep, something—anything—that

Francis had written in his own hand. Yet as much as Brother Leo wanted it, he could not bring himself to ask.

When he was preparing to leave the hermitage, Francis called Brother Leo to his side. "Little Lamb of God, I want to write. Would you please bring me a pen and paper?"

Leo did what he asked and waited while Francis wrote a prayer which he titled "The Praises of God." It began, "Thou art holy, Lord, the only God and your deeds are wonderful. Thou are strong, thou art great, thou art the Most High . . . thou art love . . . wisdom . . . humility . . . endurance. Thou art all our riches, and you suffice for us. Thou art beauty . . . gentleness . . . and our guardian. Thou art our haven and our hope . . ."

When he finished, Francis said, "I want to give this to you, Brother Little Lamb of God." Then he turned the paper over and wrote on the back, "A Blessing for Brother Leo. God bless you and keep you. May God smile on you and be merciful to you. May God turn His countenance towards you and give you peace." At the end of the note, Francis added, "God bless Brother Leo—you!"

Francis signed the paper with a Tau cross and skull, a sign of the victory of Christ over death. Brother Rufino, Brother Illuminato, and Brother Angelo came in next to say goodbye.

"Live in peace, dearest sons, and farewell!" Francis said to them all. "My heart remains with you! Brother Donkey awaits me," he said with a smile. "I am going with Brother Little Lamb of God to the Portiuncula and I will never return to Mount Alverna."

It was a long, slow journey for the two friars over the mountain passes of Southern Tuscany. From atop Mount Casella, Francis took his last look at Mount Alverna's rocky ridges and spruce-flocked slopes. "Farewell, holy mountain where God is pleased to dwell," he said. "I will not see you again. God bless you." He made a sign of the cross over the vast landscape, then they began the final descent into the valley against an icy November wind.

When they finally reached Assisi, Francis was intent on getting to work despite his weakness. So after only a few days' rest, they set out on a missionary journey through Umbria and the Marches of Ancona.

In the town of Foligno, late in the spring of 1225, Francis encountered Brother Elias. The vicar was distraught at the sight of Francis. He was only forty-two years old but the flesh had all but disappeared from his diminutive frame. "Return to the Portiuncula at once," the vicar commanded. "You must have medical attention."

Francis objected. "A friar minor must not seek too eagerly for a cure when God has given him sickness. "'Whom the Lord loveth, He chastiseth,'" he said, quoting Saint Paul.

Unmoved, Brother Elias retorted, "Saint Paul also tells us to 'Persevere in discipline.' For you, Brother Francis, that means to submit to your vicar."

Chapter Twenty-Two

CANTICLE OF BROTHER SUN

Francis agreed, and returned to the Portiuncula with Brother Elias at his side. When they arrived in Assisi, Francis asked to visit San Damiano one last time before seeking medical treatment. Clare had built a wattle and daub hut near the chaplain's residence for Francis.

No sooner had he arrived at San Damiano than his condition grew much worse. He was almost entirely blind; only a little light penetrated his darkness and even that caused him pain. *I must be the worst of sinners that God has allowed me to suffer in this way*, he thought. He could not rest or find any peace because he feared so much that he must have offended God. Some nights he would cry out in agony, "Help me, Lord, help me so that I can bear this sickness with patience!"

Then, one night he heard a voice. "Francis, would you bear it willingly if these sufferings of yours purchased for you a treasure so great that the world itself and all its riches were as nothing in comparison?"

Francis knew the voice. His answer was charged with love. "Yes, Lord!"

"Then rejoice and sing, Little One, for your suffering and weakness have bought you the kingdom of heaven."

In the morning, Francis called the brothers to him and said, "I have composed a song of praise to God on high. It is a canticle of all God's gifts of which the sun is the most brilliant and by its light gives the greatest glory to God." The brothers listened while Francis sang.

"Most high, all-powerful, all good, Lord!
All praise is yours, all glory, all honor
And all blessing . . .
All praise be yours, my Lord, through Sister Earth, our mother,
Who feeds us in her sovereignty and produces
Various fruits with colored flowers and herbs.
Praise and bless my Lord and give Him thanks,
And serve Him with great humility."

Brother Pacifico took up the lovely tune and joined Francis as he sang a second time. Soon more of the brothers joined in. Sister Clare and the other Poor Ladies could hear them from the cloister. Later that day, Sister Clare visited Francis in his tiny cell while Brother Leo dressed his wounds with clean bandages. She brought him bread and water and read the day's Gospel to him. "Father Francis, your voice is strong and joyful today," she said.

Francis looked serene. "The mice were at their worst last

night. They never ceased running all over me and disturbing my prayers. I thought the devil had sent them to torture me for my sins."

It was not surprising that there would be mice in a hut made of rushes that stood beside the open field, but Sister Clare was sorry that Francis had to endure mice on top of all his other torments. Francis reassured her. "It has been an unspeakable blessing, Clare. To comfort me in my suffering, the Lord has promised me the greatest treasure of all—the kingdom of heaven! Is it not fitting, then, that I should rejoice in my trials and praise God?"

Tears of joy welled up in Francis's inflamed eyes and streamed down his sunken cheeks. Clare rejoiced with him; never doubting that what he said was true.

The day finally came when Elias insisted that Francis get medical attention. Cardinal Hugolino had summoned Francis to Rieti to visit a reputable eye doctor. Preparations for the journey were interrupted, however, by news of strife between Assisi's chief magistrate, the Podesta, and Bishop Guido of Assisi. There was a stalemate between the two powers and the town was divided in allegiance. Factions were forming and violence had begun to erupt.

Francis heard this news with a heavy heart. "Brother Elias," he said, turning to the vicar, "Tell the Podesta to gather as many of the city's magistrates as he can in the Piazza del Vescovado, and ask Bishop Guido to preside."

Brother Elias sent one of the brothers to attend to the details.

Francis quickly scribbled on a piece of parchment then gave it to Brother Pacifico with instructions to read the message he had written at the time he would designate.

When everyone had gathered, Brother Pacifico and Brother Illuminato stood and a hush fell on the crowd. With all eyes upon them, Brother Pacifico explained, "Blessed Francis, in his sickness, has composed a hymn that he calls 'The Canticle of Brother the Sun.' It is written in praise of the Lord and he has asked that you all listen to it."

The two friars then sang the canticle Francis had composed. At the end they added the few new lines which Francis had written on the parchment that day:

"All praise be yours, my Lord, through those who grant pardon
For love of You; through those who endure
Sickness and trial.
Happy those who endure in peace
By you, Most High, they will be crowned."

The Podesta, whose conscience had been troubled, understood the point at once and declared, "I solemnly assure you all that I hereby forgive the Lord Bishop and acknowledge him as my lord." He walked over to the Bishop, seated upon the dais, and knelt, saying, "For the love of our Lord Jesus Christ and of His servant, blessed Francis, I offer any amends you require."

The bishop lifted him to his feet. "I am quick-tempered," he admitted, "but my office demands humility. Please, forgive me, I beg of you."

Brother Pacifico and Brother Illuminato reported the scene to Francis later in his hut at San Damiano. "Thanks be to God," said Francis.

Francis left his hut at San Damiano then. After he was gone, Sister Clare found a parchment on the straw, signed with the Tau cross and skull. She picked it up and read aloud to the other sisters.

"'I, little Brother Francis, wish to live according to the life and poverty of our most high Lord Jesus Christ and His most holy Mother and to persevere in this to the last. And I beseech you, my ladies, and I exhort you to live always in this most holy life and poverty. Keep close watch over yourselves so that you never abandon it through the teaching or advice of anyone.'"

By this time, Francis and a few of his brothers were well on their way to Rieti, eighty miles away. As he rode on the back of a donkey, Francis consoled himself thinking, *Our Lord rode to the city of His execution on the back of an ass.*

The doctors in Rieti treated his eyes with salves and herbal plasters. Francis apologized to "Brother Body" for having treated it so badly over the years, but it was clearly too late.

Next, he went to the hermitage of Fonte Colombo outside of Rieti where more physicians came to treat him. They determined that the most extreme measures were required—to cauterize his face from the temple down to the jaw with irons heated by fire. They hoped this would draw the diseased humors away from his eyes.

Brother Elias ordered Francis to submit to the treatment. When the red-irons were handed to the surgeon, Francis made a sign of the cross over them and said, "My Brother Fire, noble and useful among all the creatures, be courteous to me in this hour. I pray our Creator who made you to temper your heat now, so that I may bear it." When the iron touched the flesh of his temple, a stench of burning flesh filled the room. The doctor asked Francis how he was doing.

Francis replied, "If more is needed go ahead, for I have not felt any pain yet."

During the next weeks, the doctor checked Francis for signs of infection or improvement. "I am sorry to tell you," the doctor ruefully admitted after a couple of weeks, "the cauterizing has made little or no difference to your condition." Francis nodded; he himself could tell that this was true.

"I need no further treatment, Doctor," he said, "since the Lord allows me to suffer sickness for my soul's sake."

Brother Elias disagreed and insisted on sending Francis to Siena where he endured the attention of some new physicians. They tried piercing his eardrums to relieve the pressure from his inflamed eyes. This treatment also proved ineffective.

By spring Francis had begun to hemorrhage, drifting in and out of consciousness, and his lower body began to swell. He begged Brother Elias to allow him to return to Assisi. After some deliberation, Elias decided it was fitting that the Saint of Assisi should die in Assisi, so he agreed to move Francis again, but he required some time to arrange the trip. He had heard a rumor that the Perugians were plotting to capture Francis in the hope that the sainted man would die within their walls.

With Brother Elias in charge, the friars took Francis to the town of Gubbio, and from there, directly south to Assisi. An armed guard was sent to accompany them into the city. Despite his request to go directly to the Portiuncula, Francis was brought to the palace of the bishop, who was away at the time. Brother Elias said it would be easier to keep him under guard at the bishop's palace, and to obtain medical care in the town.

The physician in Assisi was Doctor Bongiovanni. When Francis met him for the first time, he objected laughingly to his name, which means, Good John. "Surely you know that only God is good," Francis joked. The doctor smiled and apologized that he could not alter his name.

"That's alright," Francis laughed, "from now on I shall call you . . . Bembegnato instead. That is close enough? Tell me, Bembegnato . . . how long do you project that Brother Body has to live?"

Doctor Bongiovanni took Francis's emaciated hand and looked at him steadily. "It is not likely that you will live beyond the end of the month, Francis. At most, you may live to the beginning of October."

Francis was quiet for a moment then suddenly raised up his arms as if in praise and burst forth with a new verse for his canticle:

"Praised be Thou, Oh Lord, for Sister Bodily Death,
From whom no living man can escape!"

"Bembegnato, listen!" Francis said, and he sang the whole "Canticle of the Sun" adding these last two lines. Brother Leo and Brother Angelo came in to sing with him. They all rehearsed it together until they knew it by heart.

"What is going on here?" Brother Elias stepped into the room in alarm. Doctor Bongiovanni explained with amusement that Francis had composed an addition to his song and that the friars were rehearsing it.

"Bembegnato here has wonderful news, Elias," said Francis. Elias looked confused. "You mean Doctor . . . Bongiovanni?"

Francis smiled. "Yes. He promises that I shall soon meet Sister Death. How can I help but sing in praise and thanksgiving? By the grace of the Holy Spirit I am so closely united to my Lord and God through my suffering that I must be glad and rejoice in Him. Do you know the melody yet, Brother Elias?"

Francis again began to sing. Outside the door of his room, Brother Leo and Brother Angelo joined in. Even Doctor Bongiovanni by this time knew the tune and hummed along. Brother Elias left the room frowning with disapproval, discreetly closing the window as he went out so that no one on the street would hear. A few minutes later, however, the window was open again, "to allow the patient fresh air," the doctor explained with an impish grin, and the song poured out into the streets of Assisi.

Chapter Twenty-Three

THE FLIGHT OF THE LARKS

Over the next few days, Francis experienced excruciating abdominal pain. By this time, it was clear to Doctor Bongiovanni that besides malaria and a rare form of conjunctivitis in his eyes, Francis had developed stomach cancer. After one particularly difficult night, Francis told the friar who was caring for him, "Brother Benedict, I want to make my last testament before it is too late. Can you write what I tell you?"

Brother Benedict, who had been a lawyer, took his pen and transcribed Francis's words into Latin. Later that day, he read aloud the last testament of Francis, while all the brothers listened with heads bowed.

"This is how God inspired me, Brother Francis, to embark upon a life of penance. When I was in my sins, the sight of lepers nauseated me beyond measure. But then God himself led me into their company, and I had pity on them. When I had once become acquainted with them, what had previously nauseated me became a source of consolation. After that I did not wait long before leaving the world.

"God inspired me, too, with such great faith in priests who live according to the laws of the holy Church of Rome, because of their dignity. I revere them because in this world I cannot see the Son of God with my own eyes, except for His most holy Body and Blood which priests receive, and priests alone can administer to others. Above everything else, I want this most holy Sacrament to be honored.

"When God gave me some friars, the Most High himself made it clear to me that I must live the life of the Gospel. Those who embraced this life gave everything they had to the poor. We made no claims to learning and we were submissive to everyone.

"God inspired me to write the Rule and these words plainly and simply so you must understand them plainly and simply, and live by them, doing good to the last. And may all who observe this be filled with the blessing of the most high Father, and with that of His beloved Son, together with the Holy Spirit. And I, Brother Francis, your poor worthless servant, add my share to that most holy blessing. Amen."

When Brother Benedict finished reading, the friars sang "The Canticle of the Sun" in unison. This time Brother Elias sang with them.

One night soon after, when Francis was in pain, feeling hot and cold by turns, and writhing in bed, he noticed a look of weariness on the face of the friar who was caring for him. In a flash of understanding he said, "Care for me as you would for Christ himself, my son, for it is not I but the Lord who you must always see in the sick. And when you are weary, keep always before your eyes that the Lord will reward you for all that you do for me, the least of your brothers."

The next morning Francis announced firmly to Brother Elias, "Death is not far off and I do not want to die in a palace. I want to return to the Portiuncula where God first showed me the way of life."

Late the next day, the knights who had been guarding him, and about twenty friars, stood outside the bishop's palace to accompany Francis back to the Portiuncula. Brother Elias borrowed a litter from the leper hospital for Francis to lie on since he could no longer hold himself upright.

A wind rippled the flags of the guards, and the friars' robes flapped around them. Slowly the procession moved out the gates of the city and onto the Via Francigena. Outside the hospital of San Salvatore, Francis asked his bearers to set down his litter to face Assisi. Two men supported him so that he could look on his hometown for the last time. It was beautiful, like a jewel atop the hillside. While he strained to see it, Francis raised his hand in blessing and said, "Blessed be thou of the Lord, for He has chosen thee to be a home and an abode for all those who in truth will glorify Him and give honor to His name."

The litter was lifted again and the procession moved on toward the Portiuncula. Outside the Church of Saint Mary of the Angels, some larks were scuttling about, pecking at the ground. One of the small brown birds alighted on the edge of Francis's litter and cocked its head at him. Francis smiled and reached out a finger to stroke it. Francis had often told the friars they must look to "Sister Lark" as an example of a good Friar Minor.

"Sister Lark has a hood like a Religious," he would say, "and she is a humble bird, for she walks contentedly along the road to find grain, and even if she finds it among rubbish, she pecks it out and eats it. As she flies, she praises God sweetly, like good Religious, whose minds are set on the things of heaven, and whose constant purpose is to praise God. Even her humble plumage resembles the earth and sets an example to Religious not to wear fine clothing."

When at last Francis was placed onto a straw mat on the floor of a hut behind the church, he sighed with relief. "My brothers! See to it that you never abandon this place. If you are ever driven out from one side, go back in at the other. Here when we were but a few, the Most High gave us increase. Here He enlightened the hearts of his poor ones by the light of His wisdom. Here He set our wills afire with the fire of His love."

Later that day, Francis turned to Brother Leo beside him with a question.

"Brother Leo," Francis said, "consider two friars who are walking to the Portiuncula after a long journey, weary from their travels. Consider also that one knows the way and the other does not. I ask you, Brother Leo, out of love of his brother what should the friar do who knows the way when his brother, who does not, strays onto the wrong path? Consider also, that the path this friar has chosen in error ends with a steep cliff above a pit of vipers and other wild beasts that would tear the friar to pieces. What, then, Brother Little Lamb of God, should the friar who knows the way, say to the friar who has chosen the wrong path?"

"He should show him the right path," was Brother Leo's answer.

"Just as I was thinking," Francis nodded. "And it is far worse to be separated from God's goodness for all eternity, than to fall into a pit of vipers. Brother Little Lamb of God." Francis said after a brief silence, "I have composed a fitting ending for my 'Canticle of the Sun.' Will you call in Brother Angelo and Brother Pacifico so that you all may hear it and sing it with me?"

When the three friars had gathered around,

"Praised be Thou, Oh Lord, for Sister Bodily Death,
From whom no living man can escape.
Woe to those who die in mortal sin!
Happy those She finds doing your holy will!
The second death can do no harm to them.
Praise and bless my Lord, and give Him thanks,
And serve Him with great humility."

The friars repeated the new verse and then sang the entire canticle. Francis slept for a time, but he awoke with a start and said to Brother Leo, "Brother Little Lamb of God, the Lady Jacopa de Settesoli, who is so close to God, will be grieved when she hears that I have died. We must write to her now to tell her to come at once." Brother Benedict, hearing him, took a pen and parchment to write while Francis dictated.

"To the Lady Jacopa, Christ Our Lord has let me know

that the day of death is near at hand. If you would find me still alive you must come at once. Please bring with you cloth for my shroud and the cloth needed for my burial. And if possible, please bring some of the honey almond pastries that you made when I . . . "

Francis was interrupted by a commotion outside. Brother Matteo came in. "Father, I don't know what to do. There is a noblewoman here who wants to speak to you. I told her that women are not allowed at the Portiuncula but she said, 'I am a brother!' Naturally, I did not believe such a thing, yet she spoke in all seriousness, and she said, 'Tell Francis that Brother Jacoba is here—he will understand.'"

Francis smiled. "It is the Lady Jacopa de Settesoli! Brother Matteo, you may allow her entrance, for it is as she says. She is a friend and has traveled a long way to visit before I die."

Brother Jacoba, who was now a widow, entered the hut accompanied by her fifteen-year-old son, Giovanni. In her arms she carried paper parcels that contained incense, wax for candles, and gray wool cloth. These she gave to the porter for the burial. To her old friend she exclaimed, "Dear Father Francis, the Lord inspired me to come and to bring the things that will be needed for your burial."

She sank to the ground beside his mat, kissed the bandages that covered the wounds on his feet and began to weep. Francis laid his hand on her veiled head in blessing. Wiping away the tears, she rose and asked the porter where she could cook.

"Cook?" Friar Matteo repeated, thinking he must have misunderstood.

"I have with me what is needed to make honey almond pastries for Brother Francis. It is his favorite food," she explained. Taking a small wooden box from Giovanni, she opened its lid to show the friar earthen pots sealed with linen and beeswax. Inside were honey, almonds, and a flour mixture. Giovanni then reached into a small bag from the crook of his arm and brought out four round eggs. The three visitors smiled broadly. Friar Matteo could not help but laugh, and showed them to the clay oven outside.

Soon Brother Jacoba returned with a platter of the warm almond confection. She knelt beside Francis, handing him one. He admitted that he had been thinking of these when he was writing to her that very day.

After his visitors left, Francis slept fitfully. Early the next morning, while it was still dark, he said to the brothers, "Let us read the Gospel of Holy Thursday."

Brother Leo read aloud the Gospel that recounts the evening of the Last Supper. "'Jesus, knowing that His hour was come, that He should pass out of this world to the Father, said to them: For I have given you an example, that as I have done to you, so you do also.'"

Francis was at peace. He asked to be laid on the bare ground, covered only in sack cloth, and sprinkled with ashes because he said, "Soon I shall be nothing more than ashes and dust." As evening fell, the friars watched and prayed beside him. Suddenly, Francis opened his eyes and said aloud, "Welcome, Sister Death."

He began to sing the Psalm of David. "'*Voce mea, ad Dominum clamavi voce mea* . . . I cried to thee, Oh Lord: Thou art my hope . . . Bring my soul out of prison that I may praise thy name; the just wait for me, until thou reward me.'"

After this there was no sound in the hut. The candlelight flickered against the walls and the friars felt their hearts beating, but nothing else stirred. Then, there was a faint rustling outside. All at once a flock of larks began to sing their joyful song, flapping their wings and rising to the sky as one.

Brother Francis had met Sister Death.

Afterword

The funeral procession from the Portiuncula grew by hundreds as it moved along the Via Francigena. Noblemen, peasants, beggars, dignitaries, prelates, men, women and children of every age from Assisi, Perugia, Terni, Rieti, Spoleto, Siena, Viterbo, and Rome joined the cortege with olive branches in their hands as a symbol of peace. Their hymns rose to the sky where the larks soared far above the litter that held the body of Friar Francis, the little poor man from Assisi, herald of the Great King.

The sound of voices united in song alerted the nuns of San Damiano that the cortege was drawing near. The iron grille that separated the holy women from the world had been removed so that they could behold the body of their founder before it was consigned to the earth. Sister Clare came forward to kiss the wounds of Christ in the hands, feet, and side of her mentor, protector, and friend. Francis and Clare had been of one mind and heart in life, and so they were still. The tears that splashed onto his tunic when she bowed her head over his body were not tears of sorrow, but the earthly expression of the joy that Francis now had perfectly.

Francis was buried that day in the crypt of the Church of San Giorgio in a plain stone coffin. Two years later, when Cardinal Hugolino ascended the papal throne as Pope Gregory IX, he declared Francis a saint, "for we have seen it with our own eyes."

Four years later, Brother Elias insisted that the body of the saint be transferred to the magnificent Basilica di San Francisco d'Assisi, built under his direction as a testimony to the glory of the Friars Minor.

About the Author

Margaret O'Reilly attended Thomas Aquinas College in Santa Paula, California. After graduating in 1984, she earned catechetical certification from Our Lady of Peace Pontifical Catechetical Institute in Beaverton, Oregon. She taught high school theology and Church history at St. Agnes High School in St. Paul, Minnesota. Mrs. O'Reilly and her husband have twelve children whom they teach at home. Her articles on theological and apologetic topics have appeared in Catholic publications including *Homiletic and Pastoral Review*, and *The Catholic Response*. She is the author of *Humble Servant of Truth: A Novel Based on the Life of Thomas Aquinas*.

Building Wealth 101
How to Make Your Money Work for You
by Robert Barbera

Christopher Columbus: His Life and Discoveries
by Mario Di Giovanni

Dark Labyrinth
A Novel Based on the Life of Galileo Galilei
by Peter David Myers

Defying Danger
A Novel Based on the Life of Father Matteo Ricci
by Nicole Gregory

The Divine Proportions of Luca Pacioli
A Novel Based on the Life of Luca Pacioli
by W.A.W. Parker

Dreams of Discovery
A Novel Based on the Life of the Explorer John Cabot
by Jule Selbo

The Faithful
A Novel Based on the Life of Giuseppe Verdi
by Collin Mitchell

Fermi's Gifts
A Novel Based on the Life of Enrico Fermi
by Kate Fuglei

First Among Equals
A Novel Based on the Life of Cosimo de' Medici
by Francesco Massaccesi

God's Messenger
A Novel Based on the Life of Mother Frances X. Cabrini
by Nicole Gregory

Grace Notes
A Novel Based on the Life of Henry Mancini
by Stacia Raymond

Harvesting the American Dream
A Novel Based on the Life of Ernest Gallo
by Karen Richardson

Humble Servant of Truth
A Novel Based on the Life of Thomas Aquinas
by Margaret O'Reilly

Leonardo's Secret
A Novel Based on the Life of Leonardo da Vinci
by Peter David Myers

Little by Little We Won
A Novel Based on the Life of Angela Bambace
by Peg A. Lamphier, PhD

The Making of a Prince
A Novel Based on the Life of Niccolò Machiavelli
by Maurizio Marmorstein

A Man of Action Saving Liberty
A Novel Based on the Life of Giuseppe Garibaldi
by Rosanne Welch, PhD

Marconi and His Muses
A Novel Based on the Life of Guglielmo Marconi
by Pamela Winfrey

No Person Above the Law
A Novel Based on the Life of Judge John J. Sirica
by Cynthia Cooper

Relentless Visionary: Alessandro Volta
by Michael Berick

Ride Into the Sun
A Novel Based on the Life of Scipio Africanus
by Patric Verrone

Rita Levi-Montalcini
Pioneer & Ambassador of Science
by Francesca Valente

Saving the Republic
A Novel Based on the Life of Marcus Cicero
by Eric D. Martin

Soldier, Diplomat, Archaeologist
A Novel Based on the Bold Life of Louis Palma di Cesnola
by Peg A. Lamphier, PhD

The Soul of a Child
A Novel Based on the Life of Maria Montessori
by Kate Fuglei

What a Woman Can Do
A Novel Based on the Life of Artemisia Gentileschi
by Peg A. Lamphier, PhD

For more information on these titles and
the Mentoris Project, please visit
www.mentorisproject.org